TRAVEL DIARIES OF THE DEAD AND DELUSIONAL

LAUREN NICOLLE TAYLOR

Travel Diaries of the Dead & Delusional
Copyright ©2019 Lauren Nicolle Taylor
All rights reserved.
Printed in the United States of America
First Edition: February 2019

Clean Teen Publishing
WWW.CLEANTEENPUBLISHING.COM

Summary: Langley is crazy. She knows it, but clings to visions of her dead sister anyway—she just can't let go. Tupper's life is charmed, but he sidesteps his planned future and starts his journey where his mom's ended—following her hand-drawn map from Kansas to Canada. It puts him on a collision course with Langley, and their bond is palpable from the start. But two ghosts could tear them apart....

ISBN: 978-1-63422-320-1 (paperback)
ISBN: 978-1-63422-321-8 (e-book)
Cover Design by: Marya Heidel
Typography by: Courtney Knight
Editing by: Cynthia Shepp

COVER ART
© NEOSTOCK: BILLIE-URBAN-FANTASY-13

Young Adult Fiction /Social Themes / Mental Illness
Young Adult Fiction / Social Themes / Self-Esteem & Self-Reliance
Young Adult Fiction / Coming of Age

For more information about our content disclosure, please utilize the QR code above with your smart phone or visit us at WWW.CLEANTEENPUBLISHING.COM.

FOR MY PARENTS, BOB AND RAELENE.
NOT ONCE DID YOU TELL ME I COULDN'T DO
SOMETHING.

THANK YOU.

1. LANGLEY

Maka Mani Psychiatric Hospital, UT, 2015
WEATHER: CLEAR AS CUT GRASS

**I'M THE GIRL WITH A SECRET NO ONE WANTS TO HEAR:
I'M CRAZY, LIKE *GET THE ST*RAIGHTJACKET AND READY THE
PADDED ROOM KIND OF CRAZY, AND...
I WANT TO STAY THAT WAY.**

SARAH'S TWIG-LIKE FIGURE RUSTLES up behind me. A wisp of smoke swaying in an invented breeze. I wonder how long before she taps my shoulder and tells me to turn around. But today, she simply follows two steps behind. Not pushing forward, not pulling back, just watching as I creep down, down, down, the wet grass burning into my soles like acid.

Shards of glass wiggle in my skin, sending small shocks of pain rippling up my legs. Standing on my toes to ease the open cuts, I wipe my fingers on the sides of my pajamas. The smears of red over happy toaster cartoons cause Sarah's mouth to twist into a silent *ew!* expression.

Ducking, I hide in the dip between the fence and the lawn, then press my weak hand into the wet mud. My arm shakes under my weight like a branch about to break. I squat closer to the ground, hiding in the shadow of the dinner-plate moon. Down here, it's as dark as the bottom of a lake. It feels cool, comforting, in the dirt.

Maybe I'll stay here, let the earth claim me.

Sarah halts in the white light, afraid of the shadows and shadow-less. Hands on her hips, she stares at me huddling in the ditch. The breeze sweeps her dark hair from her face to reveal a disapproving scowl.

"I know, I know," I explain, hand talking. "But I can't stay here. Everyone thinks I'm crazy." I roll my eyes around and try to smile, though it's not very funny.

1

She just gives me a look that means, *Well, you are crouching in the ditch like a dying frog.*

I laugh, or more like cackle, and I do sound crazy. "Even a couple of hours break would be nice," I plead, my mind playing tapes of the *crazy* people who never change out of their pajamas, milling around laminate tables, bumping into each other, muttering nonsense. My shoulders pull in, recalling the drag of chair legs across the linoleum floor as we take our places in Group.

Sarah dips her head in contemplation. *She gets it. She understands.* Skirting the shade, she jerks her head to the locked gate. I rise with hope, but then fall as if the shadows have thrown a weight around my neck. The sounds of many legs brushing grass and the flurry of colliding torchlight scanning the gnarled orchard tell me I've missed my window. Sarah purses her lips, frustrated. She wanted me to wait.

I couldn't wait.

A pour of white cloth and hairy arms flies down the hill, cornering me against the wall. Thick and menacing, Johnny lunges and stabs me in the arm with a syringe, whispering, "Not this time, honey."

Feeling the flutter and dimness that comes with the needle every time, I'm almost grateful for it. It's the only time I get to be alone.

When I slump in the orderly's arms, the last things I see are my dark feet churning up the lawn as I'm dragged back inside and Sarah waving before she jumps on to the stone wall. She squeezes neatly between the fence posts, which are made to look like feathered arrows. They point to the sky like a tease.

———⌘———

I STRAIN AT MY wrists like a broken puppet, even though I know it's futile. I've got at least twenty-four hours before they will loosen these restraints. My eyes adjust to the bright lights inside the infirmary, and I gaze down at my legs. I think the nurse went a little overboard with the gauze because they look like Q-tips, the expensive kind with wood for the sticks. Wiggling them, I chuckle, but my amusement then hits a dam, brims up, and pours out instant panic. *Where is she?*

I scan the clean lavender room frantically, and see her

head peeking out from behind an instrument trolley. Grinning, she motions for me to cover my eyes with my hands. She laughs cruelly when she realizes I can't because they're bound to the bed.

"I'll close them instead," I say, closing my eyes and counting. "One, two, three…"

When I open them, my view ticks over scenes like the arm of a clock. A nurse sits at her station staring at a computer like she's in a trance. The vacant intermittent click of the mouse is audible, but nothing else. Empty bed. Empty bed with a bedpan on it. Instrument tray. Something sticky and yellow on the floor…

The curtain to my right billows slightly, two tiny feet poking out from underneath.

"Found you," I exclaim, stretching my neck and shoulders against the straps to turn toward her.

"Found who?" asks a voice like scrunched-up paper.

2. TUPPER

KANSAS CITY, MO, 2015

WEATHER: A WALL OF DUST TO BREAK THROUGH

**I'M THE GUY YOU HATE, THE GUY WHO WAS OFFERED EVERY-
THING AND DIDN'T WANT IT.**

I KNOW I'M IN over my head. It crashes down on me the moment I step out the door. But I can't stay. Someone's driven an acme missile through my stomach. There's a gaping hole there. I don't know whether this will help fill the space, but I need to try. I need to understand Anna. She's somewhere between the scribbled thoughts and highlighted routes on that old road map.

I have to do this before my life becomes a plan.

Mom waves frenetically from the window, a big, plastic grin smashed on her face. They didn't want to come outside. They stay caged in the living room. Afraid people will see just how much I've hurt them and how disappointed they are I haven't made the *right* choice. I should be leaving with the others.

Dad's shadow pulls Mom back until all that's left is a hand smear in the fake snow that's still there from last Christmas. He's already said his goodbyes, so I understand him not wanting to do it again.

Today I will leave the endless dust behind.

Swinging my keys around on my finger mindlessly, I'm thankful I don't have anyone else to say goodbye to. Everyone has left for college or is starting new jobs. I raise my eyes to the house across the road, noticing Kris is home. Her shiny new SUV is crookedly parked in the driveway. A gift for getting good grades.

I consider it, but it would just be rubbing salt in the wound or something. I've hurt her enough.

4

I can't be what she wants me to be, talkative, sharing my feelings. That stuff makes me ball up. Even as I think about the last time we spoke, sitting cross-legged across from her like eight-year-olds at a sleepover, my chest caves in and I shudder. She looked at me with her big blue eyes, and said she'd wait for me. And I knew it so strongly and all at once that I didn't want her to. And then she kept saying 'what's wrong?' and 'tell me how you're feeling' and the caving-in sensation became more of a setting-like-cement feeling. I told her I was sorry, really sorry, but I couldn't ask her to do that. She'd cried, soaking my shirt, and when it was over, all I could think was, *I can finally leave.*

It was pure relief, flying like a banner. So it must have been the right thing to do. But when I look over there, I feel the pain I've caused her, the time I've wasted, how unfair things are.

I think she thought I was the strong silent type with a surprise center. But I'm just the silent type. There's nothing in my middle except more quiet.

Throwing the keys high in the air, I squint at the pale sun as they come back to me. I catch them, pop the trunk, and throw my bag in, slamming it shut. It marks the end of my life here. Even if I come back, things won't be the same. *I hope they won't be.*

The car grumbling to life brings me home, like the noise comes from inside me. Gas fumes fill my chest, and it settles me. Here on the old vinyl seats, the grit and ancient crumbs wedged between the creases, I'm comfortable.

I unfold my giant map. Dad asked me to take a GPS, but I wanted a real map, one I could draw on, track my route in big red marker, and circle all the spots I planned to visit. Just like Anna did. I quickly write in pencil over my hometown—**LEFT IN THE MORNING. NOT SAD. APRIL 22**. I draw a happy face next to my comment. He looks upward, his hopeful eyes tracking the mass of intersecting roads, twisting together like veins.

Folding the map down to my immediate journey, I lay it on the bench seat. I love the way the road ahead is short and then cuts out, so I don't know what's coming.

Adjusting my mirror like Dad always tells me to, I snap my seatbelt on and I'm gone.

3. Anna

Kansas City, MO, 1997

WEATHER: DEVASTATING, UNCONTROLLABLE, ALL THE
BAD THINGS, ALL AT ONCE

ANNA'S END WILL BE TUPPER'S BEGINNING.

ANNA COULDN'T HAVE KNOWN her story would finish like this, but part of her is unsurprised. After all she's been through—endlessly driving with baby Tupper from her beautiful, safe home in Canada to the hot, suburban dustbowl of Kansas City—it shouldn't be this predictable.

She thought this place would save her. But if there is beauty in this town, if there is redemption, she hasn't the energy to find it.

Anna has come to the end of her journey, and it's like the end of her arm.

Bruised, pricked, and wasted.

———✐———

IT TOOK A LOT, but the pain of losing her parents has subdued. It still throbs there in the darkness surrounding her heart, but for now, she is numbed.

As she stumbles back to the car, her memory of how long ago she left baby Tupper has blown away with the smoke and been punctured by the needle. It could have only been hours. But where was the sun? She stares up at the offensive ball of fire. When she dragged her painful limbs away from Tupper to find a hit, the sun was setting. Now it's high in the sky, blaring on her head and burning her pale skin.

Laughing, she thinks, *Time is a funny thing.* It just keeps going and going until it stops. Then time means nothing. Life means nothing. Now she has nothing.

She flaps her arms jerkily, a wounded bird dancing in aimless circles on the baked pavement. People stare.

She laughs at nothing.

She has *nothing*.

She is weightless. She could fly away, and no one would care.

Something pushes up, tries to break through the bubble of carefully cut chemicals. Tupper would care. Her baby. The only person she has left in the world. She strains to clear her head, shake it free, so she can remember how long it's been. How. Long. Ago. Since she left him in the car? The thought skips like a needle on a record, but it can't make its point.

Picking up her pace, she drags three tons of baggage behind her. She's sure it leaves oily stains on the pavement in her wake. She tries pressing deep into her hazy brain, managing to pick out the hours. The answer is devastating. It has been a day. Anna has left her baby in the car for... One. Whole. Day.

Running up the street and around the corner, she slams into a pedestrian staring at the ground as he walks. "Sorry, Miss," he mumbles.

Shifting to the side to let him pass, she sees the yellow tape wrapped around her car like it's a sweet sixteenth birthday present. The words *crime scene* are her greeting card.

She is plugged into the ground. Her breaths leave her hollow. Her mouth twists around words she dares not say out loud...

She killed him. She is a sickening excuse for a mother. She is trash, dirt. A selfish junkie.

The gavel comes down. It's final. There *is* nothing left. She is released from caring about this life. Set free in the worst possible way. Someone has grabbed the end and tugged, causing her to twirl and unravel. Naked, there is nothing she likes when looking down at herself.

She walks past the car and then back again, hoping beyond hope it's a cruel joke. That he's there, sleeping peacefully. But as she looks through the window, she sees the car has been emptied. There is no cardboard box and blanket, no map. All that's left are shards of glass glinting on the seat from a broken side window.

The flap of paper grabs Anna's attention. A woman and man stand in front of a coffee shop holding a newspaper. Pointing at the car, the woman says sternly, "Yes, that must be it. What kind of person abandons their child in a hot car for hours?" She tsks and purses her shriveled mouth. "You know it says here the baby remains unclaimed."

"He's alive?" Anna asks, getting way too close to the couple, who lean away from her in fear. The man sniffs like he can't stand the smell of her. He doesn't answer, so she snatches the paper from his hands, reading the article with eyes goggled by drugs and grief.

It tells her a detestable person abandoned a nine-month-old baby in a cardboard box in a hot car. Thankfully, the coffee shop owner heard screaming and broke the back window, rescuing the child from certain death. Police were called shortly afterward. The authorities are searching for the owner of the car, a one Anna Barrymore, who hasn't returned to the crime scene. She will likely face charges of criminal neglect and child endangerment.

Each word slams Anna like a hammer. She is so ashamed. Her parents would be so ashamed if they were alive to see this. And again, they would *be* alive if not for her. If they hadn't loved her so much they'd chased her across the states to bring her home. All the bad things are because of her. She causes nothing but pain. She may love Tupper, but she is no good for him. She will *never* be good enough for him, for anyone.

She backs away from the car like it's a bomb about to explode. She has lost everything, but it's better this way. He'll be better off without her.

When she turns her back to the tape-wrapped Chevy, her eyes sting and her heart pounds so hard she swears she can hear it punching against her ribs.

The needle calls. The secure feeling flowing through her veins like warm honey is all she needs. It's all she's good for.

She'll let Tupper go. Let it all go.

And if she never comes back, it won't matter. There is no one left to grieve her. There's peace in that knowledge.

As Anna slides away from the scene, she has the comforting and shattering thought that maybe her end will be Tupper's beginning.

4. LANGLEY

I'M NOT SURE HOW to proceed. My options are crazy Langley or sane Langley. Sane Langley's good at getting the restraints loosened early, charming the doctors and making them wonder why she's here in the first place. Crazy Langley is good at distracting people while she crushes her meds under her heel or slips them into the band of her pants.

I go with sane. They've got me captive, so I figure I might as well play nice.

So when he asks who I found, I say, "Found you, of course. I was wondering when someone was coming to explain why I'm tied to the bed."

Dr. Thera gives me an unconvinced look, though the term doctor is a tad too conventional for Thera. He's more of a therapist slash horticulturalist who thinks all our problems can be solved with a bit of 'outside' time, reconnecting with Mother Earth or some crap. I work that angle.

"Yeah. I went outside to get some fresh air *and* to check on the orchard—I'm real concerned about the state of those apples—when Johnny sedated me without warning." I say 'sedated' instead of 'slobbered in my ear and stabbed me with a syringe' because it sounds less crazy.

Sarah emerges from her hiding place. She pokes her tongue out at me, blowing silent raspberries at the mention of Johnny's name. She hates him as much as I do.

I hear the tap, tap, tapping of Thera's pen on the side of his coffee mug that says in solemn black writing, *Do what you love. Love what you do.* I look up at him, which takes some effort since I'm tied down. So essentially, I have to strain to touch my chin to my chest to make eye contact.

"Are you still seeing the girl?" he asks, ignoring my apple

concerns and going straight for the obvious question. I can tell he's not in a believing mood. So I nod, flipping the card over to crazy Langley.

He raises his eyebrows at my honesty before writing something in his notebook. I imagine all he writes is, *still sees girl,* underlining it a few times.

Sarah looks worried. She picks at the hem of her dress and sucks on her lower lip. I want to tell her not to stress out, but that always rings alarm bells. The 'crazy girl talking to her dead sister while strapped to the bed' routine won't help me right now.

"Can you see *the girl* right now?" Thera asks in a leading kind of way, his eyes searching the room. Like if he squinted hard enough, he might see her, too.

"No." I wince. I hate that he calls her 'the girl' like she's a random ghost without a name. She's not random. She's my only family. "Doctor Thera," I say, trying to be flattering. "Can you please loosen these for me? They're rubbing the skin clean off my wrists." I try to cry. It's always been hard for me, so I go for wide, watery eyes by refusing to blink.

Thera clucks his tongue and inspects my raw skin. "Of course, dear. You know we're only trying to help you. This *is* for your own good."

I nod. They all say that. They say it until they are blue in the face, to me at first, and then to themselves like they're trying to convince their consciences that treating me this way is 'helping'. I don't fit into their classic models. I'm not schizophrenic. I'm not paranoid delusional. I'm something else. Eventually they get angry, throw their hands in the air, and get rid of me. Again. Then I'm someone else's problem.

"Can you get her to take these?" The nurse, who is pressed up behind Thera, drops some pills into his hands and rolls her eyes as if to say, *Good luck with that one.*

His kind eyes, sunk deep into tanned skin, run over my face. "Will you take these willingly?"

"I will," I reply. The nurse's pothole mouth opens in shock, and Thera can't smother his surprised gasp. I part my lips like a good pet, and he places the two pills on my tongue. I very rarely take my meds without a fight, but I swallow them this time. Sarah's horrified expression wobbles like a mirage. Little pieces of her fall away until there is nothing but clean air in her place. I can't help but stretch my tethered hand out to where she was standing.

I want to tell her I did it for a reason. There's a plan. But for my plan to work, I need to be the model patient.

5. TUPPER

KANSAS CITY, MO, 2015

WEATHER: PROMISING

LEAVING THIS DUSTBOWL FEELS like taking a deep breath after holding it for a really long time. So much so, I almost choke on the release of all that pent-up oxygen from my lungs.

The Chevy passes chocolate brick villa after brick villa. Wailing eighties arches shade sagging screen doors. Suddenly, suburbia falls away and I'm staring at vast expanses of red dirt and defiant clumps of rock. It feels good, fresh. The untouched un-messed-with dirt is cleansing. The blue sky is cooling; the pale sun hanging like a cough drop from a string above me, spreading vapors. Like the kind Mom always gave me when I was sick, but Dad said were a waste of money and would only rot my teeth. Thinking of them produces a slight ache in the middle of my chest, but for the first time in as long as I can remember, I feel relaxed.

Sinking deeper into my seat, I put one arm across the back and lean into it.

It shudders and bucks, but the old Chevy seems to like the open road. Soon, we are roaring along. Traveling backward through time. Because this is my mother Anna's car; it's her journey plotted out carefully that I follow. This is the reverse trip she took to leave me. And now I'm taking it to get her back.

I have two maps on the seat beside me. One I bought from the gas station about a month ago and the other found shoved in the dash of this old Chevy Impala the day they found me. A skinny, screaming, and kicking baby in a cardboard box on the backseat of a hot car. Abandoned.

When I whir past a cactus, I almost squeal in unmanly delight. I don't know why, but I screech on the brakes and shove the car violently into reverse. It resembles a lopsided man, his arms at right angles, one shorter than the other. He grows around some old barbed wire that doesn't seem to be keeping anything in or out, and it presses into his stomach.

A spiky beacon.

I find where I am on the map before spreading it out over the hood of the car. Pulling a pencil from my pocket, I quickly sketch the cactus. I add sunglasses and a cowboy hat, like people see on every souvenir mug from here to the Grand Canyon.

In a speech bubble over his head, I write two sentences. **THIS IS WHERE IT GETS GRITTY. YOU SURE YOU WANT TO GO ON?**

I switch the maps over to read Anna's thoughts from eighteen years ago. She also drew a cactus, but he welcomes her. **YOU MADE IT! YOU FOUND YOUR COURAGE**, he says, a spiked smile across his face.

She was at the end of her journey. I'm at the beginning of mine. I'll take what courage she left etched into this map and try to find my own.

Kansas City, MO, 1997
WEATHER: PROMISING

THE SUN RISES FAST. The purple and pink snapping shut and giving way to stark, bright sunlight.

Anna glances down at her map. She is so close now she can feel *his* mouth on hers, his strong arms wrapping around her and lifting her from the ground.

She taps the street map and glances at the broken screen door, propped up with a brick. She hopes the address she has is the right one. It has been a long time since *he* wrote this down, pressed it into her palm, and whispered, "When you find your courage, you come find me." His breath hot and sweet on her neck.

She touches her skin there, a brand he left. It has been almost eighteen months and she has so much to tell him, to show him, to share with him. Her eyes fall to little Tupper sleeping in the backseat. He looks so much like his father. She just knows *he* will love him the moment they meet.

She takes a deep breath, steeling herself and pushing down the nervous excitement, then knocks on the door of the man she drove thousands of miles to see. Tupper's father.

———————

THE TIRES SQUEAL AS Anna anxiously speeds away from *his* house before *he* hears, driving in circles until the baby calms down. Soon, her arms feel like aching spaghetti strands and she pulls over. She forces courage into her chest and exits the car, walking quickly toward the phone box before she changes her mind.

Her hand steadies as she starts to dial. She can barely see the numbers as the sun begins to set and the buildings slant over her thin form.

All those reasons for leaving her parents, for cutting them off, all that love she thought she was saving, is gone. She touches the corner of her eye gingerly, feeling the bruise *he* gave her deepening, the swelling rising. Tupper's father's voice vibrates in her soft head. She sees his demanding fist threatening her when she shook her head *no* to joining him on the filthy floor. Said *no* to squatting on a stained mattress sucking in fumes so strong she'd held her sleeve to her nose.

She'd found her courage. She wanted to join him so badly, but she stepped back. Finally, she could see in him what her parents had. Someone in trouble, someone they couldn't save, so they took what they could carry—her—and ran from him.

Anna understands that what they did was out of love, for her and for her baby.

Tupper's little red face is finally at peace after miles of screaming. She didn't tell *him* he was a father. She couldn't. No good would come from their meeting.

Smiling sadly, she watches him sleep peacefully in the backseat of the Chevy.

She thinks of Tupper's father, wild and unpredictable, violent, and she wants to believe he will pull out of it. She wants to believe he loved her, could still love her if not for the drugs ripping every muscle from his body, the light from his eyes.

A tear slides down her purpling jaw.

The phone begins to ring.

She composes what she might say. *I want to come home. I'm sorry. I couldn't see clearly. Now I can. I want to try to make this work. I want you to be in Tupper's life… I need your help. Please.* The phrases pulse with every long ring. Just when she thinks her heart can't take one more empty bell sound, someone answers.

"Hello?"

"H-h-hello," she stutters. This is harder than she thought it would be. But then falling to her knees was never going to be easy.

The voice sounds familiar, but it's not her father speaking. "Who am I speaking with?" the man asks in a calm, solemn tone.

Unsure, she's worried she called the wrong number. *Could her parents have moved?* "It's Anna," she manages to whimper, tears flowing freely and pouring into the holes of the receiver.

A deep regretful sigh pushes through the phone. Grabs her by the throat. "Anna. I'm sorry. It's Charlie… er… Freeman, your neighbor."

She whispers the words, knows they aren't true, but she has to say them anyway. "I must have the wrong number." Her voice sounds dead, her spare hand picking at the aged stickers on the window of the phone box.

She can almost see him shaking his head sadly as he speaks, "Anna. I'm so sorry to be the one telling you this, but your parents were in an accident this morning."

She gasps. She knows the answer, but she asks it anyway, "What do you mean accident?"

He doesn't want to say the words, but she forces him to. "They, er, died. Your parents are dead."

Covering her mouth, she says, "No," into her hand. *Dead, died, accident.* Each word is pointed, stabbing her between her ribs like a repetitive beak.

She wants to hang up, to run from the phone box. As it is, she feels like she's hanging from the receiver, the ground disappearing beneath her feet.

"They were on their way to Williams, in Arizona, and they were in a car accident." Charlie coughs, makes a strange groaning sound, and then continues, "I-I guess they were speeding or something. Told me they were on their way to visit you, asked me to water the plants." These stupid details are making it real. She doesn't want it to be real. "I'm so sorry, Anna."

She knows she should say something, let the poor guy know she's still on the phone, but she's frozen and broken. Parts of her are shattered ice. The rest is melting.

"They were coming to find me?" she asks.

Another sigh. "Er, yeah, I guess so. I'm here letting the solicitors in, you know, since I have a key and all. You let me know when you'll be home, and I'll open the house for you. I think the funeral's going to be in a few days…"

Limply, she hangs up the phone. Dazed and aching, she walks straight past her car, past Tupper. Her eyes are dry, her blame is insistent. This is her fault.

The pain is too strong. It pervades her bones. It shrieks like a howling ghost inside her.

She hails a taxi and heads away from Tupper, the baby still asleep in the car.

Away from life and into the arms of oblivion.

7. LANGLEY

Maka Mani Psychiatric Hospital, UT, 2015

WEATHER: BREWING

THEY LET ME OUT of bed after twenty-four hours. I haven't seen Sarah that whole time. Biting my nails, I start the process of worrying. The question that has no answer plagues me.

Where does she go when she's not with me?

I worry she won't come back, that I'll be alone. That's when shadows lean in. I feel like the bed will rise and crush me to the ceiling.

My new room is within sniffing distance of the nurses' station. Since I smashed the window of my old room, they've moved me to a highly supervised area. This is where the potential suicidal and homicidal patients reside.

The muffled, loony chant of one sails through the small window in my door. "Git over here, purtty girl," he says with his face pressed to the glass. I move closer to my window and flatten my palms against it, framing my indifferent expression.

"It's 'get', you hick," I say playfully. It's Acorn. He's harmless. I don't really have friends in this place, but he's always been nice to me.

"Langley! I didn't know that was you. What are doing up this end with all the unsavory characters?" His voice changed from redneck to gentleman in seconds.

"Misunderstanding," I reply, flicking my eyes to the nurse who's pulling the dinner trolley down the dimly lit hallway.

Acorn grins at me, showing all his rounded teeth. "Oh, yeah. Me too! I'm Miss Understood. Miss Congeniality, too."

I laugh. "Congratulations." Acorn's a woman trapped in a man's body, or sometimes a bear or a butterfly, depends on the day. He causes so many eye rolls from the staff I'm sure it's only a matter of time before someone's fall out.

"Thanks, I was robbed of the top prize by a Vaseline-toothed Barbie doll." He bats his eyelashes at me, slicking his eyebrows down with a licked finger. "Some people can't appreciate true beauty."

"You're right," I say. "Maybe next time?"

Acorn claps his hands together loudly. "Hurrah for next time! That tiara will be mine for sure," he shouts, dancing around his room in the moonlight like some deranged Peter Pan shadow.

The nurse manning the dinner trolley rolls toward my door. She waits for me to step back and then pushes a tray through a slot at the base, watching patiently. This one's not too mean; the younger ones usually aren't. She needs to make sure I take my meds, but with less staff on, all I have to do is put them in my mouth and then open it, poking out my tongue. The nurses can't be bothered coming in and checking at night. Besides, they always check properly for morning meds, squeezing my cheeks together and making me lift my tongue. I'm locked in my room. Even if I haven't taken my meds, there's little damage I can do in here. The bars on this window are much closer together. I have no hope of getting out tonight.

Putting the pills in my mouth, I push them into my gums with my tongue and open for the nurse.

She nods. "Goodnight sweetheart," she whispers.

When she's gone, I wrap my tranquilizer in a napkin and tuck it into my waistband.

Sitting down on the bed, I clasp my hands together anxiously. Now that the meds from earlier have worn off, I wait for Sarah to return. *I miss her.* On these nights, when the crazies are howling at the moon or rattling their cages, she helps me sleep. She sits at the foot of my bed, making shadow puppets for me until my eyes get heavy. I watch her braid her dark hair into a side plait before gently unwinding it and teasing it out with her fingers. It's a comfort. It was the first and only comfort I had in those early days.

I blink groggily and rub my eyes. It's six o'clock. Too early for a Saturday. I close my eyes, pulling the quilt over my head.

"Go away, Sarah," I groan. "Aren't you supposed to be at your stupid gymnastics meet?"

I brace myself. Usually she'd be hitting me with a pillow by now. I pull the covers down and open one eye, my heart beating wildly in my chest. I'm scared, but I don't know why. Sarah sits on the end of my bed wearing her costume. She looks up at me, her eyes impossibly sad, and shakes her head slowly. Noises push around the barriers of sleep. Beeps, heels on hard floors. The sound of other people breathing.

"Where's Mom?" I ask, sitting up, panic rising from the floor and building like flames. Something's trying to choke me. Sarah does nothing but shake her head, dark hair falling over her face. "Where's Mom?" I shout. "Sarah, talk! What's wrong with you? Talk!"

Dad stumbles into the room, his face gray and lit with fluorescence. "Shh! Langley, why are you screaming like that?"

"Sarah's teasing me, Dad." I point to the end of my bed accusingly. "She's pretending she can't talk," I whine, blinking, confused as the room sharpens around me and I realize I'm not in my bedroom. I'm in a hospital bed. Sarah's still sitting there, shaking her head.

Dad looks at me quizzically, but then sadness pulls his expression down to the ground. "Langs, Sarah and Mom... they're gone."

Gone.

Gone?

"To, to the gymnastics meet? B-but they were supposed to wake me up." I stumble over my words. I don't want to pick up the ones that matter. The true ones lying bloodied in the road.

He shakes his head, running a palm over his tired face.

Sarah mouths, 'I'm sorry.'

Please, please, please...

8. LANGLEY

Maka Mani Psychiatric Hospital, UT, 2015
WEATHER: ICY

I SHIVER. MY BLANKET has slipped from my feet, and they're ice. I wriggle my toes and groan. Something light grazes my pinky toe. I mumble, "Sarah," before pulling my leg in under the covers sharply.

"Nope, not Sarah, darling." Johnny's dark voice climbs the walls like a slick shadow.

Opening my eyes, I'm now fully awake. I sit up quickly. Johnny's hand is on my leg, his white teeth shining like a Cheshire cat in the moonlight.

"Get the hell out of my room, you sicko," I warn.

Johnny's quiet laugh sounds like air hissing from a punctured tire.

"Or what?" he challenges. He pulls the blanket away from my legs. "C'mon. Why're you always fighting me? You know you want to."

Now it's my turn to laugh. He doesn't appreciate it, and his hand clamps down on my thigh. Hard.

"I'll scream," I warn.

Releasing me, he folds his arms across his broad chest. "Go ahead."

Narrowing my eyes, I open my mouth and take a deep breath. A white blur appears in the corner. Sarah's here. Relief closes my eyes and pulls an almighty scream from my lungs.

When I open them, Johnny is gone and the lights are on. If Sarah was here, she's disappeared again. I know she heard me, though. She sensed I needed her.

A nurse stands over me. "What are you shrieking for?" she asks, irritated. "You'll wake the others." She has one hand on her hip, the other already forming a pointed finger to tell me off.

I glance up, wishing tears would come right now. Maybe then they'd believe me. "Johnny was in here. He put his hand on my leg. He was trying to, trying to…" I start, but I can tell I've lost her already. No one believes the crazy girl.

Patting my arm, she says in a very un-soothing voice, "You just had a bad dream, dear." She does a cursory sweep of the room. "There's no one in here. Go back to sleep."

She's right about one thing. This is a bad dream. It's a nightmare. And I need to get the hell out of here before it gets worse.

"Dad, please," I beg, my hand disappearing inside my sweater as he drags me across the parking lot.

"I'm sorry, honey, I don't think I can handle this anymore. Handle you. If your mother was here, she'd know how to help you." He runs a hand through his hair, straightens his shirt. "I'm just not good at this. I'm not fit to care for you at the moment, not with all your… issues. Maybe if we have some space from each other, things will get easier. Right now, it's just too much for me."

My hand is on my heart. His hand is tugging on an empty sleeve.

I drop to my knees. "Please! I'll tell her to go away. I'll stop seeing her."

He crouches and takes my face in his hands. "We've tried everything else. I wish it were that simple, sweetie, but you're sick. You need more help than I can give."

Like that, he drops his hands, stands up, and forgets who he was. Forgets me.

"It's going to be easier for both of us this way."

My throat hurts. I want to cry. Why can't I cry? I glance to my left. Sarah is balancing on the brick wall, arms out at her sides, dipping her feet like a gymnast. She knows I can't fight this.

I stand. "When will I see you?"

He scratches his chin, looks past me, over the hoods of cars. "Well, you know I've just started this new job, but as soon as I'm settled, I'll come visit you. As soon as I can."

I bite my lip.

He'll come as soon as he can. And I'll be better. Then he'll take me home.

Sarah jumps from the wall. She beckons me with her finger.

21

9. TUPPER

SUPERIOR, CO, 2015

WEATHER: CALM AND CONFUSING

ANNA'S HANDWRITING IS EERILY like mine. I imagine her pressing down, her thoughts pouring into the ink and lead and onto the page. She writes in thick, round font, comic-book style, like me. She describes things in sharp one-liners. Some things I understand, some I don't.

I trace her words with my finger, feeling the indent from the pen eighteen years later. Words from the grave. Her thought on our first stop, on the tiny, mostly deserted town of Superior.

BEER'S BETTER THAN A HANDSHAKE.

I frown. I don't know what that's supposed to mean.

It's around lunchtime when I pull into the one and only street, feeling like I'm on the set of a movie because this place seems unreal. I can't help but grin at the charm and the insignificance of it. Standing over the dilapidated, made-for-film-looking buildings, like stony guardians, are red rock formations that dwarf this old mining town. It's beautiful and scrabbly and ancient.

I'm sure this place is a pop-up. If I push hard enough, the shops with just the right amount of peeling paint and cobwebs dancing in the breeze will fall with a creak and a puff of dust.

I approach an old bar, tempted to give it a shove, and peer in the window. It's barred up, but hanging behind it is a framed cross-stitch with the words, *Beer's better than a handshake*, neatly stitched into once-white linen.

Stepping back, I feel a little like I might be sick. It hits me, an obvious boxing glove on the end of a spring, that my mother probably looked at that picture. Maybe she had a beer in that bar with me tucked in the crook of her arm. Or did she pass it while walking me up to the supermarket-slash-liquor-store-slash-post-office, and think it was funny, cute, quaint?

I don't know.

These memories are just as real as the ones I made up when I was a kid.

I'll never really know what happened to her. All I'll ever get is a postcard scrubbed of all meaning.

Pushing up the street, I buy myself some bread and a soda, then trek back to my car.

I sit in the car a long time, just staring out the window at the huge mountains behind the western buildings. Trying to picture people wandering in and out of that bar, music playing, loud drunk voices clashing against each other.

I sketch a quick figure next to the place name on the map. A miner with a mug of beer for a hand and a pickaxe in the other. I caption it, making the man speak.

I CAN'T SHAKE YOUR HAND, BUT YOU CAN DRINK MINE.

The dirty old man winks. It's not funny. It's gross. But I don't feel very humorous right now. This place is dead, and it gives me the creeps.

I've spent two hours peering in windows, trying rotted doors, and searching for remnants in this town. It's now too late to drive to the next one. I book myself into the El Portal Motel, then collapse on the bed to watch crappy TV and eat a cheese sandwich.

10. Anna

Superior, CO, 1997

ANNA FEELS THE SMALL tug that was missing before. The one reminding her that her parents are sitting at home worrying about her, waiting for her to call. She knows she couldn't stay, but she does regret some of the things she said. The way she left.

Her hand lifts the receiver of the phone in the scummy hotel. Each number she dials pushes pain through the cracks of her messed-up chest. She watches the dial rotate back into place. Each time, her thoughts spiral with it. *They won't understand. They're the ones who pulled him from her life, told her he wasn't good enough, forced him to leave her and leave town.* There are too many reasons not to call and only one reason to call. Her hand shakes as the phone begins to ring. If they pick up, what will she say? She hears a click and stops breathing. Panicking, she slams the receiver back down. She knows they'll say they love her, that they want her to come home. Those words hurt. They are too tempting. Guilt rises and she stands suddenly, stomping on the uncomfortable feelings.

She needs something to slice through the pain writhing inside her. Again, she touches her chest. A burning sensation pulsing under her skin. She checks on Tupper. He's sleeping soundly in his box. She laughs, thinking she'll have difficulty getting him to sleep in an ordinary cot when the time comes. Or maybe she'll just have to find a bigger box.

Sneaking out the door, she heads for the store on the main street.

The man at the counter smiles as she enters, giving her a wink. He looks harmless, old and smudged with grease. She feels as if bugs are crawling under her feet, threatening to inch under her skin. Quickly, she grabs the first six pack in the fridge without even looking at the label. She clutches it to her hip, holding it as she would her baby.

Gently, she places it on the counter, avoiding eye contact with the friendly old guy.

"Nice choice," he crackles. "You know I just bought a carton of this for my son-in-law? It's his favorite. And you know what they say here in Superior—beer's better than a handshake."

She glances up, sees a man desperate to talk. Watery eyes and bristled gray moustache lifted in a hopeful smile. He reminds her of her neighbor back in Chilliwack, of another life that got lost somewhere on the road.

She tries to smile back. A tip jar sits to the side with only a few lousy pennies in it.

"Thanks," she mumbles, breaking a beer from her pack and placing it inside the tip jar.

She hurries out before he can say anything more.

———✦———

THE BEER CLUNKS SADLY down on the dresser. She sits on the edge of the bed and reaches for it, pulling each can out of the plastic rings one by one and lining them up.

She snorts. A family of beer cans.

She taps the top of the first one. Her dad. Loving. Disappointed. Desperate. He wanted so much for her. She wanted things, too, but…

Her finger coasts over the next can. Mama. Protective. She had it together. Until Anna pulled her apart.

Her fingers wrap around the can and squeeze. The cold bites into her hand, and she releases the beer. The alcohol promises forgetfulness. It doesn't promise a solution.

Tupper squirms in his sleep, and she gazes down on him. Her hands are wrapped together to stop herself from reaching for a drink.

It shouldn't be this hard. It shouldn't mean as much as it does.

Her family of beer cans stand like sentinels, watching and waiting for her to mess up. Like Dad and Mama, they shake their heads. They make her feel not good enough. One beer would numb it, even if just a little.

She understands now why she wants it. Yet, it doesn't

stop her from needing it.

Tupper wakes and she kneels, stroking his head and watching his eyes roll back into sleep again. He is her family. He needs her.

She gathers up the beers. Throws them in the trash. Letting them sit for a moment before she grabs the trash can and takes it outside, she then empties it into the large industrial bin in the alley.

She knows she is weak. Her promise to herself is to be stronger.

11. LANGLEY

Maka Mani Psychiatric Hospital, UT, 2015
WEATHER: GETTING WARMER

"I'M REALLY IMPRESSED, LANGLEY," Dr. Thera announces, pointing at his notepad with his pharmaceutical gift pen. "You've made a great deal of progress in the last few sessions." I think he's more impressed with himself than me, but I don't say anything. "If we could just get you to truly let go of your emotions so you can experience your grief in a healthy…"

Sniffing, I wipe at the corner of my eyes. It's the best I can do. "Thank you, Dr. Thera," I reply, my eyes on Sarah. She's dancing against the backdrop of diplomas and heavy textbooks, spinning in circles. Holding out her hands to me, she begs me to play 'Ring Around the Rosie.'

To Thera's amazement, I talk to her in his presence. "Sarah, sit down. I'm trying to concentrate on my session." She glares at me, silently defying my request, and begins scaling the bookcase. My heart becomes a lump creeping up my throat. "Wait. You could fall." I reach out my hand to my delusion/hallucination or whatever they're calling her these days. She ignores me, digging her toes into a shelf that houses books on schizophrenia in teenagers.

Thera turns around, attempting to follow my gaze.

"What's happening?" he asks in a guarded yet curious tone.

I gasp as her foot slips. "She's, uh, climbing the bookcase," I answer, barely making eye contact with the doctor, turning my attention back to Sarah. "Seriously, get *down* before you break your neck," I shout. Her head snaps in my direction. She pulls a book from the shelf and throws it to the floor, climbing quickly after it.

"Is she all right?" the doctor asks, slowly getting pulled in. "Did she fall?"

I shake my head. "Why don't you sit down and read that

book you just *had to have* while I finish my session?" I suggest, my eyes widening when I see the title.

Sexual Dysfunction in Males with PTSD.

Thera shuffles to the edge of his seat. "Langley, can you please tell me what you're seeing?" he almost begs. It must be intriguing and kind of isolating wanting to see the crazy theater that's going on without him.

I snort, rolling my eyes. "It's um, well…" I turn to Sarah. "Choose something else."

Smirking, she holds the book above her head, the pages fanning out and revealing what I'm sure is extremely inappropriate content for a ten-year-old. She scrunches up her nose at the words as she reads them. I smile but take on the disapproving mother tone. "Choose something else now," I demand.

Throwing the book on the floor with a flourish, she stands up to peruse the shelves for something else to read.

She behaves for the rest of the session.

"Langley, I've managed to get your yard privileges reinstated and I think we can return you to your old room," he says proudly. "Took some convincing, but…"

I lean forward, hands clasped together. "Thank you so much, Doctor Thera. I really want to check on those peas I planted."

He nods, suddenly flustered. "Use them well," he says, standing and showing me to the door.

I feel bad. He's probably going to get fired after this.

———— ✆ ————

I'M WITH THE CRAZIES today, and we're planting tomatoes. Thera explains we're like seeds. We just need the earth to nourish us, and we will grow.

"And then what? You'll eat us?" someone yells out. "I don't want to be canned and sold at Walmart!"

Acorn pats the yelling patient on the head, talking down to him, "Wholefoodzzz, honey. We're all organic here." His face is so serious that I snort.

Thera ignores them, and continues his earth, growth, and healing speech. I'm finding it hard to concentrate, though. Acorn is impersonating a bee today. I can't help but crack up at the unfortunate orderly who wore a yellow shirt to work and is now trying to avoid being 'pollinated'.

It's hot, and the communal hats we've been given stink more than usual. Sarah leans against one of the raised garden beds, staring up at the clouds. She used to find the weirdest pictures in the sky. I could never see them. She'd drag me onto the roof of our house and we'd lie back on the shingles, me gripping the wood in fear.

"Look, there's a ballerina dancing with a turtle," she would say in her sweet voice. I would squint and turn my head, but all I could see was a cloud. She'd pat my arm condescendingly. "You've got no imagination, Langs." Then I'd kick her legs, and we'd fight until I started to panic I'd fall off the roof. That was before, when I was actually scared of death.

She stares at me questioningly with her deep blue eyes. *What are you thinking about?*

I don't answer, but I think, *God, I miss your voice. Why won't you speak?*

Sarah pats her pocket and holds one finger to her lips, reminding me of what I'm supposed to be doing. I pat my own pocket, feeling the lump of several sleeping pills gathering lint.

Johnny leans on a shovel, pretending to work whenever Thera looks at him. But the doctor's attention is on Acorn and the disruption he's causing.

Plunging my hand into the loamy soil, I scoop out a shallow grave for my tomato. I drop it in, and hear the airless giggle of Sarah behind me. She knows I hate tomatoes unless they're in ketchup form. I smile as I rake the dirt over the tiny seed.

Johnny's boots appear in my peripheral vision. "You've got a beautiful smile," he rumbles. I glance up, squinting into the light. Shielding my eyes, I get the full impression of his leering face.

I'm at the right height to punch him in the crotch right now, and my fists clench. "Thanks, Johnny," I manage, swiping my forehead with the back of my hand. "Would you mind getting me some water? It's so hot out here, working in the garden. I mean, you should know. You work so hard every day." I'm laying it on thick, but so is Johnny. I run my gaze up and down his arms appraisingly. He seems to like it. After he runs over to the cooler, he brings me back a bottle of water, holding it over my head. A cool drip of condensation lands on my lip, and I lick it.

Johnny raises his eyebrow. "For a kiss?" he asks with a wink, holding the bottle out of my reach.

I smile sweetly, wanting nothing more than to punch him. "Not here." I wink. It feels awkward, but he seems to buy it.

Grinning, he gives me a knowing look. "I knew all yer defensive, leave-me-alone bullshit was just an act," he whispers when he drops the water bottle into my lap.

A bitter taste swirls under my lips, rinsing my teeth in acid.

All I can manage is a light nod.

"Now that you're back in low security, I can come visit you tonight without people getting suspicious. Then we can have some real fun," he murmurs, touching the back of my neck with his sweaty hand like he has a hundred times before. This time, though, I restrain my shudder.

Sarah stares at me with giant eyes rippling with sadness that grow and grow. She's wondering if it's worth it. Wondering what it will cost me to keep her.

12. TUPPER

EL PORTAL MOTEL, CO, 2015

WEATHER: TUMULTUOUS

I WAKE UP IN a tangle of sheets and regret. This all seemed like a good idea in the planning stage, the part before real life. But yesterday surprised me. I wasn't expecting to feel like that. Empty. And then *angry*!

Sitting up in the bed, I snatch my mother's map from the nightstand. The next stop on her road trip is Moab. Her note reads:

THESE WINDOWS ARE ALWAYS OPEN. THEY'LL NEVER CLOSE.

What the hell does that even mean? My hand scrunches a little over the eighteen-year-old paper, but then quickly relaxes when I realize how delicate it is. A large part of me wants to destroy the only link I have to her. This map full of strange phrases and anecdotes. But the weird tightening in my chest tells me I shouldn't. It tells me I've only just started this journey, and I have to push on and against my fear.

I force myself to get out of bed to take a lukewarm shower. The faucet stutters like my thoughts.

When I finally check out and pay the extremely grateful owner, it's already eleven-thirty. Moab is over three hundred miles away. After a sigh full of red dust and cartoon clouds, I start the car.

13. LANGLEY

Maka Mani Psychiatric Hospital, UT, 2015
WEATHER: UNCOMFORTABLE

I'M PACING. SHE'S PACING. We pass each other in the middle of the room before turning in our respective corners. I want to tell myself this is the hardest thing I'll ever do.

I want to believe it.

I don't believe it.

Someone rubs their palms over the outside of my door. It's a rough sound, their skin like sandpaper.

I want it to be him.

I don't want it to be him.

Sarah stops dead in the center of the room like that one square tile under her feet suddenly contains her. I shuffle timidly toward the door, feeling elastic and tied to the outside window.

"Psst! Langley," Johnny whispers harshly. I don't like the way his voice slices through the glass embedded with metal, the spit spraying the pane. I tense, roll my crackly shoulders, and try to force myself to relax.

His hand curls into a fist against the window.

I move closer until he can see me. "Johnny," I say breathlessly, hand on my heart. "What are you doing here?"

His fingers relax and slip down. "I, uh, I thought..."

I swallow. "I'm so glad you made it," I whisper, glancing up into his shadowed face.

"Oh, you are, are you?" His voice is greedy, slick with desire. I gulp.

Stepping back from the window, he looks left, then right, and the lock slides open. The door parts, and he squeezes his muscular form into my room. Sarah retreats until she's flat against the wall, her baby bird chest rising and falling quickly.

Johnny advances, and I threaten myself to stand still. *We've been here before*, I tell myself. *You just need to play along this time.*

He puts his hand in my hair and leans down, inhaling deeply. "Mmm," he murmurs. I want to laugh at his enjoyment of my standard issue antibacterial shampoo. A soap dispenser that announces it can be used as shampoo, body, and face wash, screwed to the shower wall. It smells like dishwashing detergent.

Distracted, I'm not prepared for his other hand, which goes to the small of my back and pulls me against him.

Sarah is a shadow flat on the wall, shivering like grass in the breeze.

I can feel him, *all of him*, through his thin uniform and it's disgusting.

"Johnny, not here." I pull away, still caged in his arms. "Can't we go somewhere more…romantic?" I ask around my want to vomit.

He pauses. Thinks. "Where?" he grunts impatiently.

I tap my finger on my chin. "How about the greenhouse?" He doesn't seem to like that idea, his face contorting into a dissatisfied scowl, until I say, "That way we can make as much noise as we like."

He loves that idea and grabs my hand, practically dragging me out the door. My free hand lingers, calling for Sarah to take it. She does. Together, we sneak down the hallway and outside.

My bare feet touch the wet grass, and I exhale loudly. Johnny turns back toward me. "Excited, are you?" he asks, salivating.

Biting my lip, I nod, wondering how he could possibly be buying this act. After all the times he reached for me and had his hand slapped away. After all the times I complained to the doctors, nurses, anyone who would listen, about his repulsive behavior… He's so deluded that he belongs in here more than I do.

We reach the greenhouse, and he uses his large set of keys to unlock the door. "Ladies first," he says, arm out like he thinks he's a gentleman. I glance at Sarah. She's released me, her hands clasped in front of her. Her eyes are on the ground, and she won't look at me. She's not coming in, and I don't blame her. She doesn't need to see what comes next. It's better if I do this alone.

I nod to her and say, "Thank you," to Johnny.

We walk inside. He closes the rickety door, but doesn't lock it. It's dark, and he fumbles around for the light switch. "I'm glad you finally came to yer senses," he says. "Things could be a lot easier for you here if you learned to get along with me. I help all the girls who help me."

He finds the switch. Low lights flick on one by one. A greenish haze settles over the building. The tart smell of to-mato plants grows stronger as the lights heat up the room. Johnny's eyes find mine, and I tilt my head. He could have been handsome if he wasn't such a pig.

He stalks me like a tiger stalking a deer, inching closer as I stumble back toward the far wall. My back clatters against garden tools. He thinks he's got me cornered. But I know I'm exactly where I need to be.

14. TUPPER

SUPERIOR, CO TO MOAB, UT, 2015

WEATHER: STARK, COLD

THE WOODEN SALAD BOWL *spins on the table. At least it fills the silence. I watch the green, red, and orange-colored vegetables spiral together as it twirls and then slows to a stop. I meet their eyes. Kind eyes. Loving eyes. Eyes nothing like my own.*

"When?" Dad asks gruffly. He stares down at my hand, my pencil drawing random triangles on a napkin.

"As soon as school's finished," I reply.

Mom gasps, shakily dishing out clumps of salad onto our plates. "What about college?"

Triangles are coming together to make a man, a man made of triangles.

"Mangle," I whisper. Part triangle, part man… Powers…? Maybe he could throw triangles from his body like ninja stars…

The alarm in Mom's voice grows. "What?"

"Nothing," I mumble. "Look, I can defer my scholarship if I decide I actually want to go."

Dad scrunches his hand into a fist on the table, a yellow napkin trapped in his grasp. It's a bad sign. "We can't pay for this trip. You know that, right?" he says, hope laced through his voice.

I nod. "I'm going to use the money they left me. Who knows? Maybe that's what it was meant for."

I hate creating those lines in Dad's forehead. I don't want to cause them pain. "You won't go, Tup. I just know it. If you put off college, defer, you'll decide you don't want to go."

I shrug. "Maybe. But I have to do this, Dad. I need to."

Dad lets go. The napkin falls from his grasp in the shape of a flower. "Your body was made for football, son. Maybe if you gave it a chance, your head would fall in line with your body. I don't want you to pass up such a huge opportunity."

I shake my head. I love him—love them both—but they don't un-

derstand. This is not me giving up. This is me finally doing what I want.

"*I'll text you at every stop,*" I say, and then we eat in silence.

My phone vibrates in my pocket.

I glance down at a text from Mom. *Are you okay? xx*

The road ahead stretches to nothing, a pinpoint I'm supposed to reach. I shrug, wishing there was a way to communicate 'shrug' in a text. Am I okay? *I don't know.*

I pull over, creating a dust cloud that swallows the Chevy and gets an angry horn bellow as a truck screams past me.

Getting out, I stretch my back and return a text. *IDK*

IDK? she replies. Now I'm wishing there was an emoticon for 'rolls eyes'.

I don't know, Mom. I'm safe, though. Just left Superior on way to Moab.

Okay, she replies.

I roll my eyes.

My body feels lazy today, like I can barely lift my feet. Maybe it's too much time in the car sitting on my ass. I lock the door, deciding to walk toward the brown sign in the distance. It looks like a national park sign, the kind with the vintage Smokey-the-bear kind of writing. Anna's map is in my back pocket, and I get it out to see whether there's a clue to where I'm headed.

I COULD BE A RANGER.

(I COULD BE ANYTHING) is written along the road I'm walking on in tiny writing. I stop and open the map up further to see if there's a visitor's center or something around here. Somewhere a ranger could be found. There is one, but I've already passed it. I curse, run to the forest sign, and tap it. Brown paint crumbles from the edges. I turn around and head back up the 191.

———❧———

You were eighteen when you made this trip. Did your parents try to stop you?

I'm driving too fast, and the Chevy doesn't like it. It shudders and strains. I ease off the gas and take a few deep breaths, looking ahead instead of inside my head.

It doesn't take too long to see what I missed, and I'm surprised I drove straight past it. I put my finger in the air and trace the skyline, the up and down of red rock that's defiantly pushing against the sky. Pillars of ochre sandstone guard the entrance to the Arches National Park.

Turning in, I park at the visitor's center, eyeing every ranger who walks near me like a creeper. They're all crusty, gray-haired bearded old men in pointy hats and neatly pressed uniforms. They appear prideful, happy. I wonder if that's what she wanted. To have a purpose, *to protect*, and then I snort, right next to a rotating stand of key chains. People look my way, and I avert my eyes. If she wanted to protect things, she wouldn't have left me in a cardboard box in a hot car.

I flick lazily through the names. Thomas, Taylor, but no Tupper. There's never a Tupper.

I don't even know why I'm here. What I was hoping to find.

As I walk toward the front desk, my eyes are on the vintage posters above the lady manning the cash register. Just behind her shoulder, I see a framed poster that looks different from the others. My eyes narrow as I read the caption next to a black-and-white sketched sandstone arch.

These windows are always open. They'll never close.

It's written in the same writing as my map. I just know it's her.

"Ahem!" The woman at the counter coughs and points her pencil at my torso, which is leaning over the counter. I slide off. "Can I help you?"

My teeth clamp shut, and I have to push them apart with my tongue. "That, uh, that picture over there, can I buy it?" I ask.

She glances back and then points to the wall. "All posters are thirty-nine ninety-five."

I sigh. "No, that one. The hand-drawn one behind you." I get out my wallet. She shakes her head, but I speak before she can say no. "I'll give you two hundred dollars cash for it."

Her white eyebrows rise to the top of her forehead. Quickly, and while no one else is looking, she whips it from the wall and shoves it at me, her hand open, awaiting the cash.

"Thanks," I mutter, placing the bills in her palm and tucking it into my jacket. I stalk outside with my head down, practically running to the safety of my car.

Once inside, I take out the picture and hold it in both

hands over the steering wheel. The shading is blunt, dark. It's inked in, but I can still see a stray pencil line here and there like it was done in a rush. Through the window of the sandstone arch is the Chevy, racing down a strip of road just beneath it. My heart blanks out for a moment as I squint at the tiny representation of the car I'm sitting in right now. I press my finger to the glass. *That's me in there.*

I glance at my watch. It's pretty late, but I don't care.

I drive into the tiny park that seems cradled by the dessert, yet completely separate to it. I need to climb through one of the windows. I need to see what she saw.

I FOLLOW SEVERAL OTHER tourists who are hiking up the same trail, to one of the giant red arches. I pass several taking selfies with the grand sandstone formations. The grandness and beauty are hidden behind their big heads and pouting lips, and it makes me wonder. These places, here long before we were and probably long after we're gone, what does their 'selfie' look like? When they look down on all the people scraping their feet, pulling them into their photos, what do they see?

Sitting on a boulder lining the path, I ignore the giggling teenage girls who are pointing at me and get out my sketchbook. One of the girls, wearing cutoff shorts that are not particularly weather appropriate, turns around to smile at me. I try to be polite, smile back, but it feels like a line drawn in the sand or scraped out of a clay model, flat and unappealing. She turns back to her friend, and they continue along the path.

I draw two sandstone pillars leaning into each other. One yells at the sun. *HIGHER, HIGHER, YOU'RE NOT GETTING THE ANGLE RIGHT!*

After I close the book, I walk to the arch. Its cold shadow pulls me in. Reaching up to touch the red stone, I'm surprised it feels almost wet. It's doesn't crumble under my fingers like I expect it to. It's like fired clay. Strong and immovable.

Looking through the window, I try hard to block out the hum of other people, the iPhone clicks, and general noise. I want quiet. I sigh, and even that echoes around this windswept hole.

This isn't the right one. It's too big. The view through the middle is not of a road. I leave immediately, feeling this indescribable tug to keep searching.

MY EYES ARE WORN down and carved by ancient winds.

I do like that the further into the park I drive, the less people there are. I'm not good with people. People aren't that good with me either.

Holding up the picture Anna drew to the horizon, I try to match it to the arches in front of me. I scroll across and stop. One looks right—holes shaped like two eyes, one half closed and squinting into the sun.

Jumping from the car, I run toward it, hurdling a barrier.

The holes are only big enough to hold one man. There are signs saying not to climb on them, so I get as close as I can and peer through.

Sure enough, the road lies beneath, unrolled like ribbon trailing from a sewing box.

I place both hands on the curve of the arch. It feels strange. Humming with secrets. I want to know what she meant, and it's so frustrating that I don't. I breathe in deeply and exhale. *I can't ever know.* All I can do is catalogue how it makes me feel. Not empty this time. Just small. Like I'm just a grain of sand in this landscape.

It doesn't make me feel sad. Or lost. Or lonely. *Is that progress?*

I try to interpret her words, but they could mean nothing. They could be random thoughts like most.

I tap my sketchbook with my pencil. *Just draw, Tupper. That's your language.*

I'll let peace come to me through the paper and the pen. I should know by now that I understand nothing but the page in front of me. I don't need more.

I spend the next hour sketching, emptying my head, and not noticing the slowly sinking sun.

15. Anna

Arches National Park, UT, 1997

TIREDNESS PIGGYBACKS ANNA'S EVERY move. In her whole existence, she can't remember ever feeling this exhausted and hungry. Food always seemed secondary to the views and the air. The prickle of her skin. The electricity of her thoughts. Now, it's all she can think about.

After the Grand Canyon, she craves more. There was something about it, something dominating and devastating. It made her feel small but not insignificant. Like she was part of something bigger than herself. It was a nice feeling. Getting out of her head and jumping over a cliff into the Colorado River felt…liberating.

She rolls into the small parking lot of this next park. Aware she's forking over money she shouldn't for the entry fee. But surely this is worth an empty belly. At least for her. She'll make sure Tupper has what he needs.

Pulling the baby from the car, she holds him up to the light, under his arms. His slightly scrawny form stands out pale against the red ochre rock behind him. Rocks the color of dried blood and rust. Frowning, she holds him close, scaring herself as she rubs her hands up and down his back, feeling each individual rib. She closes her eyes against the truth.

She's been so high she's not really sure when Tupper last ate. The thought opens a mouth in the ground, ready to swallow her up. She steps back from it, then turns and marches into the visitor's center of The Arches National Park.

She scans the room. Vintage art hangs on every wall, calling a name she had long forgotten, calling her hand to pick up a pencil. She stands next to a rotating stand of key rings and takes in the shapes and forms, the striking artwork inspiring her.

A small collection of energy bars and other snacks draws her attention. She grabs a handful, also buying a sketchbook with *Arches National Park* written on the front, the logo of a window punched through the rock seeming very fitting.

———————

THEY CLIMB THE SLANTED road, following other cars. She passes by every parking lot with cars, searching for a place to be alone with her thoughts and with Tupper.

Ahead, she sees an empty place and pulls in. She takes Tupper and his box from the car, then hikes the short trail to sit beneath the arches. Windows frame the view or catch it. She thinks maybe people can't catch something this wild and ancient. There are no glass panes for windows like these and she likes the promise, the possibility of windows that are always open and never close.

Setting Tupper's box on the ground, she sits beside him, breaking off pieces of energy bar and handing them to him to suck on. He seems content, watching the clouds fly past through the eye of stone.

The moment she puts pencil to paper, a calm settles over her. She realizes it's been too long. She'd lost herself. But now, maybe, she can start to draw the old Anna out from her dark hiding place.

It's a hope.

She also hopes that when she finds *him*, she can convince him this life is better. Feeling things on a normal scale is better. She smiles when she thinks of *him*. Her pencil paused and pointed on the paper. She's so sure their love will conquer anything.

She wipes the corners of Tupper's mouth, which is dribbled with drool and chocolate, then turns her head back down the path to see a ranger trudging toward her.

The old woman, with her khaki shirt tucked into khaki pants, leans down and appraises Anna's drawing. "That's very good. You have quite a talent."

"Thanks," Anna replies, shrugging. People have always said that. Her parents always believed she would end up in art school, or in graphic design.

The ranger lady casts a quick concerned glance at the baby, her eyes washing over Anna's dirty clothes and thin face. "We could use a little local art for the back wall of the visitor's center. Would you be willing to sell it to me?"

Anna gazes at the woman's kind face. She sees no judgment, and her hands wish to reach out to the woman. She knows her tiredness, her hunger, is clear in her worn, red-rimmed eyes.

"I'd settle for a meal and a place to stay for the night," Anna replies hopefully.

The woman smiles like she'd hoped that would be the answer, and she extends a soft, wrinkled hand to help Anna to her feet.

The ranger easily hefts the box containing Tupper onto her hip. She carries him to her truck like a laundry basket.

"You can leave your car here if you like. I'll bring you back to it in the morning," the ranger says kindly.

Anna nods, smiles shyly. She is happy to let someone else take the reins for a while.

She climbs into the truck that smells like coffee and roses. Her brain empties, her body retires. She falls asleep on the drive to the ranger's home. A dreamless, exhausted sleep, woken only by the sound of her baby laughing.

———⌒———

"MY GRANDKIDS HAVE OUTGROWN these," the ranger tells her, holding up a pink onesie that would fit Tupper. She also seems to have a stock of diapers, some baby food, and she shoves it all in a bag, insisting Anna take it. Anna knows the ranger is lying, and she is so thankful.

They drive back to her car the next morning, and the ranger talks about her life in the park. It sounds peaceful, rewarding. A fleeting thought rustles through Anna's brain. *I could be a ranger.* She smiles as she gazes out the window, the desert flashing past in a blur of red and stubbly green. Maybe she could now. Nothing's stopping her.

The ranger's kindness makes her think maybe she will be okay. With these new supplies, she can make it to Kansas City. She will find *him*, and her life can begin.

16. LANGLEY

Maka Mani Psychiatric Hospital, UT, 2015
WEATHER: SPRING STORMS

I FIND IT INTERESTING the way people delude themselves. They call me delusional, but here is a man who, up until now, I have fought, kicked, and screamed every time he tried to touch me, looking at me with desire in his eyes and thinking it's reciprocated. He thinks I *want* him.

My hands press into the flimsy wall behind me. My fingers spread out like spiders' legs, searching. I try to stand in an appealing way, but I'm trembling. This has a large chance of not going my way.

"What are you doing all the way over there?" Johnny croons. "Come over here." He beckons me with a finger and a malicious curve to his lips.

I smile with half my mouth. The other side protests. Pressing my foot against the wall behind me, I stick out my chest. "You come here," I say, terrified.

"You know, you girls all play hard to get, but sooner or later you always come around," he says, taking slow steps. His eyes are wayward. Breath steamy. His gaze runs from my feet to my eyes. "I've never been with an Asian chick before. Guess I can cross that one off my list."

I fight the urge to throw a pickaxe at his head. But I have to wait. He needs to come closer...

Sarah, I wish you were by my side right now. Make me brave.

Turning, I gaze across the rows of green plants, leaves glistening with artificial dew. Against the white plastic outer wall stands a silhouette. She puts her hand out—*stop*. But it's too late. It's too late and I don't want to lose her or myself to this place and this man, who, I'm sure, will never stop until he takes what he wants from me.

"Aren't you gonna speak, Langley? Though I do like your

lips all pouty and sexy like that. They're just so…" The yards between us are shrinking. "Just so…"

I gag. Clench my fists.

His face is too close to mine. He breathes, "So kissable," like he's snuffing out a candle. Suddenly, his mouth is on mine.

Pushing against me, he slides one leg between mine and pins me to the shed wall. He forces air from my lungs in a gasp, which he takes to mean 'more,' and his mouth moves to my neck. His tongue tastes my skin, which shivers with disgust under his touch.

I can't take anymore. Pushing my hands into his hair, I lead him in a shuffling circle until we have swapped positions and his back is against the wall. His teeth hit mine and I pull away, kissing down his neck, which tastes like sweat and bug spray. While his eyes are closed, I reach for the garden shears hanging behind his head, making sure I grip them tightly with my good hand. As I run my weak hand under his shirt, I bring the blades to his throat. He doesn't notice at first. Hands trembling, I push harder, his jugular vein bulging against the sharp edge.

He freezes, disconnects from my skin. "You crazy bitch," he spits.

I smile, though I don't enjoy this as much as I would have hoped. "Just like you always said," I reply, my voice lollied with fake sugar.

Keeping the shears pressed against his skin, I squeeze his mouth open. He doesn't fight me. His eyes are wide with fear, his skin sweat-sheened and pale. That's the thing. He really *does* think I'm a crazy bitch. He thinks I'll kill him.

"Swallow these now," I order. He goes to spit them out, but I clamp my hand over his mouth and nose until he has no choice but to do what I say. A rumble shakes the thin corrugated walls, and we both look up.

He gulps, eyes bugging out like a frog.

I check to make sure he's swallowed them, something I'm very good at by now. Then I release him, kneeing him hard in the groin and snatching his keys. He collapses to the ground, groaning in pain. I yank off his shoes before reaching into his pocket to take his wallet. With dry bile running across my gums, I run.

He won't make it back to the house before the pills kick in, but he might make enough noise to alert someone. I lock the door. The sounds of his wheezing and moaning disappear as I sprint for the gate.

Sarah catches up to me, and we run together. She's as light as air. I'm clomping, hopelessly, in large men's shoes. She jumps up and squeezes through the bars. I unlock the shining silver gate, the long creak sounding like a screaming chant to my freedom.

Dark clouds roll over and follow us.

The first crack sounds just as I leave the car park. Flashes of white light up the painted lines and fissures in the asphalt. Sarah stops dead as water pours from holes in the sky.

17. TUPPER

Near Moab, UT, 2015

Weather: Dark and cloudy

I STAYED TOO LONG at the Arches. Sketching until the light matched my pencil shading. I know this because now I'm in the middle of nowhere, and my eyes feel like they're melting out of my head. I'm so tired; my eyes keep doing that heavy blinking thing, where each time is longer and closer to sleep. Dad's stern voice floats through the air vents. *It's dangerous. A fatigued driver is as bad as a drunk one.*

I'm annoyed at myself for getting swept up in the red stone and the blue sky painted behind it, because now I have to sleep in the Chevy. I find a place to pull over that's not dangerously close to the road and park.

Through the windshield, I see an old gate about a hundred yards ahead. As per usual, it doesn't look like it's attached to anything. I make a note that if an axe murderer comes for me in the middle of the night, I'll run for there and hope the track leads to a house and not the axe murderer's hidden chop shop where he keeps human body parts in jars. *Great. I'll never sleep now.*

Shuddering with the car as the engine ticks over, I realize I'm starving and busting for the bathroom. The latter I can take care of pretty easily, but I don't know what I can do about food. After I flick open the glove compartment, my hand patters over pens with no ink, old receipts, and an endless nest of chewing gum wrappers. Finally, I pull out a half-eaten chocolate bar I don't remember putting there. I hold it up. I don't even like Baby Ruths. I tilt my head. *Do they even still make them?* I eye the bite marks, wondering if they're Anna's. The gross factor is high. My stomach grumbles. I'm almost tempted to take a bite, but my parents are tag-teaming me tonight. Mom's voice echoes in my head—*salmonella, salmonella*—and I shove it back in the glove compartment.

All I have is a bottle of Pepsi and some water to get me through the night.

I pull out my map, find my place on the road, and then write.

FIRST DIRE CIRCUMSTANCE: ALL I HAVE TO EAT IS A FOSSILIZED CANDY BAR.

I sketch a geriatric chocolate bar complete with cane. He waves it at me with a shout.

WHO ARE YOU TO JUDGE? MY NUTS GET TASTIER WITH AGE!

I snort at my little joke. I must be seriously tired.

The sun hovers above the craggy collections of rocks, just teasing my eyes and refusing to set. I shift uncomfortably in my seat, not even able to play the radio. I don't want to kill the battery. So I take a small swig of Pepsi and pull my sorry butt out of the car to relieve myself.

When I return, I sit on the hood. At least I can watch the sunset without squinting into it as I'm driving. I congratulate myself for looking on the positive side.

Folding my arms behind my head, I lean back against the windshield and watch.

It was clear when I started out this morning, but strings of clouds are pulling in from nowhere and pooling at the tip of a flat-topped rock. Stubbly bushes cling to the base like they're sucking the life out of it. Touching my own face, I realize my stubble has graduated to a scrabbly, adolescent beard. I resolve to shave at the next stop.

The wind picks up, but the bushes don't move. The fauna is tough out here, barely raising an eyebrow to a strong breeze. I shiver, trying to grab a sweater from the driver's seat without getting off the hood. Failing, I end up half in the car and half out, awkwardly pressing my empty stomach on the windowsill. When I try to get back to my position, I make an ass of myself and nearly fall headfirst in the dirt.

I'm so glad I'm alone right now and no one saw that.

Finally back up the right way, I return to the growing clouds and the spectacular purple and orange sunset before me. It makes the orange dirt almost red and the dark green bushes almost black. It's worrying, though, because the clouds are getting together with the others.

The sun strips the sky, and the desert goes black quite suddenly. I shiver, attempt to hug myself, and ease off the hood.

As I open the door, the first lightning strike makes me jump. It's far away, but everything is flat and you can see for miles, so it feels closer. I count the time before the thunder claps, and it's ages.

I'm about to pull into the safety of the car when I see her.

18. LANGLEY

Outside! UT, 2015

WEATHER: STORMY AND ELECTRIFYING

I WISH SARAH WOULD hurry up, but the thunder's got her spooked.

I don't mind lightning. I like the out of control nature of it, the unpredictability of where it could strike next. It reminds me there are bigger, badder things out there than me. For some weird reason, that's a comfort. But Sarah is just standing in the middle of the dirt road with her hands over her ears, conducting my irritation.

Once upon a time, I was the little sister and she was the big sister. I would crawl into *her* bed when there was a storm. Now things are different. She's trying to slow me down.

The thunder shudders through me, rumbling across my ribs in a ribbon. It finds my mouth as I shout in frustration, "Sarah! We have to move!"

She's driving me nuts. I run a few yards, then have to round back and convince her to move. She agrees and runs with me for a while. But then every time the lightning starts, she stops again, cowering and covering her face.

My feet ache from plodding around in Johnny's boots, my lungs burn from cold, and I can't keep going like this. But then I see the pathetic gate hanging from some lazy rusted wire. We must be close to the highway.

NEAR MOAB, UT, 2015

WEATHER: ELECTRIC

SHE REMINDS ME OF the roadrunner cartoon. When she speeds up, dust floats around her churning feet, but then she stops dead, turns around, and walks back. She kneels like she's praying or talking to someone, then she's up again and sprinting for all she's worth.

When she gets to the gate, she pauses and then runs in the opposite direction to where I'm parked. She moves away, getting smaller, her dark hair flapping out to the side like a shredded flag. I pull out my pencil to quickly sketch her figure. She looks like a ghost in my drawing. In thin pajama pants, hair waving wildly around her head. But her feet have these enormous boots on, and she's stomping away from me in such a determined manner I know she's real.

She's real, and she might be in trouble.

I start the car just as fat globs of spring rain hit the windshield, making a muddy mess I can't see through.

Waiting for more rain to wash the glass, I give up, jumping out and using my sweater to wipe the dirt off. She's getting away from me, and it seems important that I catch up to her. Especially now since there's a white van tearing up the driveway to the rusted gate. It really could be the home of a psychopath, and she's just escaped his clutches.

Turning the key, I speed up and catch her in no time.

Keeping the car moving slowly next to her, I roll down the window.

After I clear my throat, I start to speak. She's still running, but turns to face me. For a second, I'm taken aback by her face. She's beautiful. Not like Kris, all big blue eyes and perfectly straightened blonde hair. This girl's beauty is complicated, the features strange on their own but working in harmony.

Her warm ruddy skin is the perfect canvas for a few spare freckles across her nose, and then there are her shockingly big brown eyes. She bats her eyelashes at me once, stops running, and turns around again to walk back a few paces. Kneeling, she whispers something and stands with her hands on her hips in the way my mom used to when she caught me eating the cooking chocolate from the pantry.

Taking a deep breath, I put the car in reverse, bringing it back to meet her.

She notices the van approaching the gate, and her demeanor changes. Turning to me, she gives me a wary smile. My heart jumps a little, which confuses me, but I figure it must be adrenaline.

"Excuse me, Miss," I say. "Are you in trouble?" I sound so formal, like a cowboy from the fifties, and I'm extremely embarrassed. But she just smiles again and wipes the hair from her eyes, tucking it behind her ear.

She observes me curiously. "Maybe, but how do I know you're not a psycho with a knife under your seat and a bag full of ladies' wigs? You know, the real hair kind," she asks while flicking her eyes to the white van signaling to turn toward us.

That last part makes me laugh out loud, the sound breaking open the bubble of silence I've surrounded myself and the Chevy with. "Um… You can check if you like," I say nervously, tapping the steering wheel and jerking my head toward the mostly empty trunk.

Nodding, she goes to climb in the front seat. Her hand is on the door handle, but she stops, frowns, and gets in the back instead. She bounces around on the backseat as I drive off. When the van passes us, she shrinks down below the window. Then she pops up again and leans delicately over the front seat, her legs dangling in the air as she reaches for the glove box. She fossicks around, sifting through the paper and trash, then pulls out the half-eaten Baby Ruth bar.

"No knife," she says casually. Peeling back the wrapper, she takes a bite out of the chocolate bar before I can stop her.

"That's, um, really old," I warn, but she's already demolished it like it's the first chocolate bar she's ever had.

She shrugs and licks her lips. "Tasted fine." She slumps into the backseat, breathless. Her face has gone kind of pale since she stopped running, and I realize she might be hurt. Thinking of things to say is hard, so I just hand her the bottle of water over my shoulder.

She grabs it without a word and takes a big drink, coughing and spluttering when it goes down the wrong hole. I don't laugh, but she gives me a rueful look like I did. Although it's almost like she's glaring out the front window, not at me. Then her face softens and there's something in her eyes, some emotion I can't peg.

Right there with the dark purple clouds smashing against each other and the moon trying to push against the storm as lightning takes over, she might just be the tiredest and most beautiful girl I've ever seen.

20. Anna

Williams, AZ to the Arches National Park, UT, 1997

WEATHER: NO LOUD NOISES PLEASE!

PRESSING AT HER TEMPLE, Anna checks to see if her skull has turned paper thin. It would explain why every noise Tupper makes, every click of the blinker, makes her want to bury her head under a pile of cushions and blankets and die a quiet death.

She'd forgotten how simple and painful a hangover could be.

Licking her dry lips, she swallows. Acid burning. Fumbling around for water, she grabs Tupper's baby bottle, unscrews the lid, and skulls the contents.

She hates feeling this way. Like lightning is cracking inside her skin, burning and drying everything up. Reaching for the tin of powder, she hovers her hand over the promise of a pick-me-up. A way to speed up recovery. Tupper cries and she curses, withdrawing her hand. She said she wouldn't. She said she'd try.

The small tin of white powder vibrates next to the gearstick, calling her name in an angry, impatient way.

She shakes her head. Closes her eyes so long she veers onto the wrong side of the road.

She turns the wheel violently, shocking the baby into silence.

No.

Clicking on the radio, she winds down the window, cold air slapping her tired face. She tries to fill her brain with sounds and distractions despite the throbbing. Despite the *need.*

21. LANGLEY

Near Moab, UT, 2015
WEATHER: FLOOD WARNINGS

I'VE JUST PUT OUR fates in the hands of a stranger. I knew I would probably have to, but I'm scared my acting skills aren't up to the challenge. Especially since Sarah insisted on sitting in the front seat, and I looked like the crazy person I am for stopping at the front door and then climbing in the back like I was getting in a cab.

She turned around to me, poked her tongue out, and then wiggled around in the front making a show of getting comfortable. I wanted to tell her to get out, but then she placed her hands neatly in her lap and gave me a wide-eyed look. It was clear. *Please, I'll be good. I never get to sit in the front.* She looked so adorable that I let her.

The magnitude of what I've just done suddenly hits me. I've never gotten this far before. It is frightening and amazing at the same time.

The dash clock reads one PM, which obviously isn't right.

"What's the time?" I ask.

The boy lifts a tanned arm to his face and says, "S'about ten." His voice is short and clipped like it's an effort to say just those two words.

"Where are you headed?" I ask, trying not to sound too desperate. I don't want him dropping me at the next truck stop. He looks down at a map that's spread out over the seat. Sarah shuffles over to give him room before peering nosily over his arm.

"Williams, Grand Canyon, then on to Palm Springs."

Sarah jumps up and down, clapping her hands excitedly. I catch him staring at me curiously through the rearview mirror. I sit up straighter, trying not to look at her.

"Must be fate," I say with a chirp. "I'm headed to Palm

Springs, too!" His eyes are disbelieving, and I don't blame him. "I don't have much money but if you give me a ride, I'm sure we can come to some sort of arrangement." I try shaking my hair around seductively. It's wet and stuck to my head, slapping rather than floating sexily.

He half smiles, and I'm really scared he's going to take me up on my offer. But he just mumbles into the steering wheel, "Won't be necessary. I'll take you as far as Williams. You can find a bus that'll take you the rest of the way."

I nod gratefully. I can't argue.

My eyes feel heavy. I lay my head against the window, looking out at the clouds that are rushing away as quickly as they had come in. "I'm Langley."

"Like the fort," he says, raising an eyebrow and tipping his chin. "Tupper."

"Like the general." I give him a weary salute.

He seems surprised I know who General Tupper is, but he doesn't say anything.

"Do you mind if I...?" I yawn.

"Go ahead. You can use my bag full of ladies' wigs for a pillow," he murmurs.

"Sorry about that." I sigh, closing my eyes.

Falling almost instantly asleep, I dream about my parents for the first time in years. We are at yet another military museum. Dad's lecturing me about General Benjamin Tupper, a Massachusetts legislator who stopped some rebellion in the seventeen eighties. Sarah is bored and drags me over to the gravestones to freak me out. Before she was born, my parents made a deal—Mom could name the first child and Dad could name the next one. So Sarah got the normal name, and I got named after a fort in British Columbia.

Walking down the rows of dilapidated stones, all I can think is they were all so young. Even the adults died in their twenties and thirties. Sarah drags me to the children's graves. Those are even worse, babies and kids my age or Sarah's. Then she stops talking and I feel it, even though I'm in a dream. The scene is taking a dark turn. She stands over one grave, and traces the letters on the headstone.

Sarah Penelope Cross
Beloved daughter and sister

1994- 2004

Sarah pulls at her hair, and her skin goes gray. It's like one of those TV movies where the girl is dead, but she doesn't realize until she sees her own grave. And then it all makes sense. Except, there's nothing entertaining about this. She's not going to learn some lesson or help someone and shoot up to heaven. She's just dead.

The memory is not worth this. I want nothing more than to shake out of this dream before the earth opens and swallows me like it always does. The TV movie descends into horror movie. I watch her body disintegrate into ash before my eyes as she screams silently. Her mouth becomes a dark hollow as her face falls away around it.

I scream and scream and scream.

Something's shaking me. *Someone.*

"Who's Sarah?" a worried voice asks.

22. TUPPER

MOAB, UT, 2015

WEATHER: COOL AFTER THE RAIN

LANGLEY OPENS HER EYES, blinking at the bright white lights of the Walmart parking lot. My neck cracks as I turn back and ask again, "Who's Sarah?"

Yawning, her eyes focus on my arm resting on the back of the bench seat. "What?" she asks softly, fear in her tone.

"You yelled 'Sarah' in your sleep," I say, getting frustrated with how many times I've had to say the same thing.

Her face falls to her lap. "Oh, um, Sarah's my sister. She lives up in Canada. I'm hoping to hitch a ride up there," she confesses.

I swear under my breath, folding the map in half so she can't see the end destination of my road trip. "So you're not heading to Palm Springs? Grand Canyon isn't even on your way…"

Shaking her head, she looks up, giant cartoon brown eyes blinking at me with tiredness and sadness. She presses her lips together. I stare, waiting for an answer, but she doesn't say anything.

"What were you running away from?" I ask, watching as she picks at scabs on her wrists. I look away, too scared to ask her why she has scabby lines running around both her wrists like rope burn.

"A bad place," she answers lightly, like she's ready to dump that memory and forget about it.

"Am I going to get in trouble for helping you?" I ask.

She smiles. "Not with me." The smile is fragile. Temporary. And I find myself not wanting it to go away.

"You an axe murderer?" I ask grimly.

"No, I prefer bows and arrows. Are you?" she quips, forcing a miniscule smile out of me.

"No," I reply.

Turning to the front, I grip the steering wheel with both hands and count to three. I have questions for her, but asking them means talking and I don't really want to do that.

"Clothes," I say, eyeing her in the rearview mirror. Her pajamas are filthy and the boots, well, they're obviously not hers.

"Huh?"

I fish out a fifty and hand it to her.

"What's this for?" she says, holding it flat in her palm like it's heavy gold.

"Go into Walmart and get some clean girl clothes." Did I just say *girl clothes*? She doesn't take the money. Just hunches down, nervous and small in the backseat.

"I, uh, can you come with me?" This is not what I thought I'd be doing on my journey of self-discovery or whatever this is. I shrug, which she understands to mean yes. She touches my shoulder and murmurs, "Thank you."

SHE HOLDS UP A striped sweatshirt with something French scrawled across the middle. "Am I a size fourteen?" she asks.

I chuckle awkwardly. "You don't know your size?"

"Of course I do." Flushing pink, she snatches the sweatshirt from the hanger and puts it in her basket. I don't tell her its miles too big.

She grabs a pair of jeans—which she thankfully tries on—and some other essential stuff, the whole process seeming to be overwhelming and stressful to her. I'm not sure she's even looking at what she's buying. Soon, it becomes stressful and overwhelming to me, too, so I leave to grab some food, coming back to find her standing bewildered in the aisle.

"It's bigger than I remember," she whispers, hands hanging limp at her sides, addressing the middle row of socks.

"I hate them, too," I manage.

She gives me a small smile, turning to follow me to the checkout.

When the woman gives her the total, she seems completely surprised. Flustered, she counts the cash in her hand and then starts to pick items up to take back.

Money is not a problem for me. The day I turned eighteen, my bank account suddenly had a lot more numbers in it. "I got it," I say, pushing the sweater down on the counter.

Langley winks at me, tucking her auburn hair behind her ear. "I'll find a way to pay you back."

The cashier arches an eyebrow. I stare at my feet, so she can't see my red cheeks.

This girl is confusing. Distant and then all too familiar. I wonder what I've gotten myself into.

23. LANGLEY

Moab, UT, 2015

WEATHER: CLEAN STREETS, FRESH START

HE'S LIKE A GENTLEMAN *or something. At least I hope he is. I'm treading a skinny little line here, though, trying to be friendly, trying to convince him to help me without offering too much. Things I can't actually give.*

I'm relieved when I see him still standing there. He's waiting for me next to the Starbucks. I come out of the bathroom dressed in my new jeans and enormous sweatshirt, then stare down at my thin, denim-clad legs. I haven't been shopping for clothes since I was eight. I chose the plainest things I could since I don't know what's 'in' anymore. I'm assuming it's not flannel pajamas and straitjackets.

He looks uneasy as people pass him. A young woman in a cute dress and ankle boots checks him out as she glides toward the counter. His broad shoulders pull in like he's trying to make himself smaller, like he doesn't want to be noticed. He runs a hand through his sandy-blond hair, moving closer to the wall like he'd like to disappear into it.

Sarah seems to like him. She stands at his side, looking up, up, up into his strong face. She grins and sways, playing with her hair. I give her a stern look as I approach, stomping in my too-big boots.

Turning slowly, he hunches over me when he says softly, "Coffee?" I nod. His eyes crinkle, almost painfully, as he holds up a brown paper bag, pushing it in my direction. "Here."

I open the bag. Inside are a pair of bright red sneakers with polka dots on them. When I hold them up high, Sarah jumps at them, trying to tug on the laces. They are so pretty I might just cry. I bite my lip and smile. "Thank you so much, Tupper. I love them."

He barely tips his chin in response.

Sitting down on one of the Starbuck chairs, I try them on. I feel like Dorothy. They fit perfectly. I'm tempted to click my heels together.

Tupper hands me a coffee, the name on the side says *Thumper*. "Thumper? Ha! Like the bunny from Bambi?"

He smiles sheepishly. "They never get Tupper right."

I knock my heels together and look up. "Hey, how'd you know my shoe size?" I bump his hip with mine as we walk outside. "You got some sort of foot fetish or something?"

He chokes on his coffee, and Sarah scowls at me. I shrug at her. "Um, what? No. My, er, I guessed."

I consolingly tap his shoulder. "I was kidding!"

He rolls his thumb and index finger together, quiet for a while. Slowly, a chuckle builds in his chest. "Good one."

As we pass the trash can, I shove Johnny's boots in, punching them down on top of old coffee cups and muffin wrappers.

"What did those boots do to you?" Tupper says with an unsteady smirk.

I try not get sucked back into the recent past, but by the look on his face, I've failed.

"They're not my style," I reply, trying to leave my legs alone as I feel Johnny's ghost of a hand sliding up my thighs.

He opens the door for me when we reach his ridiculously cool old car. I race to the front seat before Sarah gets in, laughing triumphantly when I beat her.

Tupper looks at me peculiarly, but he doesn't say anything.

I push the map into the center as he slides in. "Let's go," I say enthusiastically.

"Hang on," he says, picking up the map. There's another older one folded neatly underneath. He picks up a pencil and starts drawing. I don't know what he's doing but I leave him to it, my eyes turning to the endless morning procession of people buying things.

While he's drawing, he is serenely focused. His shoulders relax. His breath is steady. I watch him from the corner of my eye and wait.

He places the map down, starts the car, and turns to me expectantly. "Ready?" I think he expects me to ask him what he was doing, but I don't. He's a little weird. I'm a lot weird. I figure if he wanted to tell me he would.

24. TUPPER

MOAB, UT TO WILLIAMS, AZ, 2015

WEATHER: IT'S RAINING SECRETS

CLICK YOUR HEELS THREE TIMES. I sketch a quick likeness of Langley in her new red shoes. Her huge eyes glance off in the distance. I mentally trace them. She has the most intense, mirror-like eyes.

"Williams is about 360 miles away," I tell her. "That okay?"

She turns her head lazily toward me, her neck still resting on the back of the seat. "I'll go wherever you want to go, handsome." She takes a quick sip of her coffee, frowns, and tucks it into her side.

Gripping the steering wheel a little harder than necessary, I stare out the window. When I turn back, her eyes have fluttered closed, her hands, pulled inside her sweater, rest neatly over her chest.

I switch maps after about half an hour, when I'm sure she's really asleep. My mother's handwriting glows black and steely over mountain ranges.

Shifting my gaze briefly from the road, I regard the girl sleeping next to me. I have questions, and I think I'm going to have to force myself to ask them. Starting with why is she all alone?

———————

SHE SNORTS AWAKE AROUND lunchtime, giving me a groggy half-smile and scratching her head. "Where are we?"

"Somewhere in the desert," I reply, turning back to the road. "Where are your parents?"

She jerks upright. "No easing into it, huh?"

I frown. "How old are you, like eighteen, nineteen? Are you homeless or something?" I ask. She nods on the second number.

She laughs. "Oh, yeah. I lived on the street. Singular. The

only street in that crappy town."

"So…"

"So…" She sighs, tapping her finger on her leg and staring at the back corner of the car. "I escaped from a loony bin. I can call it that because I am a loon who lived in said bin, but you regular folks would call it a mental health facility or psychiatric hospital."

A sharp disbelieving laugh escapes my lips. I check her expression; it's dead serious. "Seriously?"

"Seriously. Look, my mom died kinda suddenly when I was a kid. And well, I didn't handle it very well. After a while, and because of lack of trying, my dad couldn't handle me, so he stuck me in an institution." Her earnest expression frames the plea in her eyes. *Please, please, please believe me.* "I couldn't stay there anymore. Like I said before, it was a bad place."

I believe her.

"So you're *not* crazy?" I ask nervously, my fingers running along the bumps of the steering wheel cover.

She pauses, takes a deep breath, and says, "I never said that. But I promise you I'm harmless. I will never hurt you or anyone else for that matter."

I believe her twice.

And I decide I don't need to know anymore. At least not right now.

"You don't seem crazy," I say, like this is supposed to reassure her.

She dips her shoulder, then grins all toothy and dramatic. "That's coz you don't know me very well."

It makes me smile. It shouldn't, but it does.

Ahead, rows of red dust canyons rise, dotted with dark scrub and exposed history. The scars are there for everyone to see. I like that I can hide mine.

SHE ROLLS HER EYES, looks behind her at the backseat again, and huffs. "Okay," she snaps in an irritated tone. I turn my eyes back to the road, watching the ribbon fall and flutter ahead. "General Tupper, why do you have two maps?"

I cast my eyes down. The corner of the older map is poking out from under the new one. My jaw tightens, my voice retreats. I rub my chin with one hand, working the joints like that could get it moving.

"It's personal," I reply. She seems unfazed by my answer.

"I figured," she says.

I glance down at her, surprised there are no follow-up questions, and she smiles. I like her smile. It's one part devil and one part nervous. She'd make a good super villain.

I'm used to people pushing, trying to open me up.

This is new.

She shrugs and says, "Eyes on the road, soldier," as she kicks off her shoes and puts her feet up on the dash.

"Feet off the dash," I grumble. She pulls them down and crosses her legs so her knee is poking into my side. The touch sparks something in me, and I open my usually wired-shut mouth.

"You know I'm headed to Canada, too," I confess. "I mean, I'm taking my time getting there, but my final destination is Chilliwack."

Her eyebrows rise, and she giggles. "Chilliwack. Love that name."

I laugh and tap the wheel. It *is* a weird name.

"Well, maybe I can convince you that I make an awesome travel companion," she says expectantly. I click the radio on. It's some old bop song, and she taps along on her leg with one hand.

"Yeah, maybe."

She hums for a while before turning to me with a more serious expression. "I'm only kidding. You've done more than enough for me. You can drop me anywhere. Drop me here on the side of the road and I'd be grateful." She grips my arm, and I tense. Not because I don't like her touching me, but more because I do. I don't want to say goodbye to her just yet.

"I said I'd take you as far as Williams," I say.

She seems to be relieved by that and sinks into her seat.

"Are we going through Flagstaff?" she asks.

I nod.

"Okay, good."

25. LANGLEY

Flagstaff, AZ, 2015

WEATHER: COOL, CUTTING WINDS, SHARP SUNLIGHT

THE STREET NAME AND number from the faded postmark that smudged some of the words are stamped in those cold, lonely places inside my head. I clench my teeth as I build up the courage to ask.

Sarah seems indifferent to this choice. She draws spirals, turning them into snails in the condensation of the side window.

"Tupper?" I ask, wondering how much information I should give.

"Mmm." His lips are so set in this dented line. I imagine if I really wanted them open, I'd have to get those Jaws of Life and pry them apart forcefully. I shudder at the memory, curling my arms around my middle and hugging myself. Tupper's eyes flick sideways, noticing. He thinks I'm cold and leans across to switch on the heat.

Sarah is bored, rubbing sections of her hair between her palms, creating dreadlocks. She knows I hate it when she does that, and I scowl in her direction. She turns away, knees up, locked in her own world for the time being.

He's waiting for me to speak.

"Tupper, when we get to Flagstaff, I need to make a stop." I blurt the words in one breath.

A long, drawn-out "Okaaaay..." is his response.

"Fifty-three Willow Tree Avenue," I chant, the words spinning barbed off my tongue, because I don't really want to go there. I pick at my fingers as I wait.

"What's at fifty-three Willow Tree Avenue?" he asks, his eyes switching between the speedometer and the horizon. I stare at his fingers, stained black like he's dipped them in motor oil.

"My passport," I reply, hoping he doesn't ask me any more questions.

"Your passport?" he repeats like a question.

I shuffle to face him. "Yes. I'm going to need it if I'm going to get across the border," I answer anxiously.

He thinks. Runs his hands across the leather steering wheel. "Big *if*. Since you escaped from a mental health facility …" He makes sure he gets each word in the right place with the right emphasis. "They may stop you at the border."

"Damn it!" I say slapping my hand on my forehead. He's right. Sarah hangs over the bench seat and winks at me. She holds her long hair in two bunches, wanting my opinion on her hairstyle. "Not now," I whisper to her.

Tupper takes the exit for Flagstaff, casting me one concerned glance as he pulls over. "Fifty-three…?" he asks, his hand out like he expects me to drop a tip into it.

"Fifty-three Willow Tree Avenue. I know right? It sounds like a giant frog or rat's going to answer the door," I babble, my lips humming with nervousness.

He doesn't react to my *Wind in The Willows* reference, saying only, "It's ten miles away," while looking at his watch.

"I won't be long, Tupper, I promise. In and out," I assure.

He nods, starting to drive through the main part of Flagstaff. Clasping my hands, I try not to hyperventilate.

———❧———

IT DOESN'T LOOK ANYTHING like our old house. But why would it? We've been parked for a few minutes. I'm just staring at the black-lacquered front door like it's a mouth ready to swallow me.

Sarah grows impatient and flips onto the front lawn. She does a few cartwheels but when a lazy-looking cat strolls past, she freaks out and runs. Reluctantly, I get out of the car, following her as she streaks down the side of the house and into the backyard.

Tupper calls after me, "I'll wait here."

Putting a hand up to signal I've heard him, I disappear between the narrow shadows.

I twist my nose in disgust at the climbing flowers hanging over the fence. They are far too normal and cheery. The neatly lined-up trash cans. The recycling separated. It's all an empty laugh. A mocking tribute to my old life. I wanted to think his life was a disaster without us—not that he kept on being the same guy with the same 'save the earth one soda can at a time' attitude. No. He's supposed to be different. Messed up. Like me.

I stare at the bins for a long time, an angry feeling stretching my skin and pulling at my arms.

Sarah grins devilishly, and I open the lids. Like the nutcase I am, I start pulling the stacks of old envelopes, cereal boxes, and toilet paper rolls out of the paper bin and dropping them into the plastic bin. Then I dive into the other bin and pull armfuls of plastic milk containers and soda cans out, scattering some on the ground and shoving others in the miscellaneous bin.

The stale, cheesy smell of old milk fills the immediate space. I stop, growing colder in this shadow, this imitation of my old life.

"Great raccoon impersonation." Tupper's constrained voice freezes me in place, wobbling on my toes as I ready myself to plunge into the bin again.

"I, uh…" Sarah laughs hysterically. Bent over her knees, drawing in deep breaths I can't ever hear.

Tupper takes another step closer. I drop my armfuls of trash and fall back. He catches me before I slam into the fence. "What are you doing?" he asks, his hands lightly on my hips as he steadies me.

I blink up at him. His sandy hair touches the sun, gold and leafy. I huff and slam the lids down one by one. "Revenge," I say in seething quiet, my face reddened and plastered with vacuum bag fluff.

26. TUPPER

FLAGSTAFF, AZ, 2015

WEATHER: LIKE A TORNADO'S COMING

"REVENGE," SHE SAYS MENACINGLY, an upside-down smile on her face. If she's trying to be funny, she's failing. Whatever's going on inside her head, it's not a prank. It's obvious she's hurting.

Outwardly she's furious, but when she blinks up at me, I see softness in her deep brown eyes. I see the reflection of a girl running through dark streets, black inky rain pelting her upturned arm as she tries miserably to shield herself. After I release her waist, I bend to scoop up the rest of the trash, sorting it carefully into the assigned bins she seemed so intent on rearranging.

"Why are we here?" I ask as I stupidly, blindly, follow her down the side to the backyard.

"I told you," she says. "To get my passport."

There are other reasons. I should ask... My mind goes to the inky rain, my hand to my pencil.

Pretty late in the game, I register that this is her dad's place, the dad who couldn't 'deal with her'. And as I watch her crawl around in the garden beds, flicking her auburn hair back like a wild animal, I feel equal parts understanding and anger toward this guy.

"Ah ha!" she shouts lifting a rock.

I think she's found one of those hidden key rocks, so I stand there waiting for her to unlock the door. Instead, I watch in shock as she smashes the back window, alarms blaring so loud I cover my ears.

Bewildered, I dart my eyes to the side gate, the escape route I should be running toward right now. But I don't move.

She reaches through and unclicks the lock, turning back to me before she slips inside. "You can leave if you want." She doesn't say it like a challenge. It's more an expectation. And it makes me want to stay.

Dancing from leg to leg, I hover for about two seconds and then follow her.

Inside, she faces the keypad, fingernail between her teeth. She quickly types in some numbers and frowns when the alarm stops. "Nothing changes," she whispers before storming up the stairs two at a time.

I'm a statue turning on a Lazy Susan, slowly taking in the sparse home. One armchair facing a small TV, one unwashed coffee mug in the kitchen sink. Stranger still is the kitchen table with only one dining chair. This is a sad place. *A fortress of solitude*. I roll my eyes at my reference, and they land on the shelves behind the table. There is one old family portrait sitting on the dusty shelf. The frame is coated in a fine layer of dirt. I pick it up, wiping the glass with my sleeve.

Two little girls—maybe eight and ten—dressed in period costumes smile cheesily at the camera. A proud father grasps the waist of his beautiful wife. She's holding a parasol and wearing a bonnet, her dark hair escaping the hat. Her eyes are that same deep brown. Langley looks just like her mother. The other older girl—her sister, I guess—looks like Langley and their mother, but she has her dad's blue eyes. She's beautiful, too, in a subtler way.

A weird pang of jealously hits me like a swinging ball to the chest. It was always obvious to me that my parents were not my real parents, even before we had the painful 'you're adopted but you're still our son' talk. We look nothing like each other.

I start wondering whether I look like my mom or my dad when I hear a lot of stomping over my head. Carefully, I place the photo back in its mound of dust before climbing the stairs.

SHE'S NOT BEING VERY careful. Boxes are scattered all over the bed and papers all over the floor. Langley rakes a hand through her hair, breathing quickly. Her eyes practically pop out as she paces the room, muttering to herself.

"Where do you think they could be?" she asks, staring at the wall. She pauses, puts her hands on her hips. "But I looked there already…"

When she notices me standing in the doorway, she jumps.

"Christ! You scared the shit out of me, Tupper. I need to tie a bell around your neck or something."

I try not to panic at the mess she's made, but she's totally trashed her dad's bedroom. Again, I ask myself why I'm even here. The answer—pretty simple. I obviously want to be, or I wouldn't be standing here thinking about how I'm going to convince Langley to leave before someone finds us.

"Have you found it?" I ask, my feet crunching over bills and typed pages.

She gives me a disdainful look. "What do you think?"

I think you're going to get us both arrested.

Walking over, I put my hands on her shoulders. They're thin but not bony. "Stop and think," I say, using my dad's words.

Take a deep breath. Stop and think. It's never as bad as you think it is.

Her chest rises and falls really fast. She blinks, shakes her head, and sighs like she's releasing thousands of pent-up notes from her chest. "Did you see this place? Look at it," she shouts, gesturing around the room, pointing to the drab quilt and the single sad pillow sitting in the middle of the bed. "It's just so…so normal. He's fine. He's just the same as before. Except without me. It's like I never existed." She pushes on my chest weakly. "He just left me there, Tupper. Alone. With *him*. With all of them."

I try to understand what she means, but all I can see is the home of a solitary, lonely man. Someone who wants no reminders of the past.

"You're not alone, Langley. You have your sister. When you see her, all of this won't seem so bad."

She bites her lip, face falling like she might cry.

"Did I say something wrong?" I ask, dipping to catch her downturned face.

She waves me away. "No. I'm fine. You're right. I have Sarah." Her eyes light up with mischief, and she beams. "I've got you too, right?"

I laugh awkwardly, feeling like I've swallowed some of the notes she just released. She might be right on the money.

"Now, Tupper, where do you think he might have hidden my passport?"

27. LANGLEY

Flagstaff, AZ, 2015

WEATHER: THE AFTERMATH OF A TORNADO

WE FIND THE PASSPORT in a box in his wardrobe. I stare at the expiration date. It runs out in a few months. I breathe relief mixed with poison. Coming here was a lot harder than I thought it would be. Sarah rubs my back softly as I try to slow my breathing. I need to get out of here, but there's just one more thing I need to do.

"Tupper?"

He stands in front of me stiffly, made of metal and rivets. "Yes?"

"Can you give me some privacy, please?"

He nods and leaves, his heavy frame creaking down the stairs.

Searching the nightstand, I find a pen and paper among his Civil War biographies.

Dear Dad (though I'm not sure you want that title any more, right?),

I've taken my passport. I'm crossing the border into Canada in a few weeks, and I want you to call off any search for me. (If there is one)

Tell Maka Mani I'm okay. That you've sent me to live with a relative in Canada or something. I don't care—just make something up that sounds convincing. You washed your hands of me a long time ago, so don't attempt to get them dirty now.

You owe me this at least.

I can't threaten you, since I have nothing to hold over your head. But if you do this for me, I promise I will never bother you again. We will never bother you again.

Stupid thing is I still love you.

Langs x

P.S. I'm not sorry about the mess, and I took your emergency cash. (I can't believe you still hide it in the same place!)

I pray to the Holy Ghost of crazy people it's enough.

Folding the note into a tent, I leave it in front of his pillow.

I steal the money he stashed inside his leather-bound Civil War history book. Third shelf, five in from the right.

When I close the door, I whip around, searching for Sarah. She's sitting in the front seat waving at me over Tupper's lap, her happy expression in contrast to his concerned one. But he's here, waiting for me.

I'm starting to wonder if he's as nuts as I am.

I go around to the passenger side and open the door. "No way!" I shoo Sarah out of the front seat. Tupper raises an eyebrow. "Fly," I say as I slide into the now-vacant spot.

He tips his chin and seems to relax into his chair.

"So are we staying in Flagstaff?" I say hopefully, knowing full well he hasn't agreed to anything.

He flips the corner of his map up, glances at something, and then says, "Nope. We have to stay in Williams."

"Have to?" I ask, desperate to peer under the map to see what he's looking at.

He nods. If he can get away with it, I'm learning a head nod or shake is his preferred way to communicate.

Pulling the scrunched-up bills from my pocket, I put them on the dash. They slide toward him like trash blowing across the sidewalk as he turns the corner. "For gas and the shoes and stuff."

He goes through a roundabout, and the money scuttles back my way. "Keep it. I don't need it."

I look around the old car, at the patched seats and door missing a window. "You sure?" I ask doubtfully.

He just nods again.

Taking the money, I shove it back in my pocket. I may need it later.

28. TUPPER

WEATHER: CLOUDY AND CONFUSING

THE ROAD TO WILLIAMS is part of Route 66. When Langley stares out the window, I steal another look at my mother's map. Along the short stretch of road, she writes, **GET YOUR KITSCH ON ROUTE 66.** Then she's drawn an old-school Mickey Mouse strolling down the road with a cane. **IT'S LIKE DISNEYLAND FOR OLD FOLKS (CREEPY MUSIC AND ALL!).**

Pine forests crowd the roadside, the trunks lining up so I can see small frames of the inner woods as we speed past. It's so fast I can't really register what I'm seeing until it's too late and I've moved to the next part. I'd like to freeze it. Draw a border around the scene and keep it pressed between paper pages.

"Deer!" Langley shouts, her finger pressed to the window. I don't even turn my head, and she huffs.

"Don't you like deer, Thumper?" she asks with a flat, cheeky smile.

"Like 'em fine, but I don't think they're anything special," I say.

She gazes dreamily out the window. "That's the first one I've seen in a long time. Do you see them a lot where you're from? Is that why they're not 'special'?" She uses air quotes.

"In Kansas? Not a lot. Just don't think they're very interesting."

"Bunny!" she squeals excitedly as the damn rodent tries its best to be a bunny-pancake under my tires.

I brake and swear.

"Are you having some kind of fit?" I ask with irritation

She pretends to think about my question and then ignores it. "Lemme guess, you don't think they're interesting either?"

I shrug and shake my head.

She pulls her legs up, resting her chin on her knees. "Tupper." *The way she says my name, soft like she's being careful with it.* "Everything is interesting in its own way. If you don't see its value, you're just not looking at it right."

One side of my mouth tugs into a half smile.

I swallow. "I think *you're* interesting," I say, staring at the line in the center of the road, the wheels bumping over the reflectors when I coast too close to the middle.

"I know," she says on a sigh.

There's a long silence filled with sweeping pencil lines in which I wait for her to say, *I think you're interesting, too.* But she doesn't say anything.

The exit for Williams is up ahead, and I indicate my turn.

"Ever been to Disneyland?" I ask. I've never been. I want to know what Anna might've meant with her old Mickey Mouse picture.

She shudders. "Random question but yeah."

"What's it like?" I ask.

She narrows her eyes, making them look more normal sized. "Geez, you're chatty today. You've said more in the last hour than you have in the past twenty-four!" I wait for her to answer my question. "The rides are cool, but those people-sized characters freak me out."

I laugh.

"I have what you'd call an overactive imagination, and ain't nothing funny about picturing a naked dude wearing some poor cartoon character's skin."

I cover my mouth. "Thanks for that visual!"

She giggles. "Aw man. Now I can't stop picturing it either!"

We laugh together. Mine, low and reluctant. Hers, high and kind of spectacular. It's a strange feeling because it's not something I remember doing in a long time.

We pass under a large wrought-iron archway. The name Williams threaded through the arc.

"Tupper, I think you're very interesting, too," Langley says, giving me a wry smile. "Fascinating even!"

I shove her shoulder gently. "Shut up."

29. LANGLEY

Williams, AZ, 2015

WEATHER: UNPREDICTABLE

I'M ALWAYS WAITING FOR the other shoe to drop. Though in my case, it's usually less of a shoe and more of a piano from the sky. I know things work out for some people. I just don't think 'some people' is me.

We drive up the main street of Williams in the fading daylight. The neon signs look kind of depressing in the daytime, all this dazzle and nowhere to go. Tupper is distracted looking for something, though I'm not sure what. He winds down the window, letting in the ice-cracking air, and narrows his gray eyes. His fingers tap on the steering wheel. Every now and then, he taps the brake, sending Sarah and me lurching forward. Sarah thinks it's a great game, purposefully slapping the back of my head every time he brakes.

"Ouch!"

Tupper snaps back to reality. "Sorry."

"Are you looking for something in particular or are you just reliving your Driver's Ed classes?" I ask.

He runs a hand through his hair and sighs. "Not really."

Informative!

"Maybe we should try to find a bus stop?" I suggest.

He makes a show of glancing at his watch, staring at the sun, and then back at me. "It's late," he says warily. "Stay with me tonight, get some food, and then we can find the best way for you to travel tomorrow?"

I nudge his side. It's hard and kind of ribby. "That's a lot of words for you, Tupper. I know that took a lot of effort," I say, drawing it out so he has to wait for my answer, like he always does. "Soooo... how could I possibly say no?"

We both sigh. Mine is with relief. I don't know whether it's the same for him or if he's disappointed.

We drive a bit further, and he points ahead. "What about

there?"

I smile. "Perfect."

We pull over in front of The Grand Canyon Hotel. Gathering up my stuff, I put it in a Walmart bag. Tupper grabs his gear from the trunk. Sarah gives me a brief smile and leaves, running down the street with no shoes on, dragging her hands across the glass windows and leaving greasy streaks that only I can see. I watch her dart around a dark corner, startled when Tupper takes my arm and steers me toward the door.

Dumping the bags at the counter, I eagerly ring the bell. I bounce on the balls of my feet, having a hard time containing my excitement. I haven't slept in a hotel in years, and the last experience was nothing like this.

Tupper nudges my side and points at the photographs on the walls. I realize this is one of those themed-room hotels, and I let out a little squeal of delight. Tupper folds his large arms over each other and leans on the counter.

I point at the different options. "Giraffe room. Awesome!" I say, elbowing his very still form. His eyes are searching artwork hanging on the back wall, his expression flat.

Dinging the bell again when no one arrives, I then start to punch it at half-second intervals until suddenly a two-foot-tall old lady comes shuffling out from the office.

"Sorry, I didn't hear you," she mutters, flustered with voice crusted and cottony. "Welcome to the Grand Canyon Hotel. Do you have a reservation?"

I instantly feel awful I've disturbed this ancient woman. Tupper clears his throat, gazing down at her. "No, we don't."

She puts her glasses on and fires up the computer, shaking her head solemnly. Leaning over the counter, I'm suddenly very invested in the Giraffe room and am worried I might miss out. Tupper stares at me like I'm his annoying younger sister, rolling his eyes.

She looks at me and then at Tupper. "Is it just the two of you?"

Tupper nods. "Yes, but we need two rooms."

I frown. It's bad enough he's paying, but paying for two rooms is too much. "No, no. One room is fine." I sigh, defeated. If he wants two rooms, he's definitely not going to want a double. I release my dream of staying in the Giraffe room.

"Uh. Okay. Do you have any twins available?" Tupper asks.

The old lady blushes under what I think must be talcum powder or that white stuff used to dust for fingerprints at a crime scene and scans her screen. "We have the Three Sisters or the Bunk room."

She starts to explain the different rooms. I interrupt her, pumping my legs and vibrating with excitement. "Bunk room! Bunk room!"

Tupper chuckles, then hands over his credit card and ID. "The Bunk room for two nights, thanks."

I glance at him, confused.

"Taking a day trip to Grand Canyon tomorrow."

WE REACH THE TOP of the stairs and I stop, blocking Tupper's way. He glances up at me, his perplexed expression mirrored in the plate glass of ten different and stunning photographs of the Grand Canyon. I take both his wrists in my hands, opening my mouth to speak.

"Is this where you push me down the stairs and take all my money?" he asks with a smirk.

His skin is warm. I squeeze. "I just wanted to say thank you," I say, catching his eyes and getting stuck in the leaded sincerity of them.

He shrugs. "I'm just doing what any decent person would do."

I want to laugh, cackle at the beauty and ridiculousness of his statement. But I restrain myself.

"Tupper, your idea of the average person hasn't evolved yet." He looks to the side and then back at me.

His gray eyes are plays on shadows, watercolor paintings. "Didn't say average. I said decent."

Pursing my lips, I think about how many 'decent' people I've come across in my life. Some…not many. Not one like Tupper.

Leaning down, I kiss his cheek. He is as still as a fence post and as immovable. Though I hear his hand scrunching the bag of groceries resting on his knee. "They must grow em' real decent in Kansas," I say, putting on my best Southern accent.

He gives me a taut smile. "Langley?"

"Yes." I pause in the middle of my hoedown.

"Can I come up now?"

"Oh shit! Yeah sorry." I cover my mouth.

I let him pass and follow him down the hall.

"Langley." He says my name like it's two words, long and drawling and always like a question. Laaang Leeee?

"Yes," I say to his back.

"It helps that you're cute," he says to our hotel room door.

I snort, not actually believing him. I have this feeling he would have helped me even if I had three warts on my nose and a lazy eye. Maybe even if I had two lazy eyes. Pausing, I wonder how 'cute' that might look until the door opens, then I scream, "I call top bunk!" and bound into the room.

30. TUPPER

WILLIAMS, AZ, 2015

WEATHER: A BIT WARM

LANGLEY'S NOT KIDDING. SHE scrambles up the ladder and plonks down on the top bunk, her arms spread out on the mattress, claiming it like she thinks I might take it from her. I chuckle and throw my bag on the bed underneath, sitting on the third single bed squashed in the corner. I don't like sleeping with something over my head.

The bathroom is shared with another room, but it doesn't seem to be occupied.

"Do you want to shower?" I ask.

Staring down at me from her bunk, Langley's eyes shine with childish excitement. "With you?" she asks, and I swallow dryly. She lifts her face and laughs. I can see it spreading like laughing gas over the ceiling. "I'm kidding. Geez, Tupper, you can resume breathing."

Jumping down, she grabs her Walmart bag and strolls into the bathroom. I gape like an idiot as she passes me. When she closes the door, I manage to breathe again.

Hearing water splashing the tiles, I take the opportunity to get out my two maps. Spreading my mother's out first, I find Williams, Arizona and read Anna's caption again. Disneyland for old folks doesn't make a lot of sense. And the music? Frowning, I fold the map back up. I want to reach her, but in some ways these words and pictures drag me further away. I try not to think about the fact that most likely, the random doodles of a dead woman are just that. Random, not a mystery to be solved.

Bringing out *my* map, I circle Williams, tapping the Route 66 symbol with my pencil. My ear tunes to the shower, and a fleeting thought dashes across my mind like the road runner. I could… I shake my head. I don't even know this girl. I knew

Kris. I knew her so well, but we never did what I'm thinking of doing with Langley. I knew her, but she didn't know me. It never felt…right.

I write all over the state of Arizona.

THINGS I KNOW ABOUT LANGLEY:
1. ESCAPED FROM A MENTAL HEALTH FACILITY.
2. MIGHT BE CRAZY.
3. SAD AND BEAUTIFUL.
4. ALWAYS DISTRACTED.
5. HAS SECRETS.

I don't know much at all. That's partly my own fault. If I could actually bring myself to ask her questions, I might know more.

I write one last fact.

6. I WANT TO KNOW MORE…

Dropping the pencil, I pull my hands through my hair, sighing. This took a turn I wasn't expecting. But I guess that was the point. An adventure.

Standing up, I catch my reflection in the mirror. I look tired and confused. I need to shake myself out of it.

The door clicks open just a fraction, and steam pours from the opening. Langley's warm brown eyes find me, and I freeze. She blinks, water dripping from the end of her eyelashes. I watch that lucky drop wind its way down her neck and beneath the towel she has clutched to her chest.

"Can I borrow a shirt?" she asks.

I stammer. Actually stammer like an idiot. "Sh…sh… sure," I say, unzipping my bag and pulling out a long-sleeve checkered shirt. "This do?"

She nods, extending her naked arm through the door and snatching the shirt.

Her lips quirk, and she closes the door. When she opens it again, she's wearing just my shirt, which is almost to her knees, and the shoes I bought her. She is flushed from the shower, her wet hair dampening the collar.

I'm hating myself right now. Hating that I can't seem to get myself together enough to lift my thoughts out of the gutter.

"Your turn," she says slyly.

Grabbing my bag, I enter the bathroom, eager to get

some space from her. As the door closes, she yells, "Wear something pretty, Tupper. I'm taking you out tonight."

I don't answer.

———❧———

"**WHAT DO YOU HAVE** of the deep-fried persuasion?" Langley asks in a posh voice, holding her menu up to her nose and peeking over the top at the waiter.

He smirks at her and leans in, dragging his finger up and down the items to point out the various deep-fried options, of which there are many. When her hair moves from his breath because he's that damn close to her face, I clench my fists under the table.

Langley notices my tenseness. I try to relax, pulling my pencil from my pocket and twirling it in my fingers.

"I'll have the…" I start, but he puts a hand up to my face. *Rude bastard.*

"Ladies first, dude," he says without looking at me. If he did, he would be vaporized by my laser vision.

Langley twists her hair into a loose ponytail. "And this may seem like a strange question, but…can I order from the kids' menu? I mean, I know I'm twice the age," she says, lying and tapping the part that says twelve years and under. "But I'm happy to pay adult prices."

The waiter laughs, putting his hand on her back. She shrinks away, just slightly, from his touch, her eyes moving to the memorabilia on the wall. "Tell you what. I won't tell anyone if you don't," he says, and then he fucking winks at her.

I groan loudly. His eyes flick to me, narrow, and then go back to Langley, stupidly cute as a button in my shirt, cinched in at the waist with the curtain cord from the hotel and her red sneakers. She crosses her legs and glances at me, her eyes half closed.

"Great…" She takes the waiter's name tag between her fingers. "Dylan. Well, I'll have the kids chicken fried steak with an extra serving of fries, and I'd love to try one of your local beers. You want a beer?" Her eyes are steel rimmed as she leans away from the greasy waiter's touch.

I nod, my eyes on the growing pile of crushed-to-dust peanut shells on our table.

He gives me a dubious look but takes our orders, returning shortly with two beers. When he puts them down, Langley reaches out and touches my hand, ignoring Dylan the waiter with the too-long hair and the dirty apron. "You okay there, Tupper?"

Taking a sip of my beer, I attempt to smile. "Fine."

Dylan seems happy when he walks away since he thinks we're fighting. I clench my teeth.

Sweeping over the brewery slash restaurant, I wonder whether Anna came here. But then I see the *Established in 2008* sign and frown.

Langley nudges my shin gently under the table. "Do you want to leave? You don't seem very comfortable."

I take a deep breath, then a long swig of my drink, and shake my head. "That Dylan guy seems like a douchebag."

Tipping her head to the side, she looks confused. "We got the beers, didn't we?"

She lifts her glass and clinks it with mine, sipping it slowly. Her nose screws up as she swallows, and she looks confused.

I laugh. "Is this your first beer?" I ask, feeling myself relax just from watching her face.

Dipping her finger in the beer, she then points at me accusingly, delicious beer droplets hitting my face. "I was led to believe it was the tastiest, most refreshing drink on the planet." Her hands fall to her sides, her body limp with disappointment. "It tastes like dirty sponge mixed with raisins," she murmurs to the sticky table.

"Dirty sponge and raisins?" I say doubtfully.

She nods definitively, as if to say, *Of course it must taste like that because I said it and how dare you look at me with doubt in your eyes!*

She pushes it toward me with a disenchanted expression.

Wrapping my fingers around the glass, I drag it across the table. "Who *led* you to believe this anyway?"

She sighs. "Acorn."

"Acorn...?" Like *An acorn?* I have my first real panic about her being truly crazy.

Sighing, I want to punch myself when she says, "He's a patient. He said if we ever got out of there, he would take me out for my first beer and that he couldn't wait to see the look on my face when I took that first sip. He said that first sip of beer was like heaven," she says sadly. My heart crumples like paper at her voice. At all the things she's missed out on.

"How long were you in that place?" I ask, taking a sip from her beer as mine has magically disappeared. I kind of have to agree with Acorn about the heaven part. The first, second, and third sips all taste like heaven to me.

Rolling her eyes to the trussed ceiling, she taps her chin. "That one? About three years."

I know that's where I'm supposed to say, *That one! How many others were there?* but the question doesn't *need* asking. I don't want to ask it.

She looks at my two empty glasses enviously, and I signal the waiter. "A peach cider and another beer for me?" I ask, twirling my finger around and pointing at Langley's hopeful eyes. Girls usually like those fruity kinds of drinks, so I hope she'll like it. "Apparently, the beer was a little too spongy for her taste."

Langley snorts, dipping a fry in aioli. Popping it in her mouth, she makes what could probably be described as an orgasmic face. I smile goofily, reaching for a fry. She slaps my hand.

"If you wanted fries, you should've ordered some," she snaps.

I take my hand back. "Anyone would think you haven't had fries for years," I say, instantly regretting it. "Shit. Sorry." I put my hand over my mouth. This is why I shouldn't be allowed to talk to people.

Shrugging, she pulls the basket to her chest possessively. "I haven't." Then she carefully places three fries on a napkin and slides them over to me, clearing a path through the peanut shells. "Here," she says, giggling.

"So generous," I mutter. I go to dip one in aioli, and she slaps my hand away again.

"My, aren't we presumptuous?"

My beer and her cider arrive. I wait to see what she thinks, my hands clasped on the table, my eyes on her lips.

The fizzy pink liquid reaches her mouth, and she scowls.

"Oh, gross!" she exclaims pushing yet another glass in my direction. "That is the worst thing I've ever tasted. It's so sweet."

I take a sip. It tastes fricking delicious to me. I lick my lips. "I thought girls usually liked this kind of thing," I say in confusion, taking another long drink.

"Girls and tall, *usually* silent, cowboy types," she quips.

I roll my eyes.

Grabbing the drinks menu, she peruses it looking like she often does, a child playing grown up.

She walks to the bar, props her elbows up, and waits.

While she's gone, I flip the paper kids' menu over and sketch her standing at the bar. In my drawing, the bar is really high and she's standing on tiptoes to get the barman's attention.

"EXCUSE ME BARTENDER, DO YOU HAVE ANYTHING LESS SPONGY BACK THERE." She hands her beer back to the bartender.

In the next frame, the bartender hands her the dish towel in a highball glass.

I cram the picture in my pocket when I see her returning, giant brown eyes expectant. It looks like she's carrying an empty glass. I peer at it as she takes a delicate sip and smiles. "Mmm." Her hand shakes, and she transfers the glass to the other.

Grabbing her wrist, I lift the glass to my nose. "You're drinking whiskey?" I ask incredulously.

She raises her glass to the air and shouts, "Hallelujah! I've found my drink!"

Dylan breezes past us, whispering in her ear, "That's badass."

And I wobble on my stool.

31. LANGLEY

Williams, AZ, 2015

WEATHER: ENLIGHTENING

I WOULDN'T SAY HE talks more when he's had a few drinks. It's that the things he says are stupider, more average. I don't mind it, though. Some of the restraint he so often seems to be wrapped in has dissolved. It's entertaining at the very least.

I take another small sip of the whiskey. It's smooth, honey-ish, and glides down my throat with a delicious burn. Sarah looks up from her coloring and wavers. I guess, like the meds, alcohol dulls her. She's concerned, so I put my hand up, waving slightly to reassure her. She nods before returning to her detailed drawing. Always in the lines. Beautiful shading. Such a show off.

Sipping very slowly, I watch as Tupper plows through his fourth drink in less than an hour.

When dinner arrives, we eat quickly. The manager has started paying attention to us, probably realized we are well underage.

Paying the bill, I leave a meager tip for Dylan, the overly touchy waiter. I shudder when I think of his hand on the small of my back.

I shuffle through the peanut shells. Tupper lumbers.

My cheeks feel pink from the heat and the whiskey. The cool outside air is a relief. "Where are you going?" I say as Sarah hops down the path in a determined manner.

"The hotel?" Tupper asks.

Sarah really wants to explore. She beckons me with her thin hand, her pink plastic bangle slipping down her arm. I mouth *okay*. "Shall we go for a walk?" I ask Tupper, offering him my elbow.

He links his arm through mine clumsily, and I lead him down the main street.

Neon lights cast colorful shadows on our faces. We look in the windows, making fun of the kitschy gifts and catchy slogans.

I press my face to one glass pane. Plastic number plates with every name run from floor to ceiling, and I sigh. I have one eye on Sarah and one on Tupper, who's wobbling a little after downing all my rejected drinks.

She points out her name. There's always a Sarah plate, but she wasn't allowed to have one because of me. There's never a Langley. Never.

Tupper stares through the shop window like he's searching for something specific. Grabbing his shirtsleeve, I drag him into the brightly lit store. Behind the counter, a woman is talking on the phone. Her eyes are red, and she whispers into the mouthpiece, "But isn't there something you can do?" while dabbing at her nose with a balled-up Kleenex. I have the Sarah number plate in my hand, but I put it back and start to leave, giving the woman some privacy. She shouts, "Wait!"

Turning around, I give her an awkward smile. Tupper lingers in the doorway, quite obviously desperate to get out.

"I can come back later," I say.

Shaking her head, she holds out her hand for the piece of plastic.

She scans the plate, and I pay. I leave thinking about how little I know. How everyone I pass in the street—every shop owner, waiter, tourist—is going through their own crap just as I am. And maybe if we all stopped and thought about that for just one second, the world would shift. The way we look at the world would change.

Tupper bumps into me at the door.

"That was weird, huh?" he mutters. "I feel bad for her." He grips the doorway in his strong hand, shifting his weight from foot to foot. "Uh, can you... uh... I'll be back in a minute." He runs away from me more gracefully than a guy who's had too much to drink should be able to.

Leaning against the window, I clutch the plastic nameplate and wonder where the hell he's gone. Sarah followed him, so it's one of those rare moments where I'm alone. Smoke twirls to the sky from some sort of meat on a spit on the corner. I sigh, breathing my own solitary smoke.

It's peaceful being alone, but it's also boring.

Ten minutes later, Tupper's large form approaches holding a tray of hot drinks. He hands me one before entering the shop. I poke my head through the door, but don't enter.

He approaches the woman behind the counter, placing a hot chocolate in front of her. I crane my neck to hear what he says.

"You've had a bad day," he says. It's not a question because we know she's had a bad day; it runs down her face in rivers. Stunned, she stares at him and takes the cup. Slowly dragging it across the counter and into her hands, she then clutches it to her chest. "Drink up, Miss, before it gets cold."

Her eyes light up when he addresses her as 'miss'. I think that made her day even more than the hot chocolate.

When he walks toward me, his expression is neutral. He doesn't seem pleased with himself or looking to me for approval. But I more than approve. I'm in awe of what he just did.

Tears prick my eyes like silver needles. Tupper leaned one way, and a tiny little part of my world just shifted.

Sarah gazes up at him adoringly. Like he's Superman.

I'm inclined to agree.

———✦———

WE WALK THE MEAGER street in under twenty minutes. Sarah looks unsatisfied as she tugs my arm, dragging me in the direction of the train line.

I shiver.

"You cold?" Tupper asks, his gaze off in the distance. He's searching for something. I just don't know what.

"Uh-huh," I manage through chattering teeth. We cross the train line, the dark suddenly closing in on us. The one strip of neon lights now a distant glow behind us. A streak of white rises before me, and I realize Sarah has climbed the vintage black train. As I get closer, I see a perky sign.

Please Don't Climb!

I glare up at her and she just waves happily, clambering into the roped-off engine room.

Tupper's large arm comes to rest on my shoulders. "Is this okay? I'm sorry. I don't have a jacket to lend you." It feels good and warm and scary.

A crackle overhead makes me jump, and the warmth I was feeling is yanked away from me as creepy music starts to play in the dark. Tupper breaks away and runs forward, hands out like he's trying to catch the song.

He disappears into the dark. I'm left standing and shivering, trying to get Sarah to come out of the train. "Sarah," I whisper through gritted teeth. "Get down from there." I stomp my foot, but she pokes her tongue out at me, refusing. "Fine, stay there!" I snap, turning away.

I follow the noise of gravel crunching. Up ahead, one solitary floodlight shines on a portion of the tracks. 'Lollipop' plays from speakers on poles. I begin to worry I've stumbled into a horror movie—soon, an army of cracked porcelain dolls will rise from the dirt and hack me to death with their miniature parasols.

"Tupper," I whisper through the dark, my shoulders hunched and tense.

"She was here." He sighs. "Can you hear the music?"

I turn around suddenly at the sound of his voice. His broad shadow takes up a significant portion of a park bench. His head is bowed, his hands clasped in his lap.

"You're a bit drunk, aren't you?" I say teasingly.

He laughs, but it lacks any form of joy. "Guess so."

Sitting next to him, I'm unable to stop myself from huddling close to his side for warmth. He doesn't shift away.

The music changes to a softer song. It's the Everly Brothers.

"She said there'd be music. And here it is. Music." He points at the sky.

Dream, dream, dream plays, and I'm thoroughly confused. "Tupper, you're not making a lot of sense right now. Who said there'd be music?" I ask, kind of scared he's as crazy as I am.

Leaning his head against mine, he sighs. His breath smells unpleasantly of beer and fermented peach, but I like being this close to him. I shouldn't, but I do. His jaw moves against the top of my head as he speaks. "My mom did. My birth mom. I'm kinda doing this trip because of her." His voice disintegrates at the end of his sentence, like he wants the words back.

I look down at my red shoes. They dance in the every now

and then light. "You mean she told you to take this trip?"

Again, he gives a joyless laugh. Bluntly, he says, "She's dead."

I look to my left to see Sarah balancing on the railway tracks as she walks toward us. "I'm sorry."

"Don't be. She's always been dead. To me anyway. She died a long time ago. I don't remember her at all. She never gave me the chance to know her." He sounds angry, bitter.

"I'm sure she didn't die just to put you out," I blurt before thinking.

"Ha! Yeah, it was very inconvenient of her to do that to me," he mumbles. "Anyway. I'm taking the trip she took before she abandoned me, only in the reverse. It's the only way to get close to knowing who she was."

I imagine my mother, the way her cloaked arms used to open and fold Sarah and me inside. "I'm sure she didn't just abandon you; maybe she didn't have a choice," I say, trying to reassure him.

He shakes his head. "She left me in a cardboard box in a hot car. A store owner found me after a couple of hours. He smashed the window to get me out. They waited for her, and you know what? She never came back, not even to get her car. Believe me when I say she *abandoned* me."

I drag in a shocked breath.

Silence.

Sarah tapping on the railway line sends small metallic sounds our way.

More silence.

He shrugs hard. "It doesn't really matter now." He squeezes my arm. "Thanks for bringing me here. I don't know how you knew, but you knew," he says quietly. Three long breaths of quiet air and then, "I like this song."

I gulp. Sarah pretty much forced me to walk this way. It gives me the creeps. I don't like to think of her having thoughts, a direction outside of me. "You're welcome, I guess." I shake it off, like I do with so many things. "You know, Tupper, you're getting more and more intriguing." I knock his shoulder.

And I have to leave tomorrow. A wave of loss crashes over me, the grief of losing something I didn't really have climbing up my throat. *Am I losing the only friend I've ever made?*

Tupper seems lost in the music, his head moving slightly from side to side, a light hum balancing on the edge of his lips. "Do you think maybe we were meant to find each other? You know, like I was supposed to help you and you were supposed to help me?" he asks, totally confirming he is drunk.

"This isn't a movie," I say flatly. I don't believe in *supposed to*, fate, or whatever. That would mean that what happened to me, to my family, happened for a reason, and I can't believe in that. "So what happens tomorrow?" I ask, attempting to change the subject.

Slinging his arm around me, he pulls me close. "Let's talk about tomorrow, tomorrow."

32. LANGLEY

Heston, NV, 2004

WEATHER: DRY, SAFE. PERFECT DRIVING CONDITIONS

As I lean my head against the car window, my drowsy eyes watch cows turn to brown and black blurs in our wake.

Sarah whines at Mom, who is hastily applying lipstick and driving one handed, her eyes creased with tiredness. "We're going to be late!" Sarah crosses her arms over her costume. The performance is Toys Coming to Life *or something, which is why she looks like Bride of Chucky.*

Mom looks at me sympathetically in the rearview mirror, but replies to Sarah, "It's all right, honey. We have plenty of time. It's only…" She glances down to check the clock on her phone because the clock in our old Volvo stopped working years ago.

I roll my eyes. Dad is lucky he had to work late last night. He has a valid excu—

Tires screech. I can't tell if it's us or someone else, only that we're spinning around. Mom's eyes are frozen open, and Sarah is screaming silently with a mouth so wide she could swallow the world. And I am trying to say something, anything, to change this moment, move it out of frame and into another.

Glass shatters inward, and my head is punched to the side. I look to Sarah's seat, her empty seat, because she's gone. She's part of the door and Mom is part of the windshield, her long black hair catching beads of glass like a net. And I'm just bleeding and screaming and trying to undo what just happened.

We tumble down, cradled in the arms of the trees. I'm grateful for the darkness, so grateful, because I know, I know, I know no child should ever have to see this.

33. Anna

Williams, AZ, 1997

WEATHER: A FREEZE OUT

ANNA HANDS THE CLERK her ATM card, holding her breath like she always does. This time she doesn't get the relief that comes when the small piece of plastic is approved.

"I'm sorry, Miss, your card has been declined," the teenage clerk says in a monotone that makes her want to crack open his pimply face with the jar of beef jerky sitting on the counter.

Placing Tupper on the floor, she fumbles around in her bag for cash, handing the clerk a wad of bills that he has to sort through and count.

He doesn't give much back to her.

Closing her dry, cracked fingers over the small amount of cash and coins, she swears. Her parents have found a way to freeze her money. She knew it was coming, but she still feels angry. *What about Tupper, their precious grandchild?* She thought maybe they would hold out for his sake.

Dumping her gear in the hotel room she can barely afford, she takes the baby and storms up the street. She wonders if she's making cracks in the pavement she's stomping so hard.

She wipes her sore nose. This was the final string, and now it has been cut. She thought she was being clever, moving all her trust fund money into an account in Tupper's name. But not clever enough. They found it. Somehow, they've suspended it.

At the closest ATM, Anna checks her balance, her heart plummeting as low as the zeros that greet her. They've cleaned her out. Now she has nothing but the cash in her bag.

Her head swings this way and that, hinged on pointed shoulders, taking in her surroundings. The neon signs and old folks in leather jackets make her sneer. This place was made for people like her parents. Kitsch and creepy, with fifties-style diners and old-time music playing through megaphones by the train station. Her body brews with hate. She feels like she could climb up one of those poles and the rip the speaker from its anchor.

Breath coming in quick, angry bursts, she strides to the public phone on the platform, dialing the number before she can talk herself out of it.

Her father answers, "Hello?"

"You took my money away," she says in a low, dark tone. One she is sure must be someone else. One her father knows well.

"Anna? Is that you? Where are you? The last time we checked, you were in Palm Springs, but it's been days... How's the baby?"

"I'm in Williams, Dad. You'd love it here. It's perfect for boring burnouts like you and Mom." He doesn't respond, which makes her even more furious. "I can't believe you did this. What about Tupper? What about me? That was *my* money. I'm an adult, you can't just take away all *my* money," Anna says, all intended drama gone from her voice. Now she sounds like a child. A pleading child.

Her father's voice is so sad, making her feel guilty. She doesn't want to feel guilty. "That money was for your future, for college, a life—not to pay for drugs and some insane trip to find that loser. Please, Anna, come home. You can have all the money you want. It will sit in the account for Tupper until you come back. We'll get you help. We'll do whatever is necessary. Just come home." They're words, the same as before, carved into a rubber stamp they use every time they speak to her.

"I don't need your help," she says unconvincingly, her hands shaking, violence spreading to her fingertips as she slams the phone down. She picks it up again. Slams it harder and harder still. She hears a crack in the plastic. Suddenly she stops, scared someone is watching and will reprimand her.

Tupper gazes up at her. He's stunned, his gray eyes blinking and counting the ways in which she's crazy. She claws at her neck, wishing there were better words, ones that made sense to her. The burn of fear creeps up her throat. This is too hard. But she can't go home, not until she has tried to make it work with *him*.

Her heart stutters unhappily in her chest. She just needs a little lift. A little something to help her get through these overwhelming feelings.

Anna blames her parents. They make it too hard. It's always all or nothing with them.

The *where* to find it shines dimly at the end of the road. A truck stop with several lorries lined up like matches in a box. The *how* to get it makes her shudder.

———&———

THE TRUCKER'S PAWS GRASP for her across the seat, grabbing her hand and pulling her into the cab of the truck.

He dangles it in front of her eyes like a carrot on a stick, watching as she leans forward, her cleavage showing as she follows the swinging plastic bag with tick-tock eyes. She grabs at it, but he pulls it from her reach, teasing her. "After," he whispers, making sure he gets what he needs first. Her skin aches for the itch of that powder, and she lets him pull her closer.

The smell of old coffee and stale air seeps from his open mouth. She blinks hard. Tries to see past her *need*. Assessing him with sharper eyes, her brain ticks like a time bomb. He's not ugly. Graying blond hair combed neatly, blemish-free skin, and a cowboy shirt tucked into clean jeans. His jaw is square, and he showed all his teeth when he smiled at her kindly as she knocked on his door.

This is what it has come to—Tupper squashed in a diner highchair while she sneaks out to find her fix. And a man she doesn't know, leaning in to take what's left of her. Eyes moving to the window, she sees the waitress standing next to Tupper, hands on hips, searching for his mother. *Searching for her.*

Putting her palm to the man's chest, she pushes him backward. His eyes fly open, and the disappointment is clear.

Shaking her head, she whispers in a voice weaker than taped-together confetti, "I'm sorry. I can't do this," and shuffles out of the truck.

He smirks at her. His wide smile says he thinks he knows what kind of girl she is. That he knows she *will* do this. Maybe not now, but soon.

A neon sign flashes in the corner of her vision. It calls to her, an easier fix. A less dangerous, more acceptable risk. Wishing she could split herself in half, she follows her haphazard heart and enters the liquor store. She'll just have one beer. Two if they have her favorite. She'll be quick and be back to the baby in no time.

The pleasing crack of the can opening battles with how very low her opinion of herself has sunk.

34. TUPPER

WILLIAMS, AZ, 2015

WEATHER: DULL BUT THE CLOUDS ARE PARTING

REGRET, ALCOHOL BE THY name. I'm lying fully clothed on top of the covers, a pillow covering my head. A vague memory emerges of Langley putting it there because she said I was snoring so loud the walls were vibrating. I roll over, the pillow hitting the floor with what feels like an almighty thump. Clutching the side of my head, I try to snap my skull back together. Because I'm sure it's open, my aching brain showing like the villain from *Teen Titans*, though I don't feel very smart right now.

Mostly, I keep my eyes closed because I'm embarrassed. Of how close I was to her. Of what I said about my birth mom. Of being jealous of Dylan the waiter. Of a lot of things.

My phone dings. I open one eye to find it, squinting as the fuzzy message clears to actual words. It's a text from Mom, *Where are you? Are you having fun? I hope you're having fun <3.*
I quickly reply, *Williams, AZ and yes.*
She texts back a smiley face.

I glance at the top bunk; the corner of the bedspread hangs quietly from the edge. I start to apologize. "Hey Langley, sorry for keeping you up all night, I…" I sit up, craning my neck to find her face. The bed is just a tangle of blanket and sheets. She's not there.

My heart does this weird dipping thing like it's being pushed on a swing. She's gone.

Jumping out of the bed, I swear. *How could she leave without at least saying goodbye?* The answer is obvious—I freaked her out last night. I think back over the night. Although I was probably more talkative than normal, I don't think I did or said anything out of line. Except, I don't really remember getting back to the hotel. I try to form a memory out of my plasticine brain, but all I can remember is staring down at my feet and following them along the dark pavement because it was so hard to concentrate on even walking. I search for my shoes, determined to run after her. Surely there's only one bus stop in this tiny town. Then I see my map spread out over the dressing table. The list I made about Langley glows like it's got a spotlight on it.

"Shit!" I say, hopping on one leg as I try to jam my shoes on my feet without loosening the laces. All this does is make me fall backward onto the bed.

Taking a deep breath, I calm myself, put on my shoes, and stalk toward the door. I don't stop to think about why I'm so upset. I don't need to. Sometime between drunkenness, sleep, and the pale sun of morning, I decided Langley has to come with me.

I open the door, hoping some words will come to me before I find her. *If* I find her. The idea of not finding her sucks the air out of my lungs like a vacuum.

Thumping down the narrow staircase, I slam into hot liquid. It scalds my chest, making me release as many curse words as I can manage in one breath.

Langley stands there, crushed paper cup in one hand, coffee dripping down one arm. Her other hand holds a soggy paper bag. She holds it up with a smile and announces, "I bought breakfast."

I sigh with relief. Those words I was trying to find... they hadn't come. I don't even know if they existed. The beginnings of a sentence sit in the bottom of my stomach, unformed and not quite ready to come out. "Sorry," I say sheepishly.

She gives me a cheeky look. "I thought we could talk about tomorrow, today, over coffee and bacon and egg bagels?"

I nod. "Let's get cleaned up first."

WE EAT IN SILENCE, the smell of coffee stuck to our skin. She seems like she's delaying the conversation as much as I am.

Langley plays with the last chunk of her bagel. Her other hand goes to her mostly empty coffee cup. She pauses, switching hands.

"Why do you always do that?" I ask, tapping my pencil on my leg.

"Do what?" she asks, tipping her head and scrunching her nose, all her freckles gathering over her high cheekbones. She squeezes her right hand in a fist and then sits on it.

Her legs jiggle nervously as I say, "Switch hands. It's like you want to use your right, but you have to decide to use your left."

She arches an eyebrow. "You're very observant. You been studying me or something?" If I were a blusher, I'd blush for all the staring-down attention she's giving me with those cartoon eyes of hers. I wait for an answer. "I'm right hand-ed, but my right hand doesn't work properly sometimes. The connection between my brain," she taps the side of her head, "and my hand is not broken exactly, but it has a kink in it. At least that's the way the doctor explained it to me when I asked her to dumb it down some."

I want to ask what happened.

I don't.

Picking up the map I wrote on, she holds it up. She doesn't say anything about the list, just asks me, "So you're going to the Grand Canyon today, huh?"

"Langley…"

"I've never been to the Grand Canyon," she muses. "I've heard it's spectacular." She snaps the paper, and then pretends she's reading it like a newspaper. "You know, since your last destination is really close to where my sister lives, maybe we'll bump into each other once you get there."

"Langley…"

"Yes." She drops the paper; her eyes ready to engulf the Bunk room and its occupants.

I say three words I'll most likely regret. Three words I can't not say. "Come with me."

I count her teeth—white as piano keys—in the widest smile I've ever seen.

35. TUPPER

GRAND CANYON, AZ, 2015

WEATHER: I'M SURE THE SUN'S UP THERE SOMEWHERE

"**WHAT DOES IT SAY** again?" I ask Langley as we dip under the Williams arch and head out of town.

"It says North Rim, and it's underlined three times. Aw, that's cute," Langley croons.

"What's cute?" I ask, trying to rip open a pack of gum that's squeezed between my knees.

Langley holds up Anna's map, looks behind her, and then back at the road. "She's drawn a little squirrel perched on the edge of the canyon. He's yelling **COOEE**! Underneath, it says, **THE CANYON LISTENS. WHAT DO YOU HAVE TO SAY?** Cryptic much?"

I frown. She's right. What the hell does that mean? I picture myself talking to the canyon, and it makes my mouth feel like I've taken a bite out of some drywall. Then I try to picture Anna crouching low, whispering a secret into the abyss that no one will ever hear. Her face is a tanned blob with no discernible features. Her mouth moves, pink and cracked from the sun. I imagine she has blond hair, tied loosely at the nape her neck. Because imagine is all I can do. I groan loudly out of frustration.

"Sorry," Langley says. "I'm not dissing your dead mom or anything. I just don't really get it."

"S'okay," I mutter, bits of plaster on my tongue. "It's not you. Look up the route to the North Rim."

She smiles, puts her feet on the dash, and spreads the map over her long legs. "Why don't you have a GPS or something?"

I shake my head. "Feet off the dash!"

She slides them down slowly, the soles of her sneakers squeaking over the front of the glove compartment.

"Take this exit," she says, pointing ahead.

99

——— ✦ ———

WE PULL INTO A large, mostly empty car park. I slam the door and look up. The color of the sky matches the bitumen. Dark gray, grainy. Dirty.

Langley stretches her legs and grins. "Let's hike one of these trails," she says excitedly, holding up the map they gave us at the entrance. She points to the trail that's nearly ten miles long and takes all day.

"Little ambitious, don't you think?" I glance at my watch. If we did it, we wouldn't get back to the car before eight o'clock.

Fervently, she nods. She knows it is, she just doesn't care.

Returning to the car, I grab my backpack, water bottles, and some snacks, slinging it over my shoulder.

——— ✦ ———

IT SEEMS LIKE THERE'S nothing ahead. The sad gift shop and the small visitor's center give nothing away as we drag our feet through the loose gravel. Langley jumps up and down, shooting me a disparaging look when I roll my eyes at her. "You're taller than me," she says, like that explains her erratic behavior.

We walk a little further. All of sudden, it's there. It's there, and it's immense.

I stop in my tracks, arms outstretched like I could get a hold of her waist as Langley surges toward the barrier and is caught by it. She hangs over the bar dangerously, scaring the crap out of me. When she cackles joyfully, I thump my chest, feeling like I just swallowed one of the boulders lining the precarious path.

Soon, though, I'm too distracted to worry about her dangling her long hair into the canyon. I blink, sweeping my head back and forth just trying to process the size and beauty of it. Slowly, I approach the viewpoint, stepping to Langley's side, resisting the urge the grab the back of her shirt and yank her back to solid ground.

"Wow!" she exclaims breathlessly. And I think 'wow' is not the word. 'Wow' gets swallowed in the silence, the history, the still, watching monument. Three insufficient letters that I watch tumble and bounce down the sides of the cliff face, landing with a plop in the water below. I pat my jacket pocket, my pencil calling out to me. Langley elbows me, her arms flapping carelessly as she perches on the bent metal barrier. "Well, Tupper, what do you think?"

I shrug. *This is the earth asking for the sky.*

"I'm going to assume you're at a loss for words," she says.

I shrug again.

The colors melt into one another, stacked and sugary, like purple and orange candy. My pencil ceases calling. I can't draw this. I can't even comprehend it.

We walk back, find a seat, and sit down, breathing in the quiet.

Words are unnecessary here. For me anyway.

Langley points to the weird bends in the iron pipe barrier. "Why do you think the barrier is all twisted like that? Do you think someone really huge, like a massive circus-freak, leaned on it and it gave way? Or maybe someone tied a rope to it, flung themselves off the edge, and the sheer violent force of it made it buckle, or…"

Sighing gently, I nod along, but don't offer a theory or agree with hers. Nice thing about it is she doesn't require a response from me. She doesn't push me to talk back.

Her excited chatter soon calms. She sighs, too. It's not a sad sigh; it's a contented one. The one where the exhaled breath carries with it some of the excess stress lingering inside, and it floats out across the ravine. "You're like the Grand Canyon, Tupper. Strong. Powerful in its silence. It doesn't need to talk," Langley whispers.

Shoulders touching, we stay in a silence that could never be empty. Silence as deep and dark as the canyon. It's full. Piled high to the sky.

Minutes pass before I stand. Offer her my hand.

She takes it, not letting go as we walk to the head of the trail.

CLIMBING DOWN INTO THE canyon feels safe and sheltered, like its welcoming us to read its secrets. Giving us a very small part of what it's seen. Descending through the layers humbles me as I think about the millions of years it has stood here, and how very insignificant our impact on the towering sandstone is.

I will always remember coming here, but my footsteps will

blow away. This canyon will not remember me. It won't remember any of us.

Langley is similarly impressed, I can tell by her huge expressive eyes, her open suckerfish mouth.

Silently, we trudge the narrow path, not speaking because not slipping requires all of our concentration.

A third of the way down, the path runs under a worn-away hollow of sandstone, an archway.

Langley places her palm on the stone and puffs. "I feel so small. Do you feel small?" she asks, tucking a sweaty strand of hair behind her ear.

"Tiny," I reply with a smirk as I have to dip my head to get under the arch.

Her eyes move to the horizon, or maybe something just in front of it. Gazing out, I ache for paper and a pencil. I'm in love with the broken horizon. The fragile towers that split the sun as it starts to sink. I hand Langley some water and sit down, my back against the wall of the canyon, my legs almost stretching to the edge.

Getting my sketchbook out, I quickly draw the horizon, the sun floating above. Without colors, I can't do justice to the layers beneath. My pencil glides across the page and calms me. I breathe in deeply, scents of dust and donkey crap heavy in the air. Langley glances past me, still standing. I wait for a question, but it doesn't come. She stares down the winding path that looks like a termite has eaten into the side of the canyon, and begins walking. Moving fast like she's trying to keep up with an invisible pacemaker.

I quickly catch up, hearing her mutter, "It's not a race," as we come to a steeper, more gravelly incline.

A squirrel darts across our path and we stop, one behind the other, watching it skillfully serpentine its way down the cliff in a rodent waterfall.

I'm about to speak, make some lame joke about wishing I were as graceful as the squirrel, when Langley gasps, or more, pushes air from her chest painfully, almost like she's choking.

Suddenly, she lurches forward, grabbing at the air with her left hand, her stomach hitting the dirt and scraping the rocks that barely hold the path to the canyon wall. "No!" she shouts, her fist gripped around nothing. Nothing but air and dust.

All I can think of is the coyote. The coyote scrambling in midair and then falling, a whistling sound spiraling down to the canyon floor. But there's no trampoline waiting on the ground. *She'll die.*

Stamping down on her leg, I manage to stop her from slipping over the edge. I press down as hard as I can, and she screams in pain.

Crap! Fuck! Shit!

Her breathing is hard, shooting out in bullets of panic. Her arms and half her body hang down the side of the cliff like a ladder.

I try to breathe. It doesn't work.

Grabbing the back of her shirt, I pull her into my arms, collapsing against the rocky wall with her sweaty body pressed against my chest.

"What the hell were you doing? Christ! You nearly went over," I shout angrily.

She clutches her chest, whispering over and over, "You're okay. You're okay. Shh. Shh. Shh. You're okay." She strokes her bad hand with her good one, shakily.

As the dust settles and her legs slacken, her breath coming back to even, I'm so confused. Because I swear she was reaching for something, grasping at something, Only... There was nothing there.

36. LANGLEY

Grand Canyon, AZ, 2015

WEATHER: COOLER AS WE DESCEND

"YOU'RE SICK, LANGS," DAD states, *his words made of iron that he throws at me. "Cooperate with the doctors and then they might let you come home."*

He doesn't sound like he wants me home. There's so much doubt and blame in his voice. It hurts like a rusty fish hook dragged up my throat.

The tears I want to cry stay inside. Safe inside.

To the crowd of nurses and doctors holding my arms and legs still like I'm the chimp at the zoo that smashed the glass and bit the keeper, I desperately say, "What if she's real? What if she's a ghost? You don't know for sure. None of us know for sure!"

"Langley…" a calm, kind voice asks. "Do you know why you're here?"

I shake my head, scared. Someone holds my arm carefully, injecting me with a drug, which swirls around my brain and takes away the pain. It fills my head with something thick and cement-like, like toothpaste. It smothers me, and I can't think straight.

"Langley, honey, you jumped in front of a car," I hear my dad say from behind a thick soggy cloud.

No. No. No.

No, I didn't.

I blink slowly. Everything I do, accident or not, is because I'm crazy.

"It was an accident," I slur.

Sarah strokes my arm. I look down the long length of my body, stretching out like a gangplank, a splint on one leg.

The memory of Sarah's arm coming out to shield me moments before the car hit floats over my head like a storm. She stopped me. I'd be dead if she hadn't stopped me.

She lays her head next to mine, and I stare into her blue eyes. They tell me to breathe. Calm down. She's here. She'll always be here.

"I'm scared," I whisper into the pillow. "I want to go home."

Sarah nods. I know, she seems to say. I won't leave your side. Everyone else leaves, but I'm not going anywhere.

"Langley…" Tupper's voice brings me back. Sarah sits in my lap shaking. She's terrified. She nearly went over the edge. And I nearly followed her. Followed my delusion straight over a cliff.

I grapple with the real and the unreal, try to separate them, but it's difficult. Patting her head, I say, "It's okay." She dabs tears from her eyes. Wipes them on her rust-stained dress.

We breathe in and out together for several minutes until she believes me. Standing, she points up. She wants to go back to the car, and I don't blame her.

Tupper stands suddenly, flipping me onto the dirt. I expect an echo, but the canyon absorbs the sound when he shouts, "Answer me! Langley, what the hell did you do that for? Are you insane?" I stiffen at his angry words. *I'm used to angry.* He turns from me, folds both hands behind his head, and shouts into the abyss, "I was so goddamned scared. Ugh! I'm so fucking angry with you right now."

I try to stand, but my leg aches from where he stomped on it. Dragging myself up, I hop gingerly, not wanting to put weight on it. Tupper glances at my leg and back up to my face, the anger disappearing as quickly as it began. "I slipped," I challenge, back straight.

His expression is doubtful, voice full of regret. "Sorry about your leg. I didn't know how else to stop you."

I touch his arm. "Tupper, you just spoke to the canyon."

Slipping his arm around my waist to help me stand, his other hand slaps his face. "Jesus. I hope it wasn't listening!"

"The canyon doesn't judge," I say seriously, a smile and a wince colliding at my nose.

He grins.

Sarah tells me she wants to meet us at the car, and I'm relieved.

"We better head back to the car," Tupper says, squinting into the low-hanging sun. "Can you walk?"

He looks perfect and awkward, the light curling around his large body, the canyon eavesdropping on our conversation.

I shuffle forward awkwardly. "With your help, yes, I think I can."

"Sorry," he says again. The word surprises me. *Sorry* is not something I'm used to at all.

Making all sorts of unladylike noises, I drag myself up the path. "Pain is good," I grunt. "It reminds you that you're alive."

Tupper shakes his head, holding my waist tightly so I feel like I'm barely touching the earth. "That's bullshit."

We make slow progress. "You're right. Maybe it should be—*Pain: At least it's better than being dead.*"

He gives me a look of absolute dismay.

"Okay. Okay. Pain sucks, but then…there's joy." I curl my good hand to the sky like I'm releasing a dove.

He smiles. Sweaty, dusty, and all kinds of beautiful. "Yeah, don't mind that one. You could write Hallmark cards."

I laugh. "And you could draw the pictures!" He blushes. It is unbelievably endearing.

My ghost, my hallucination, my sister, and my friend makes dust clouds up ahead as she jogs up the path. She turns, waves, and then disappears.

37. TUPPER

GRAND CANYON, AZ, 2015

WEATHER: COOL

MY PEACE IS GONE. In its place is this mystery. A big box marked acme. A large red bow flounces and begs to be untied. I know there's a bomb in there. I know my world is about to be shredded and shattered. But just like the stupid duck, I clutch my chest, say, 'For me?' and tug on that bow anyway.

The sun is setting. The shadows that played over the red rocks now stretch, ghoulish, over us. Langley shivers and clutches one arm tightly around her body. The other is holding onto my side, her weight uneven as she tries several times to use her leg and fails.

She blows air loudly through her lips with frustration.

"Maybe I should carry you," I say, staring down at the part in her hair, strands of red, blonde, and brown mingling together as the sunlight warms them.

She shakes her head wildly, hair flapping in my face. "Don't you think you're taking this knight in shining armor thing a little too far? Nope. No way. I can walk," she mutters, then shudders. Her face is scrunched in ten kinds of pain.

I lift her by the waist as much as I can to relieve the weight.

As we drag ourselves up the path, a lot slower and wearier than we were on the way down, I again think about Anna. Walking along this path, with me in her arms. I imagine her whispering secrets only the two of us could hear. Fears and wishes.

I don't notice I've stopped moving until Langley's hair blows in my face and she says, "You and the canyon need a do over." Her arm slides out from my waist, then she tries to sit and mostly falls awkwardly. "And I need a break."

Flicking her hand in the air, she shoos me away. I let her go, wander down the path a little until I'm out of sight. "This is stupid," I yell back up to her.

"Just say what you need to say. I'm not listening," her voice urges from around the corner.

Crouching, I wipe the sweat from my forehead and exhale. Without Langley to hold onto, I suddenly feel unanchored, weightless, like the next puff of wind could blow me from the path and down to the Colorado River.

In a small voice, I whisper, "Are you listening?" I wait a full minute before I continue. "No." My voice is weak, almost childish. "Of course you're not."

I swirl the dirt in front of me with agitated fingers until I'm satisfied I've spent enough time here. When I return to a greener, paler version of Langley, she tries to get up and falls back down again.

"You didn't say anything, did you?" she huffs as I grip under her arm and pull her to standing.

I'm starting to worry I've really hurt her. Her leg drags woodenly through the fast-dampening dust as the sun disappears. "I said something," I snap defensively.

"Nothing important, I bet," she challenges, the sun setting in her eyes, making them look like there's fire burning inside them.

I shrug. "Guess not."

She nods and sighs, exhausted. Her eyelids close like curtains over her porthole-like eyes, and she whispers, "Your words are in here," she says, tapping her head. "Or on there." She pats the sketchbook that's hanging out of my backpack pocket.

I yawn. She yawns.

We need to get back to the car before it gets too dark.

Taking off the backpack, I give it to her. "And *your* words are making me crazy," I say lightly. "If I have to listen to your yapping for one more minute, I'm gonna fall asleep and then fall into the river." I jump in front of her. "Get on my back. It's less knight in shining armor and more donkey ride."

She clambers on awkwardly, scaring me with her limpness. I hook my arms under her legs and she clasps her arms around my neck, her chin resting on my shoulder.

She whispers into my ear, "Giddyup!"

Cursing under my breath, I start walking, the cold pushing me faster. The awkwardness of her body pressed so close to mine adds even more speed to my gait.

I press my hip into the side of the wall for comfort. Langley cries out as I graze her arm against the rocks but hell, it's better than me losing my step and falling. It's dark now, and Langley holds my cell phone over my head to light three square feet of path at a time.

She's slipped into quiet, which usually wouldn't bother me, but I feel like I need something to keep me alert. Something to anchor me to the ground.

"You awake back there?" I grunt, slipping a little when I jerk my head backward.

"Mmhmm," is her response.

"You can talk, you know," I whine, sounding like an eleven-year-old.

She blows warm air on my neck as she grumpily replies, "You said you wanted me to shut up."

I was joking.

I roll my eyes in the dark. "Just talk."

"About?"

I hate the way her breath feels on my skin, warm, somehow sweet even though I can't taste it. When I shake my head violently, she reacts to getting my hair in her face, huffing and sounding like she's going to sneeze. "I dunno. Anything. Tell me about the loony bin?"

She pauses. Breathes in, breathes out, and ignores me.

"She was always on the roof," she whispers.

"Huh?" My legs wobble from carrying her weight. I remind myself I'm a strong footballer. If I could knock over three-hundred-pound guys on the field, I should be able to carry one scrawny chick up an incline for a couple of miles. My mind wanders, thinking she's not actually very scrawny. She's got curves. She's built like a… I stop the train of thought before it runs right through Gentleman Station and heads toward Dirtytown.

"Who was always on the roof?" I manage through my panting.

"Sarah. We had one of those two-story houses where the upper rooms were kinda built into the attic, so you could climb straight out the window and onto the roof of the porch.

From there, she'd swing up the drainpipe and onto the roof. She'd just sit there, staring at the stars, teasing me as I watched her from the safety of the window. 'You're such a scaredy cat, Langs', she used to say. Sarah was brave. I mean she is brave. I hated climbing out and onto the roof tiles. Only did it when she forced me. I imagined they would come loose, then I'd skid off the porch and break my leg or worse…" She laughs a super sad, dreamy kind of laugh.

"Sounds like you were smart, and your sister was being a pain in the ass," I say, not sure why I feel the need to comfort her.

"Maybe."

I don't say the things I'm really thinking. *You're the knight. Linked together with armor and broad smiles. You're brave.* I think about how she's been left alone for so long. I know she doesn't want to talk about the place she was living because it's too painful. But she should know, she's a survivor. It surprises me she doesn't see that about herself.

Something cold as ice brushes my hips. I reach out and grab a metal bar. We're nearly there. The phone lights up the sign showing the hopeful red 'you are here' cross and black dotted trails.

"We made it!" Langley exclaims, jumping from my back. On landing, she makes a horrible anguished cry and reaches for me.

The guilty feeling weighs me down heavier than having her on my back.

I'm about to say sorry again, but she's fast disappearing. The circle of light from my phone shrinks like the beginning of a bond movie as she limps toward the car.

38. Anna

Grand Canyon, AZ, 1997

ANNA WANTS TO DO something good for the kid. Give him an experience. Give them both a moment they can hold onto. She steps out of the car, stretching her arms and legs. Her mouth tastes like crap and her stomach gurgles, but she can last longer than Tupper without food.

Feeling kind of gung ho, she takes Tupper in her arms and stomps happily toward the edge of the crater. She wants this to be important, to mark the beginning of a better life for Tupper and Anna.

Now the haze has cleared, she can feel more. It was a wall, stopping her from loving him properly like a mother should love her son. And now she feels that love taking her over.

They sit on the wall and watch the sunrise. The lookout is empty, silent. Tupper makes noises and nonsense and then, "Mama."

She laughs, the canyon gobbling any sound they make. Laying her head on top of his, she whispers, "You and me, kid, we're going to be okay."

It seems too small. A confession or admission like this needs to be bigger to be real. Cupping one hand around her mouth while gripping the back of the baby's shirt, she shouts into the void. "We're going to be okaaaay!"

The canyon seems to agree with her in its solemn silence. It pours colors of purple and pink and firelight-orange into the valley as the sun rises. Anna feels calm, the last of the drugs diluting in her veins.

The canyon listened. It can be her witness. She's going to break this dawn and let the colors stream through her. Sharing it with her son.

39. LANGLEY

Grand Canyon, AZ, 2015
WEATHER: SO WARM

I ENJOY IT TOO much. My chest pressed to Tupper's back, my legs wrapped around his waist. It's warm and safe and so not something I will be allowed to keep.

My nose presses to his shoulder. He smells kind of sweaty, but then so do I. Quiet as always, his unlabored breaths shoot in and out, right by my ear. His ribs expand and contract like a beating heart, and it's too comforting.

I flip the torchlight up; the dotted brown lines of the sign celebrate that we've reached the top. Sarah signaled she'd wait at the car, but I thought maybe she'd be here. The viewpoint is empty, nothing but dark swallowing dark. All spare light cocoons close to us like an unprotective bubble. The wind howls and finds its way under my shirt. Like icy hands, they drag me from Tupper's back and remind me that I shouldn't really be there. I jump from him, landing on my bad leg. The sound I make is reminiscent of an accordion being stepped on, and I hurriedly hobble away from Tupper before he offers to carry me to the car.

I hear him walking slowly and deliberately behind me.

When I start to think about it too much, my head hurts. *Lightning bolts through my skull* kind of pain. Like right now, I'm limping to the car watching for Sarah, scanning the sparse bushes for signs of her hiding. I'm holding the phone up, trying to illuminate little toes peeking out from behind a tree, dark hair caught in the brambles of a bush. But that's stupid. She's not real, right? She's *my* delusion, so shouldn't I be able to make her appear at will? I should be able to see her in the dark. But I can't. She's not a ghost. Yet, it sometimes feels like she is more than me. More than some short-circuited part of my brain.

Though I'm sure all the crazy people say shit like that about their own hallucinations.

Winding my way up the path clumsily, I worry she's probably been waiting for me for a while. I picture her leaning against the door of the car, wiggling and buffing the paint with her white dress. Counting the stars, she'll sigh deeply. She'll glance out across the empty parking lot with her young blue eyes and feel abandoned. Alone.

Speeding up, I groan with pain as my leg starts to cramp. Doing a sort of hop-walk, I feel Tupper's arm reaching for me before he even touches me.

"Why're you running? Trying to run, that is," he asks with heaped piles of concern planted in rows across his tongue. He halts me by gripping my sweater. I try to press on, but it's like I'm on a treadmill. Walking and getting nowhere.

My head follows my frantic sweeping of Tupper's phone light. My hand shakes, and I switch the phone to my left. Straightening, I take a deep breath and try to be more 'normal'. "I'm c-c-cold," I say as another sweep of wind opportunely passes between us like a karate chop, breaking us apart. Tupper steps back.

"Give me my phone," he says, holding out his hand like a teacher expecting gum.

My eyes dart back and forth. *She's not here. It'll be okay. She'll be at the car.* My chin sways back and forth slightly. Tupper watches me carefully, the light shining in my eyes like an interrogation lamp.

I swallow, wanting to slap my face a few times. *Stop acting crazy,* I tell myself. Like that would work.

He glances at the screen and curses. "It's nine o'clock," he mutters.

"And what? That's when you turn into a pumpkin?" I say, trying to grin, but my lips are quivering from cold, from panic, from pain.

Ignoring me, his expression swings to guilt ridden. "You're hurt. We might need to take you to a hospital."

Beckoning him with one hand, I throw my arm around his neck. "It's just bruised."

He seems unsure, but happy that I'm leaning on him. "I don't know, Langley. I cracked down pretty hard. Could be broken."

I laugh unconvincingly. "I know you think you're strong, but I don't think you can break a bone just by stepping on it."

He is quiet for a few seconds as we struggle toward the car. I try not to make too much noise, unable to stop myself from letting out a tiny squeal when we trip over a log conveniently placed in the middle of the path.

"Never know. Maybe I have superpowers," he says as we finally come to a streetlight. He grins sheepishly. I want to keep that grin. Save it so I can take it out later and remind myself that I met this beautiful, quiet guy who looks like a quarterback and talks like a comic book nerd.

The car glints ahead, but I can't see Sarah. Tupper seems embarrassed by what he just said, and he gently uncouples from my side. I stumble forward, my hands scraping the asphalt. Pushing myself up, I walk in a circle around the car, using the sides to hold me up. She's not here, and my panic builds with every awkward step I take around the old Chevy. Tupper watches me circle it twice without a word, then he unlocks the car and starts it up.

I bang on the back windshield. "Where are you going?"

He doesn't answer, just waits for me to get to the door.

"Where are you going?" I ask again.

He gives me a strange look. I know my eyes are wild, and my skin is seeping warmth. I feel like someone's sliced me in half. The good half is gone. The crazy half feels lost without her anchor. "Driving back to Williams. You getting in?" he asks. I hope he thinks it's just the pain causing me to act unhinged. *Hand me a tin foil hat and a shopping cart to push around my cat babies!*

He yawns widely, and I seize the opportunity. "It's like two hundred and fifty miles. Maybe we should just stay here. I don't mind sleeping in the car. Or…" My eyes find the lodge sign. "We could stay there." I point. I feel awful about it, but I play up the sore leg part. "My leg is so sore I'm not sure I could stand any driving tonight. I need to rest, keep it elevated." I try to stretch it out and wince.

Self-reproach flashes across his face.

I wait. The car warms up. He mulls it over silently, arms crossed, eyes straight ahead. I keep waiting for Sarah to appear, but she doesn't. I don't feel like I can leave here until she does.

"Okay," he concedes. "But if it's not a lot better by tomorrow, you're seeing a doctor."

I nod enthusiastically.

He turns the engine off and pulls out his phone, typing out a text to his mom. "What's the lodge called?" he asks.

"Um, The Lodge?" I reply, grinning goofily.

"Right," he mumbles.

He hits send.

"So we're staying?" I ask hopefully.

He nods, tucking his phone back in his pocket.

We walk up to The Lodge, no bags. Just a backpack, a grimace, and a missing ghost.

Sarah, where are you?

40. LANGLEY

The Grand Canyon Lodge, Grand Canyon, AZ, 2015

WEATHER: LIFE FLOATING THROUGH SPACE, COLD, DARK

"YOU'RE LUCKY," THE CONCIERGE says, not raising his eyes from the computer screen. "A couple didn't show up. Usually you have to book months in advance."

Tupper shifts awkwardly. He goes to rest his elbows on the counter, but then retreats. It's too low, and he stoops over like a nervous rainbow.

The concierge finally looks up, takes in our raked-with-a-dirty-branch appearance, and frowns at me disapprovingly. He appraises Tupper from head to toe and smiles. "That'll be one twenty-six, thanks."

Quiet and rumbling, Tupper mutters, "We need a roll away." This seems to excite the concierge, and he happily adds thirty dollars to the total. He hands us a key and gives us directions to our room.

I turn in a circle quickly, still scanning for any signs of Sarah. Nothing.

Tupper's hand goes to the small of my back as he tries to usher me forward. I tip my chin to the ceiling, holding back panicky tears. I blink. The large chandelier glows warm and inviting, sharing golden light with the dark brown timber and hefty stone walls. I blink again, my eyelids opening on an old scene.

A large chandelier hangs over my head. The light from a hundred fake candles dances across the ceiling and showers the large reception area with golden light.

"Why are we here?" I ask again. There's something in the way his eyes keep moving to the corners, like suddenly the fichus is so interesting he just can't take his eyes off it.

Dad places his hand in the small of my back and pushes me forward. "To have a break," he says. "You know, some R and R." His tone is distracted, layered.

But I'm so happy to be with him again. The last place I stayed was okay, but the endless white from floor to ceiling and the screaming kids started to wear me down. Sarah kept me sane. She's excited about this, too. Time with Dad, away from doctors and people watching us constantly.

I find a brochure stand and pick one up. "Oh my God, Dad, look!" I exclaim, my face hurting from how wide I'm smiling. "They have a Disneyland. Can we go? Please?" Sarah bounces up and down, her hands clasped in begging mode.

I hold it to his face. He nods vaguely and says, "Sure, honey. After... Yes, sure."

After what?

Sarah walks backward. Pretending to moonwalk, she hits the wall and stops. I laugh. "Ran out of dance floor, huh?"

Dad's face snaps to me. "Don't talk to her in public, Langs," he says in a tired, intolerant tone. "People will think you're crazy."

Casting my eyes downward in shame, I say, "Yes, Dad. Sorry. I'm just so excited. I forgot."

He clears his throat and stalks across the pinkish tiles to the elevator, his eyes a foot above mine and a million miles away.

THE LIGHT BOX FLASHES *spastically. It illuminates the picture of my brain I've seen many times before. A dark shadow in one corner is pointed at with the end of a pen. The word 'untangle' is mentioned, and my dad nods in agreement.*

There are other words, too.

'No guarantee.'

'Risk of complications higher.'

'Seventy-five percent success rate.'

The words float above my head, and I pick them down one after the other. "Seventy-five percent success of what?" I ask the doctor, the words gripped in both hands like batons.

She looks at me in confusion, her eyes flicking to my father. In a heavy accent, she replies, "Eliminating the hallucination and restoring full hand function."

My hand scrunches my T-shirt. The words 'I heart HK' twisting into something sour. "You want to eliminate Sarah?" I ask, my mouth as dry as the jar full of cotton balls behind the young doctor's head.

My dad sighs a deep, dark sigh, rubs his forehead tiredly, and says,

"She's not real, Langs. The real Sarah is dead." He says it so bluntly, so definitively, because he's trying to drum it in. Drill it in.

Sarah's blue eyes blink back tears as her chest heaves tight, quick breaths of panic. Shaking her head, she looks from Dad to me and back again. She starts moving away from me, edging back to the door and grasping the handle. Escape won't save her.

I reach out. *"It's okay. I won't let them hurt you."*

The doctor watches me with equal parts fascination and discomfort. Then she addresses my father. *"I thought you discussed the procedure with your daughter."*

He shakes his head. *"She would never have come if I had."*

Damn right!

The doctor turns to me now. *"Lan-gi-lee…"* She says it like three separate words. *"This procedure could improve your mental health immensely. I read your case file. I know the anti-psychotics don't work particularly well for you. The reason for that is your hallucination is caused by a brain injury, not schizophrenia. Not to mention it could also restore proper function to your right hand."*

Sarah sits cross-legged on the floor, scared. Resigned. She's sad and blames herself for this mess. But it's not her fault.

"I'm not hurting anyone, am I?" I ask, looking to my dad, who won't make eye contact. *"My hand is okay. I can use it with a little extra concentration."* I fan my fingers out, ball them into a fist.

I plead with the doctor. Her narrow brown eyes are open and if not accepting, at least understanding. *"Please don't make me do this."*

She smiles kindly. *"Lan-gi-lee. I can't force you to have the surgery. It would be unethical. But I urge you to think about it."*

I take a few seconds to pretend to think about it, staring at the white floor. Sarah's hand in mine.

"I can't do it. She needs me," I whisper.

Dad stands up suddenly, his chair skidding backward. *"I can't do this anymore,"* he says, voice full of pain. *"You don't want to get better. I can't help you. She's dead. Sarah is dead."* He yells that last part before he storms out of the office.

I can barely see the doctor through my waterfall of tears. She has become a blur, a spot of watercolor paint ready to be spread across the page. *"Not to me. She's not dead to me."*

Sarah says 'sorry'. She wishes things were different. But if different means not having her in my life, then I don't wish it at all.

The doctor pats my shoulder and picks up the phone, speaking fast *in Chinese, then she turns to me. "Stay here, Lan-gi-lee. We'll find your father."*

So much for Hong Kong Disneyland.

41. TUPPER

GRAND CANYON LODGE, GRAND CANYON, AZ, 2015
WEATHER: DISTURBING

"**NOT TO ME. SHE'S** not dead to me." Langley's lips seem pale. Her eyes far away as they stare at the ridiculously spectacular view of stars hung over the inky silhouette of the canyon. She's not really taking it in. She's frozen except for her mouth moving and her right hand stuck in a loop of tremor, squeeze, tremor, squeeze.

We're caged in circles of light, standing under the chandelier like we're caught inside an invisible force field. I nudge her, but she stays rigid. Guests look up from their glasses of wine. The soft murmur of conversation suddenly muted. Nervously, I scratch the back of my neck. I can't stand the way everyone is staring at her.

"Langley?" I say, bending to connect with her eyes. They're vacant. Almost black. I don't know what else to do so I scoop her up in my arms. She folds over me like cardboard, and just as light. When the elevator opens, I jump inside, relieved it's empty. I shake her. "Langley? Snap out of it." She doesn't respond, and it scares me in two ways. One, because there's something wrong and two, because there's something wrong *with* her. The truth climbs with every lighted number on the elevator keypad. I don't really know this girl at all, and she's acting crazy.

We get to the room, and I have to set her down to open the door. When her feet touch the carpet, she blinks and puts her hand to her heart, her mouth opening around a tiny cry.

I open the door and she walks inside, dazed but more alert.

I sit down on the bed, the old mattress creaking under my weight. Mom's reply had been 'ooh fancy!' But it looks kind of tired and old in here. I look up at Langley's unwitting face.

"What the hell was that?" I ask.

"What?" she asks innocently, and this scares me even more. She seems to have no idea of what just happened.

Dragging a hand down my face, I try to peel away some of my frustration. "You like flipped out. You went all catatonic."

Her eyes find mine. They register my anxiousness, and her expressions falls into disappointment. "I did? Oh."

"Oh?"

She sits down on the bed, rolling toward me until our shoulders touch. "I did escape from a loony bin, remember?" she says laughing half-heartedly.

"Not funny," I say flatly.

"It's a little funny." She knocks my shoulder playfully.

I sigh. "You have to give me a little more than that."

"I can't. You won't understand." She leans her head on my arm, her hair falling onto my bare skin.

"Try me," I say. "I promise I'll try to understand."

Or just lie. Lying would be okay because I'm scared of what you're going to say.

"I promise, by the end of the journey, I'll tell you everything. But please, not tonight," she pleads. "Just know I would never hurt you, Tupper. In truth, I think I'm starting to like you way too much. Tonight, I just want to rest, eat, and watch a movie. Can you let me have that?"

I know, I *feel*, that she would never hurt me. She's all papery and torn. Broken in more ways than me, but not dangerous. Still...

She puts her hand over mine. I withdraw.

"Give me something," I whisper. "How can I trust you if you're not honest with me?"

She exhales sadly. I feel bad to cause her pain, but I need to know.

"You know how I said there was something a bit broken in my brain?"

I nod.

"Well, it sometimes causes me to get stuck, kind of like a record skipping over the same bar over and over again. I get frozen on a loop. When that happens, I need someone to lift the needle so I can start spinning again. I was trapped in a memory. Living it over." She pulls both hands through her hair, clasps her head. "It kinda sucks."

I stare at my smudged fingers. My life seems so simple and easy compared to hers. "Is there anything they can do, like surgery or drugs…?"

She pauses, ticks off a list in her head. "Only if I'm happy with not being me anymore at the end of it."

What a place to live in. Stuck somewhere in between. I feel so bad for her that I suddenly feel trapped, too. The windows seem too small. The walls shrink. I stand up just for something to do. "I'm sorry."

Her words are a murmur, sounding exhausted by my sympathy. "I know you are, Tupper. Everybody always is. But I'm okay. I'll be okay. Okay?"

"Okay."

After she collapses back on the bed, she pulls the room service menu out from under the phone. "Now, Tupper. How am I going to pay you back for all the lobster ravioli I'm going to order?" she says with a wink, her hair fanned over the striped bedspread like a feathery crown.

Groaning, I point to the tiny bed I'm sure half my legs would hang over. "*You* can sleep on the roll away."

———✍———

WIND RATTLES THE WINDOWS. I watch the curtains move in tiny increments as the hundred-year-old glass tries to compete against nature. Lying flat on my back, diagonally, my feet still hang off the edge despite this being a double bed.

Langley tosses and turns. Sighs loudly. She kicks her bedspread from her body several times and then pulls it back up again.

Climbing out of bed, she moves to the window, parting the curtain and pressing her fingers to the pane. It wobbles under her touch as another gust of wind flies up from the canyon. "She must be lonely," she whispers as the moonlight punches light around her, turning her into a black-and-white graphic.

It makes me think, *If she were a two-dimensional cartoon, maybe then I'd have two hopes of understanding her. Maybe.*

She approaches the bed like she thinks she's being stealthy. Squinting at her through half closed eyes, I pretend to be asleep, scared to interrupt her like I'm watching a timid animal about to eat from my hand. Carefully, she lifts the bedspread and crawls in beside me.

I move. Pull away without meaning to. It's habit.

Sniffing, she wipes her nose with the back of her hand. "Please, Tupper," she says in a dented whisper. "I don't know how to be alone."

She shuffles back until her body touches mine. I roll onto my side, making room for her to shelter in my cage of ribs and arms.

What she said makes no sense. Hasn't she been alone for a long time? But I don't question it. I let her in, let her slot into my arms like that missing puzzle piece, feeling strangely calm about it.

Slowly, the sounds outside seem to pull back down into the canyon. The wind dies. The windows stop threatening to break. Langley becomes a soft and warm girl, sleeping in my arms.

It could be ordinary. But she's not ordinary, and I hate that I love her there.

42. LANGLEY

Grand Canyon Lodge, Grand Canyon, AZ, 2015
WEATHER: BREAKING THROUGH THE CLOUDS

I'VE BROKEN A RULE, *I guess. Ran it through my fingers and snapped it over my knee. Having sought comfort in Tupper's arms, I have probably messed everything up. That feeling of safety, that comfort I felt when I was on his back being carried through the dark, I needed it.*

Because Sarah wasn't with me, I needed it more.

Gripping the edge of the mattress, I pull myself away from the warmth. I have to pull because I don't want to go. My body aches to return to that sheltered cocoon.

Tupper breathes. *He breathes.* I pause, stretched over the bed like a lazy cat. That small recognition becomes a lump wedged in my throat. Tupper is alive. But I will always choose the dead over the living. This time, the lack of choice strangles me.

Creeping my legs to the edge, I try really hard not to disturb him. I'm relieved my bruised leg cooperates. It hurts, but not as bad as yesterday.

I grip the odd chenille bedspread. *Maybe he'll think it was a dream. It was to me.* I've not been close to anyone except Sarah. Not by choice anyway. It's a sad realization. Especially since she still hasn't turned up.

I'm just about to slide off the mattress and onto the floor when his arm reaches out, curls around my waist, and drags me back under the covers.

"Stay," he whispers, half asleep.

My body relaxes. My brain says I shouldn't. I want to tell myself, *where's the harm?* But I can't even get the words out before they fade in my head. The harm is everywhere. It's what will eventually break us apart, but I start to convince my brain I don't mind being hurt. Besides, my body has already given in and is lying happily in that safe place. Maybe that's better than nothing.

43. TUPPER

GRAND CANYON LODGE, GRAND CANYON, AZ, 2015

WEATHER: THE WIND HAS DIED

THE SUN HITS HER bare shoulder. Her shirt has slipped down. Her skin is a unique shade of desert dust and golden sunlight. Dark freckles dot her arm in a very purposeful way, like someone drew them there. They are spaced apart and lined up in some unreadable constellation. Reaching behind me for my sketchbook, I carefully slide my arm out from under her head. I dot the stars on her arm onto the paper, slope the shape of her shoulder and shade in her hair. Rarely do I add color to my drawings. I feel there's no need. In the gray, everyone is a different shade of the same color. We're all just variations of shadow—light and dark.

She stirs when I shade the darker parts of her hair. The scratch of the pencil on paper a little too loud. She turns to face me, a lazy smile on her face, and I burn five degrees hotter. Pulling my knees up, I keep drawing.

"Whatchya doin'?" she asks croakily.

I give her a look as if to say, *What do you think I'm doing?* She doesn't grab my book or try to peer over the top, she just nods, turns around, and gives me space to finish.

Closing the book, I reluctantly get out of bed. "I'm taking a shower. Do you want to order some breakfast?"

Her eyes light up for a brief second, but then she wavers. A guilty look replaces her happy one. "Okay, what's the deal? Did you win the lottery or something?" she asks, shuffling up to sitting. The quilt slips down, revealing bare legs. My eyes do a quick flick, and I flush, hoping she didn't see me.

"Something," I reply, trying to step into the bathroom before she can asks more questions.

"I'll pay you back one day, Tupper," she announces eagerly.

I shake my head. The money means absolutely nothing

to me. I was going to donate the rest to charity after the road trip. I'm about to tell her not to worry about it, but then I look into her earnest eyes, and decide to say, "Okay, Langley, but only when you can."

She nods happily. I'll never take her money. I don't need it. Stepping into the bathroom, I try to think pure thoughts.

44. LANGLEY

Grand Canyon Lodge, Grand Canyon, AZ, 2015
WEATHER: UNSTABLE

THIS DOESN'T USUALLY WORK but I try it anyway. "Sarah?" I get out of bed, my skin prickling at the cold. "Sarah, are you here?" Nothing.

This is the fear. The concrete slab-sized fear that she will disappear, and it will be the last time I'll ever see her. I won't get a chance to say goodbye. I won't understand what it was that made her go. She'll just be…gone. Like she never existed.

She never existed. She doesn't exist. Not anymore.

Tipping my head to the side, I smile crazily. Inside my brain is a maze, and I don't know the way out.

Grabbing Tupper's jacket from the back of a chair, I pull it around my shoulders and creep to the door. I peer out, just my head like a *Here's Johnny!* kind of moment, and whisper tersely, "Sarah, you out there?"

My chest tightens when she still doesn't come to me. If she's gone, then I will be truly alone. There will be no way out of the fact that she's…dead. Been dead. Closing the door, I press my forehead to the laminated fire safety sheet hanging on the back. My breath fogs up over a man climbing out a window, animated flames clawing into his back.

Come back, come back, come back. I'm not ready.

The door to the bathroom opens slowly, and I sense Tupper's eyes on my back.

"You okay?" he asks.

I turn around, hands plastered to the door, hair in my face. "I'm okay," I say unconvincingly.

He's dressed in his clothes from yesterday, his hair wet and curling around his ears. "Did you order breakfast?" I shake my head, feeling like he knows I'm a liar—that I'm an imposter. "Good. Changed my mind. I think we should go.

127

We need to drive back to Williams to get our bags from the hotel."

Be in the window. Be hiding behind the curtain. Jump out and scare me now. My eyes skip frantically over every hiding place in the room while Tupper watches me with growing concern. I try to pound the crazy into a shape I can swallow or hide in my pocket, but it's not working.

Stepping toward him, I say, "But it's so nice here. We could stay another night…"

I know that he'll say 'no'. My eyes skip to the bed. I'm looking for little hands and eyes peeking out from underneath.

"Lost something?" he asks, following my line of sight.

I shrug. "No."

He starts shoving stuff in the backpack. As he picks up the map, I snatch it from his hand. He looks irritated I just did that, and his mouth cements into a hard line.

"Where to next? I ask, my voice sounding high and beaded with uncertainty.

Unfolding the map on the bed, I find our route. Tupper comes to stand next to me. Our shoulders touch. I lean into it without realizing until he steps away. I can tell there are words in him. Reluctant ones that go something like 'so… shouldn't we talk about last night?' but he doesn't speak. He holds his words in his squeezed-tight fists. They will come out on the page later.

Palm Springs is circled, and there are words written on the road leading to it.

The desert is humming with life. Hum along. **THE DESERT IS HUMMING WITH LIFE. HUM ALONG**.

There's a picture of what looks like a gangster, hands in pockets, dark suit. His mouth is pursed, little musical notes floating around his face.

"Interesting…" I muse.

Tupper folds up the map with a grunt. "We should go," he mutters. I sit on the bed, stalling, watching him pack everything as he get more and more aggravated by my lack of assistance. When he opens the door, he has to wait a full minute for me to get up and exit. He is patient, but I'm whittling that patience down to a thin line.

"You coming?" he asks.

I feel emptied. Someone has turned me upside down, poured my contents all over the floor, and tapped the end just to make sure everything has come out.

Without her, I am…

I am without her.

This isn't funny, Sarah. We could leave without you.

45. TUPPER

GRAND CANYON LODGE, GRAND CANYON, AZ, 2015

WEATHER: THINGS HANGING IN THE AIR

LANGLEY IS BEING SUPER weird. She seemed relaxed, happy even, as we lay together in bed. But now she's agitated. Moving slowly like she's wearing concrete boots. I turn around to see her limping a little on the swirly carpet, but I'm glad to see her leg seems a lot better.

We get in the elevator. She stares at her reflection like it's another person, trapped in there. Putting her hand up to the golden likeness, she starts to smear her grubby fingerprints all over it. I'm trying to think of the right question to ask, but I'm not sure what to say. I don't want to talk about last night. And it's because it meant a lot to me. I don't want to hear it didn't mean anything to her. I also don't want to rule out it ever happening again. This is how pathetic I have become in the last few days.

Sighing, I run a hand across my face, which is scratchy with stubble. Langley breaks from the silent conversation she's having with her reflection and turns to me. "You look tired," she says, her voice pitched higher than usual. "We should stay... so you can have nap." That last part comes out in a rush.

I look at her questioningly. "Why are you so intent on staying?" I ask. She turns away from me again, glaring at the elevator buttons, her finger reaching out to push them. It's obvious she's thinking of pushing all the buttons to slow us down further, so I grab her wrist before she can. I hold it firmly but gently, winding my fingers between hers.

"We have to go," I say. "We can't leave our stuff at the other hotel indefinitely. Besides, don't you want to change?"

She ignores both my questions, pointing with her free hand at the small camera lens set inside the panel of buttons.

"Do you think someone's watching us right now?" she asks, wiggling her fingers free of mine to move closer and closer until her eye almost touches the black circle. "Hello?" she says, tapping it. "They must see some pretty interesting things. Drunks, arguments, people having sex…" She glances at me when she says that, and I shift my gaze away. "People do it in elevators all the time if you believe the movies. Makes me think it must all be over pretty quickly," she contemplates.

I laugh, embarrassed. "Yeah, in an elevator, you've got to manage your time well."

She's clever. And I wonder if she does it on purpose. I've forgotten what I was trying to do. Now all I'm thinking about is elevator sex. She moves away from the bar that runs around the edge. "Someone's naked ass probably touched that." She shudders, screwing up her nose.

I laugh again. This time, it comes from deeper inside. A rumble. "Ha! I'm sure they sanitize it every now and then."

Crossing her arms, she stands in the middle of the tiny box. I smile, leaning back on the handrail and staring up at the gilded ceiling.

When the doors slide open, she exhales a breath so deep and full of relief I find myself scanning the lobby looking for the source. There's nothing there.

She strolls out of the elevator a different person than just minutes ago, calmer. I feel like throwing my hands in the air and shouting in frustration. But I don't. Following her to the checkout counter, I watch her place her arms up on the bench and then slide over like she's making room for someone. She looks down at the floor and beams, streams of sunlight piercing through the gaps between her teeth.

46.LANGLEY

Williams, AZ to Palm Springs, CA, 2015
WEATHER: IT'S RAINING TRUTH AND LIES

THE LIES. LIES. LIES. Lies. They're bugs hitting the windshield. Small at first, but with each splat, the obstruction spreads. Soon, we won't be able to see where we're going.

After picking up our bags from Williams, we head straight back onto the highway. It's a six-hour drive to Palms Springs, and it's already one o'clock.

I put my feet up on the dash, feel the burning glare from my silent chauffeur, and let them slide back down. Sarah taps me on the shoulder, points at Tupper's weary face. His eyes droop, and his five o'clock shadow looks more like a twelve AM shadow. He yawns just to confirm my thoughts, and I put my hand on his over the gear stick. Sarah giggles soundlessly, and I roll my eyes. "Let me drive for a while," I say.

He grunts, his eyes tunneling through the windshield. The dark gray road seems endless in front of us. "I can, you know. I can drive," I say a little too desperately, like I'm trying to convince him that I'm *real people*. I'm normal. I can do normal things. "I learned it in life skills," I finish, slamming a medical file three inches thick down over any illusion I could be normal.

"Life skills?" The question mark floats in the space between us, getting pushed around by the air conditioner.

I blow my hair from my eyes. Sarah rubs my shoulders. She thinks it should be okay. Encourages me to confide in him.

"You know, in case we ever got released, they taught us life skills. Like how to drive, how to cook spaghetti Bolognese, do laundry, pay bills online. Life skills!" I don't know why I keep saying 'life skills' so enthusiastically, like it's some kind of party trick.

He raises his eyebrows, something ticking over inside that shell he lives in, but it's not getting shared with me today.

I feel embarrassed now. My life seems so sad and pathetic. Clasping my hands in my lap, I stare at them. Sarah sits back and does the same.

"I can't cook," he says, a few words puncturing the silent case he often surrounds himself with. "And laundry and paying bills, every school should teach that kind of thing."

The words are not genuine. They're said to make me feel better. But I don't mind. Kind words have always been rare. I hoard them, shove them in the glove compartment for later.

He still seems unconvinced about me driving. I smooth the maps on the seat with my palm, the tiny cartoons and phrases faded with fold lines through them. "You could draw while I drive," I suggest.

Just like that, as if my words were magic, the Chevy rolls to the side slowly and then stops. The blinker tick-ticking away like a metronome keeping time. His smile is slow and warm. His hands are eager as they dive over the backseat, rummaging around for his sketchbook. He doesn't say anything, just slides across until I have to climb over him to sit in the driver's seat.

"Sure you can drive a stick?" he asks, his fingers already flicking through the drawn pages to find the blank ones.

"Yep, sure can!" Truth is they assumed all anyone like me would be able to afford was a piece of junk thirty-year-old stick shift.

I bounce up and down on the seat a few times, the springs digging into my butt. "Seatbelt, check! Mirror, check! Foot on brake, check! Clutch in, check! Handbrake off, check! Indicator on, and here we go!" I announce.

Chuckling, Tupper sinks into his seat. One arm rests along the top, sort of behind me, the other one cradles his sketchbook, which he hunches over protectively. I notice he's written 'Life Skills!' in large text across the top of the page. I lean over, my head resting on his arm to try to see what he's drawing.

"Eyes on the road," he mumbles before turning his back to me and blocking me out.

I huff and turn the radio on, humming along to pop

music I've never heard before while wondering how long I have. How long before it all comes apart and I'm left standing, empty-handed, in the middle of the mess?

———✥———

I WATCH THE WAY he draws, my eyes darting right when I think he's not looking. His movements are fluid, concentrated and sure.

Tapping the steering wheel, I watch for the 'life in the desert' his mom was talking about. Spring flowers compete with the dark red earth, the sun is out but the air is cold. The music is accompanied by the scratch of lead on paper, and I find the noise soothing. Sarah leans over the seat. She can see what he's doing, and she thinks it's pretty funny I can't.

Flipping over the page, he takes a break, spinning his pencil around in his fingers. "So drawing's your thing?" I say quietly, observing the obvious.

He nods, cracks his neck, and says, "Sort of."

"Sort of?" I ask.

"Well, I'd like it to be, I guess. It's just…" he starts, but never finishes.

"Do you love it?"

"I do… but…"

"But what?" I challenge.

He sighs. "It's not what my parents want for me. Not what I'm *supposed* to do. I got a full scholarship to play football at like five different colleges."

I raise an eyebrow, wanting to say, *Ha, I knew it!* I knew he was some kind of super athlete.

"Everyone wants me to take one. I'd be stupid not to, right? I mean, a free ride. But there would be no time for this." He gestures at the book in his lap. "I'd have to put the pencil down." He twirls the pencil around in his fingers. I've rarely seen him without it. "So yeah. I do. I do love it, but…"

I frown, put up a hand to stop him. "Don't say it, Tupper, don't say I do…but… Say, I do… and… I've only seen a little of what you can do. And you're really good. You should do something more with it. If you don't want to play football, then don't. Become an uneducated, starving artist if you want to. It's your life."

He shrugs, his cheeks pink, his gaze on the floor. "Maybe."

Then he turns to me, his eyes staring intensely, and I shrink into the seat.

"What about you? What do you want to do?" He puts the word "do" in air quotes. And if he means with the rest of my life, then there isn't much of an answer. I don't have a future like he does. There are no possibilities, no colleges fighting over me. I don't have the privilege of turning them down to follow my passion. I am a dead end with a dead sister. My future slipped over the edge of a cliff a long time ago; it didn't even try to hang on.

I sigh sadly. "My world's different from yours, Tupper."

"Sorry," he says, flicking open his book.

Sarah pats my head, and I shrug her off. "It's not your fault."

There's no one to blame here. Not anymore.

WILLIAMS, AZ TO PALM SPRINGS, CA, 2015

WEATHER: DRY AND DESERTED

LIFE SKILLS? **I HAVE** questions, and the list grows. But my mouth, although more open than it's ever been, still mostly likes to remain closed. I look at my sketch. Langley sits at the wheel, a steaming pot beside her, a calculator in one hand and a pile of folded laundry in the other. Big lettering rolls across the top in a curled banner.

LIFE SKILLS!

I run my hand over her gray shaded face, her freckles resting on her high cheekbones. Her eyes aren't right. Erasing them, I make them bigger, sadder.

She talks about 'we' a lot. I assume she means the other patients at the hospital. I picture her in a padded room, huddled on the edge of a metal bed, crazy people shouting through barred doors, and it makes me shiver. I grip my pencil a little harder.

Langley doesn't seem like she belongs in a place like that. She seems like she should be here. I smile as I move to the next page and sketch her profile. Her long lashes stretching to the windshield.

She glances at me from time to time, and I huddle over my pictures. She'll think I'm a bit stalker-like if she sees these.

Closing the book, I roll my shoulders. Stretch my neck.

"Maybe I'll try waitressing," she announces, even though I didn't ask. "I'd look cute in one of those diner outfits. Don't you think?"

"Sure," I reply lazily, my eyes drifting over the level scene we're racing past. I see life in the form of flowers, but is that what Anna meant?

Langley hums along to another song she's obviously never heard. It's then I realize life is here in the Chevy, sitting right next to me. Humming.

———— ❧ ————

A SHARP BANG WAKES me, and my eyes shoot open. Langley grips the wheel tightly, the yellow lines of the headlights snaking all over the place as she struggles to maintain control of the car. She gasps my name, "Tupper," and the back of the car swings off the road and pulls the front with it. Red dust billows in front of the lights, making ghostly shadows as the car sits idle in a turn out.

Patting my chest, I check for injuries. I'm okay. Langley's breathing hard, staring out at the dark, unblinking, and I feel bad I checked myself first.

I think she's frozen again, like she's going to have some sort of panic attack or behave like she did in the hotel. But then she yells, "Holy shit, Tupper! I swear that wasn't my fault."

Releasing the wheel, she turns the car off and pulls up the handbrake. She turns to me and checks me over, then she glances over the backseat, gives a thumbs-up, and steps out of the car.

She shouts from the back of the Chevy. "You've got a flat." She bangs on the back window to call me over. I use the torch on my phone to look, and yes, sure enough the back wheel has a puncture. Langley hugs herself as a cold wind pushes us both in the back, then bounces up and down on her toes. "Where's your jack?" she asks, and I raise an eyebrow at her. "Life skills! Remember?"

After I pop the trunk, I try to unscrew the bolt that's holding the jack to the spare tire. It won't budge. I shine the torch over the bolts more closely. They're rusted through.

I release a string of bad words as I strain to loosen them. I should have checked that before I left.

Langley's hands go to my shoulder as she peeks into the trunk. "What's the matter?"

Shuffling back, I close the trunk. "Can't get the jack out of the tire. They're rusted together. How far are we from Palm Springs?" I ask.

She screws up her nose, her freckles communing at the bridge, and replies, "Still like a hundred and fifty miles."

I look up the number for the Roadside Assist my parents made me get and call.

They tell me it's going to be a while. Especially since I'm not entirely sure where we are, only what highway we're on. I curse the fact that I have no internet on my phone.

Langley looks excited rather than upset. Her eyes are bright, her skin flushed. "So we're going to be waiting a while, huh?"

Sighing, I shove my phone in my pocket and let my eyes adjust to the silky dark. "Might not be till' morning."

She smiles, and my heart hurts. "Cool!"

Sashaying around me, she opens the trunk again and pulls out the little survival kit my dad packed. It has matches, toilet paper, a sleeping bag, and some other essentials. No food, though.

When she grabs the toilet paper and the matches, she leaves me wondering what the hell she's doing. Then she takes what's left of our snacks and a bottle of water, then traipses down the slope, stopping at a fence. "C'mon Tupper. I want to find this humming life your mom was talking about."

I lock the car and follow her. The roadside woman said they'd call me when they were within an hour of the highway.

Langley waits at the fence. When I reach her, she throws the bag of stuff over and turns to me. She looks like a ghost in this light, a ghost wearing red polka dot sneakers. "Lift me up," she orders.

Carefully, I hold her under her arms and lift her over the fence. She is lighter than I expect, and I can feel her ribs between my fingers. She lands softly, and I climb over less elegantly.

She marches forward about fifty feet before squatting down.

"What are we…"

"Sh!" she threatens as she scrunches wads of toilet paper into little balls and lays them on the ground deliberately.

Crouching, I watch her make a teepee of sticks and bits of grass. She lights it, and it transforms into a bright smoky fire almost immediately. I'm impressed.

She lays a hand on my back. It sits there like a star, a burning star on my shirt. I feel it move every time I breathe. I breathe carefully, scared to frighten it away like a butterfly that's settled on my finger. "Listen," she whispers, a smile stretching slowly across her face, her brown eyes golden in the firelight.

The breeze has slowed and the still night opens the floor for the desert to, well, hum and then sing.

A chorus of wind through stout bushes and bugs buzzing and coyotes barking, combines to produce this low brushy hum.

Langley's hand slides from my back and her fingers entwine with mine. Gripping my hand firmly, she stares into the small fire. We sit back and I find myself laughing, just quietly, small tears forming in the corners of my eyes. Sitting here, holding the crazy girl's hand, the desert talking to me in reverent whispers, is the closest I've felt to Anna since I started this journey. I can see her here. I can *feel* her. Imagine her eyes open wide in wonderment at the sounds a supposedly dead place can make.

Langley rustles around in the bag she brought. She passes my sketchbook to me like someone would a precious artifact. She doesn't say anything. Just unwraps a candy bar and proceeds to demolish it, feeding the fire with scavenged sticks, licking her fingers and staring out at the starry sky.

She glances at me every now and then, grinning with a mouthful of chocolate. This time, I don't hunch away from her. I just draw.

———⟡———

WHEN I'M FINISHED, I sharpen the lines around her face, lengthen her hair, and then hand it to Langley. She stares at it for a while, tilting her head sideways, turning the paper at different angles, scrutinizing my work. Then she shakes her head, flipping the page over to a fresh one. "Nope! Looks like you if you were a woman, and not a very feminine one at that." Pushing the book to my chest, she says, "Try harder." Her eyes are steady, and a challenge rolls around her irises like a ball bearing.

Taking it back, I try again. This time instead of picturing Anna coming from me, I picture *me* coming from *her*. I soften her face. Change her cheekbones. I make her eyes tired, a little sunken from lack of sleep. Her top is dirty. Her bra strap hangs loose over one shoulder. Strands of hair have come loose from her ponytail, sweeping across her forehead. *This could be her. This really could be her.* I hold it back from me, as far as my hand can stretch, almost scared of what I've created. I'm looking at a ghost, her eyes, *my* eyes, stare vacantly past me into the black shadows blanketing the field. Suddenly, I turn around, feeling like someone's watching me. Ice sweeps my chest. Someone's left a frozen handprint on my heart, and I shiver.

Langley watches this performance quietly. Her eyes tracing my movements like a pencil. "You okay there, Tupper?" she asks warily.

I hand the drawing to her. "I don't know how I did that," I whisper, a little, a *lot*, spooked.

Langley stares at the picture, her auburn hair falling on either side to frame my mom's likeness. "Wow," she says. "Have you ever seen a photo of her?" She tucks some hair behind her ear so she can see me better. I shake my head.

She can see I'm freaking out a little, and she shuffles closer. "How old were you when she left you?"

You mean when she locked me in a hot car and never came back?

"Don't know. Eight or nine months, maybe…" I stutter, feeling uncomfortable. The desert dust gets in my eyes, itching my skin.

She puts her finger to her bottom lip, picking at a loose bit of skin. "You've probably just accessed an early memory. You know, like deep in your subconscious." Putting her hand on my knee, she rubs it maternally. "It's okay, Tupper."

Embarrassed, I jerk away. "I know it's okay. I'm fine. You don't need to worry about me. I'm not the crazy one."

She holds a stick she's been poking the fire with up in the air. A lonely line of smoke winds its way up to the sky. And then she points it at me accusingly. "What?"

This is why I shouldn't talk. Should never be allowed to talk. Because when I do, I say the stupidest things imaginable. I hurt people. I'll always pick the wrong word.

She stands, and I follow. "I'm sorry," I say, grabbing her shoulders.

Her eyes crush me to dust. Finer than dust. To particles that float around on beams of sunlight. "It's too late for that now," she says quietly.

Her hands scrunch into fists. She glances sideways, nods,

and stomps off further into the field. Then she comes back, grabs the matches and paper, and leaves again. And me? Well, I just stand there like an idiot, words lying in puddles at my feet, while coyotes bark in the distance.

A hundred feet away, a small orange glow appears. The light wraps around Langley's shadow as she stands over it, hands on hips, looking like a super hero ready to jump off a tall building.

48. Anna

Palm Springs, CA to Grand Canyon, AZ, 1997
WEATHER: TOO BRING, TOO WARM, TOO MUCH

ANNA FEELS LIKE IT'S chasing her. A growing, chemical cloud that wants to swallow her, keep her hungry and chained to darkness. The need claws at her will, punctures her independence. She bends, consorts with herself, bargains…

She knew it wouldn't be easy. Her strength wavers at the same time she tells herself she'll never touch the stuff again. There are ins and outs, ways around the word never, and her brain keeps poking the closed door to her sobriety, looking for a crack to push through.

Biting her lip, she tries to push her awareness out of her body and onto the asphalt, to the spreading desert meadows on either side of the car. Speeding down the highway, she is struck by the color. Stirred by the misconception she had about the desert being dead, lacking life. The flowers move in a continuous wave with the breeze. She swerves as her eyes follow the movement over paddocks, creeping up the soft hills.

Breathing slower, she tries to calm herself, but she feels the life of the desert humming through her body, sending sparks through her fingers. She curses, her whole body charged with anxiety.

The Chevy rolls to a stop. She climbs from the car like she's being pushed from it, the hum getting louder and louder until she covers her ears.

Tupper cries out, but she has to get away from the car. She climbs the fence and runs into the center of the field, prickles grazing her legs, pollen bursting from the blooms she crushes under her feet.

She releases her ears, hands out wide, and screams. Long, loud, singular screams that flare into the sky one at a time.

They scream, *Help me!* But there is no one to hear.

Anna runs her nails up and down her limbs. Her arms are itchy as hell. She wants to tear her hair out. Dig a hole and bury herself like a tooth-marked dog's bone.

Maybe then it would stop hurting.

49. LANGLEY

The Middle of the Arizona Desert, 2015
WEATHER: TOO CALM

SARAH SCURRIES AFTER ME, slipping on what smells like cow crap. She stays there, face in the dirt, until I come back and pull her up. When I yank her hand, she looks at me with her sky-blue eyes and I know she thinks I'm being silly. I just wish he hadn't said that. I didn't realize how much I didn't want him to see me that way until he said it. Even if it's true, I just... I just...

Oh, I don't know.

"Ugh!" I shout to the streaky stars, my arms tense and fisted at my sides, the blue night freckled with silver. *I'm crazy. It's true.* Sarah nods in agreement.

"Ready? One, two, three... rock beats scissors! I win," I say triumphantly. "I am the fire master."

Sarah scowls. "You always get to be the fire master."

Grinning, I turn my back to her, eagerly building my little hearth, finding stones and placing them in a circle. "Go," I wave my hand behind my back. "Go get the wood, wood wench!"

Sarah huffs and stomps through the trees.

Mom and Dad are fighting, although Dad calls it having an animated discussion, as they try to erect the tent. Sarah stops to complain to them, getting yelled at for standing on one the tent poles they're trying to pull through the nylon sleeve.

I ball up paper and start building my fire.

Five minutes later, squishy footsteps thump in the mud behind me. Sticks are thrown to the ground. Something light is placed on my head. I pat my hair carefully.

"It's a crown for the fire master, little sis," she says. "Long live the fire master!" She pumps her fist in the air and stomps in a puddle, mud flying at my clothes.

"Are you two fighting?" Dad's muffled question comes from beneath a

balloon of blue and green nylon. "If you're going to fight the whole time we're here, we might as well pack up and go home."

"No, Dad," we answer in unison.

"Jinx," Sarah shouts before I can.

I groan while she watches me shrewdly, waiting for me to slip up and speak. Now I have to be quiet until she says my name.

50. TUPPER

THE MIDDLE OF THE ARIZONA DESERT, 2015
WEATHER: THE COLD SHOULDER

I KNOW I SHOULD go over there. I should apologize. But words…words always fail me. Words are not my friends. I prefer the etch of lines on thick paper and ink seeping in, describing a fragment in time. That's my language. It's what I understand.

Sitting down with a thump, I stare at her fire while mine begins to die. A spot of orange light, growing like the sun rising.

Getting out my pencil, I start my apology.

———————

WHEN THE PHONE RINGS, I damn near jump out of my skin and into my fading fire. I glance over at Langley, who has turned toward me expectantly.

The operator for the roadside assist tells me in a very tired voice that they're on the highway, and depending on how far along we are, they should find us in about an hour and a half.

After I tear the page from my sketchbook, I follow the flames like a heavy-footed moth. Fully expecting to get burned.

The moment I leave the crumbling heat of my fire, cold air bolts around me. I find myself hurrying toward Langley's much larger and more impressive fire, rubbing my hands and sort of skipping in a very unmanly way, smashing the delicate wildlife as I go.

I'm a disaster. I don't belong here.

I reach the circle of her light and stop. She turns upward, her eyes black, her face a shadow. Handing her the piece of paper, I linger in the cold just outside the reach of the heat of the flames, and wait. Hands behind my back. Rocking on my heels.

I watch nervously as she unfolds it like she's opening my

skin and peering inside my chest to see what's ticking in there. She reads the caption and snorts.

Then she stands.

I can't move, imaginary quicksand sucking at my ankles. She holds the page up, the dark lines illuminated through the back in orange sepia. "Is this me?" she asks, pointing to the picture of Langley dressed in a kick-ass super hero outfit, her hair flying like a flag in the wind, her hand holding up my decapitated head, my headless body lying on the floor. It's captioned.

NOW WHO HAS LOST THEIR MIND!

Cartoon Langley smiles wryly, gazing at her nails nonchalantly while my head dangles from her other hand.

"Sorry," I say to the ground.

Her hand falls to her side, the picture flapping against her thigh. "It's okay," she says, her voice soft, vulnerable. "Though I do appreciate the gesture, I don't want to decapitate you. I'm all about arson, just so you know." She winks.

I chuckle, shuffling my feet closer to the fire and to her. The light pulses like a heartbeat with every shift in the wind. "I thought it might be cathartic." I take both her hands in mine, and she moves closer. Her eyes dart to the fire, a small nod like she's checking on something, and then we just stand there, hands swinging like a suspension bridge over the red dust. "I don't think you're crazy."

She looks up, the freckles on her face matching up with the stars in the sky. Langley's a galaxy. Another world. She releases my hands and wraps hers around my middle, squeezing me in a tight embrace. Her muffled voice rumbles up from where it's buried in my shirt. "Thank you, Tupper. I am, but thank you."

My hands are at my sides, pointing out stiffly like I'm an arrow about to shoot into the sky. I relax. Do the thing I've been wanting to do. I wrap my arms around her shoulders and pull her close, hunching over and sheltering her from the desert.

She breathes slowly. Big, heavy sighs that make our sides split and close.

I bury my face in her hair, my lips brushing over her head. One kiss. One simple kiss, just lightly on the top of her head, and it seems to bloom.

She feels it like I laid a rock down on her part. Her legs bow and she sinks, suddenly turning her face to mine.

"What are you do…?" she starts, but my mouth has already met with hers. She's already become soft and fluid in my arms.

She tastes like ash and salt and Langley.

She feels perfect and wrong and dangerous.

And all I can think is, *I don't deserve this. And thank God for Langley, for the desert, and for forgiveness.*

And then, *Screw it!* There are only the night blooms and the sky to witness.

AMBER LIGHTS RUN ACROSS the desert floor and meet our feet. We don't break apart instantly like maybe we should. We untangle slowly, reluctantly. Langley lets out a disappointed moan as I finally let my hands fall from her waist and take a step back, a sheet of icy air slicing between us.

Laughing awkwardly, I stare down at my hands like I'm not entirely sure they're connected to my brain right now.

Langley touches her lips with three fingers and smiles. Then she punches me lightly on the arm and says, "Now that *was* my first kiss, so I don't have a lot to compare it to, but I have to say…not bad, Tup, not bad at all."

She starts kicking dirt on the fire to smother it. I help. I'm glad it's dark so she can't see the surprised look on my face. *First kiss?*

"I didn't know," I mutter, thinking maybe I should have done something different, made it better somehow.

"Kisses are hard to come by when you're separated by locked doors, and you don't know which personality you might be about to lock lips with," she quips. "*Wanted* kisses anyway." She murmurs those last words into the smoky ashes, but I heard her.

We walk back to the car, her hand finding mine in the dark. "Don't sweat it, Tupper. It was all shooting stars and loud bangs. It was…"

I wait for her to finish, but she doesn't. Pausing at the fence, she stares at me under the yellow light of the service van. She's waiting to hear my impressions of what may have been the most unbelievable kiss ever, like in the entire history of the world.

"It was… liberating," I say, hoisting her over the barrier. It's probably the wrong word, I'm sure, but like I said, words are not my friends.

I don't tell her about all the pictures running through my brain.

Flowers opening…

Atomic bombs exploding…

Light pouring through a keyhole…

Chains falling to the floor…

She stands on the other side of the fence, hands on her hips. "Liberating, huh?" Her eyes roll around as she tests the word out. "Yep, I can see that." She grins and it has its own powerful force, like Thor's hammer splitting open the ground.

A man in a fluorescent vest comes from behind the Chevy with a lantern dangling from his hand. "So what seems to be the trouble here?"

I laugh.

Where do I start?

51. LANGLEY

Somewhere Above the Arizona Desert, 2015
WEATHER: UP IN THE CLOUDS

I THINK I'M FLOATING, my toes barely kissing the earth so they look like dusted, red velvet cakes.

He kissed me. He kissed me, and Sarah just pulled an *ick!* face and turned away from us. And then…I kind of forgot she was there.

And now I feel awful and wonderful and all mixed up in too many ways. I'm caught between the mixer blades, twirling, pieces of me getting flung against the sides. I know I'm no good for him. Eventually, I'm going to have to leave. But the part of my brain that's supposed to care about that has decided to go on vacation. As soon as Tupper's lips touched mine, that part of my brain packed a bag, said, "See ya," and slammed the door. I heard it whistling as it stepped down the path. Heard the car door slam and the tires squeal as it drove away. Further proof I am insane and should not be allowed to kiss strong, silent boys like Tupper.

I'm in trouble.

From the backseat, Sarah teases me, making kissy faces and soundlessly singing *Langley and Tupper sitting in a tree.* She draws hearts in the air, and flaps her arms like a chicken. I roll my eyes. Right now, I'm glad she can't talk.

The sun rises over the sandy stretch in front of us. Tupper drives, his eyes propped open by will. We're both so tired and confused, but sleeping in the Chevy just didn't seem practical. Besides, Palm Springs was only an hour away.

Tupper rubs his jaw in that tense, wiry way, and glances at me briefly. He keeps doing it. I'm always there to catch him, because I haven't stopped staring at him since we started driving. When his eyes find mine, he smiles, quick as a flashcard, and then it disappears like it was one of my hallucinations.

He flicks one finger at the windshield without releasing

the steering wheel. "Nice sunrise," he comments.

I watch the orange, pink, and gold paint his face. His lips pinker. His skin darker. "Yep," I reply, nodding spastically.

Light pours through the violent spray of palm leaves, wraps around their long, thin trunks, and spreads over the red dirt like rising flood waters. It is silent but not awkward. I think if we forced a conversation, then it would be awkward. Whatever is happening between us, we both seem happy to let it grow like the sunrise. Seep slowly through the barren places, warm the parts that are just starting to sprout. At least that's my hope.

The sun hits the front of the car and spirals slowly over the hood. Tupper squints, and I lean my head on his shoulder. I hear him breathe in, hold it, and then exhale loudly. His shoulders sink a little as his body relaxes.

"Thanks," he says, touching his head to the top of mine.

"For?" I raise my eyebrows.

"For not turning this into a big thing where we have to talk about it for hours, you know, debate where this is going, what's going to happen…" He stumbles over his words. These were wedged in his head like a tangle of bike parts, and he's having a hard time getting them out.

I shrug. "No point in asking questions we can't answer, right?" I ask. The palms turn from black shadows to a waxy green as the sun speeds up and races for the sky.

"Right," he replies with a nod, but he seems unsure.

Straightening, I smooth out my wrinkled clothes. "Talking's hard for you. I get that."

His jaw is rigid, his mouth clamped shut. People might think he's uncomfortable, but I'm coming to understand this is Tupper at rest. "It's okay." I nudge him with my elbow. "I get it. You like it in there. You don't want to come out from under your shell." Pinching my fingers together, I pretend I'm lifting a lid. "But maybe, from time to time, you might let me in there with you?"

He keeps his eyes on the road, unwires his jaw long enough to say, "Langley, you're already in."

My heart does this unfamiliar thing. It squeezes and hollows and hurts. I touch it just to make sure it's not actually trying to escape my chest. His mouth winds back up as if he never said anything at all, but his hands grip the wheel tighter. His cheeks are as pink as the sunrise that's slipping back like the tide.

I bite my lip and whisper, "Okay then." I talk to the windshield just as he did. "And Tupper?"

"Mhmm?"

"I just want to say, if you ever feel like doing that again, I mean, the kissing me thing. I wouldn't be opposed to it." Maybe I should feel embarrassed, but I'm not. I smile, watching his eyebrows rise. "Just so you know."

He chuckles. It lands deep in his chest. Burrows into mine. I don't want to, but I'm already starting to miss the sound.

Sarah stares out the window with a wistful expression, and I let my mind wander to that place I rarely go. It's where I imagine her grown, as my older sister. I picture talking to her about this boy I've met, her serious eyes and wicked smile filling the room. It doesn't hurt as much as it usually does. Just a small sting rather than the usually large knife wound.

I miss things that will never happen—that will always be the case—but right now, something good is finally happening to *me*.

52. TUPPER

PALM SPRINGS, CA, 2015

WEATHER: LAZY HEAT

"READ IT AGAIN," I say, pulling over at the first coffee place I can find.

"Not every pretty place provides a revelation. Sometimes it's the ditch with the trapped trash blowing through it. Ask the stars," Langley reads in a slow, mysterious tone.

"You know, I'm starting to think your birth mom was either a Dalai Lama kind of genius or she belonged in the psych ward with me. A place where she could have been properly medicated," Langley adds, tracing her finger over Anna's picture of stars set in the ground like at the Chinese Theater in LA. Anna's name is written on one, complete with handprints and high-heeled shoe prints, which kind of look like exclamation points. There's no Tupper star.

We get out of the car and stare down the long wide street, sand gathering in the gutters, the heat warping the view. Langley slams her door before coming around to meet me. "Is that what they did, medicated you?" I ask warily.

She purses her lips, her eyes on a shop window full of expensive designer furniture and one large plastic cactus covered in fairy lights. "Among other things."

I decide I'm not satisfied with her answer. If she needs medication, maybe we should get her some. "Did it help?"

She shakes her head, disappointed. "Where did my quiet artist go?" she asks, leaning against the car, her long legs crossed at the ankles. I stand in front of her, completely covering her with my shadow. She gazes up at me with her bambi-like eyes, and I momentarily forget what I'm doing. I take a step closer. She's in the gutter, and I'm on the curb. I tower over her, trying to hunch down to make myself smaller.

"It's just, if you need medication, maybe we should find

some," I say, touching her face. Her freckles are so dark, like ink spots. I feel like I could smudge them when I brush her cheek with my thumb.

She leans into my touch. "For me, being on meds means feeling nothing. No highs or lows. Nothing." She planes her palm through the air. "Just coasting along, not caring about anything or anyone. Maybe they never got the combo right, I don't know. What I do know is I don't feel like me when I'm on them. I'm okay, though. Tupper, really. I'm doing okay without them." Her voice is pleading. She wants me to understand, and I know I need to try.

Nodding, I put my hands in my pockets because I want to hold her. I want to tell her that not being her would be a travesty. Instead, I say, "Coffee?" and lead her inside.

———ɔ———

LANGLEY SWIRLS THE LAST bit of coffee left in her cup and then downs it, pulling a sour face at the last sip. "Do you think she meant movie stars?" she asks, pointing at the stack of pamphlets behind us that list tours of movie stars' houses.

"Maybe."

Or maybe she was just nuts like you said.

I feel kind of apathetic about it at the moment.

Langley yawns loudly, tapping her mouth to trap it in. It makes me yawn, too. We both stare at each other with eyes looped in tiredness. "We need to sleep before we do anything else," I say, glancing at my watch. It's eleven am. Too early to check in anywhere, but we could try.

Folding her arms over the vintage Formica table, she smiles sleepily. "Mmm. Sleep would be good."

We leave the café and stroll down the street, looking for a cheap motel. Langley holds up a pamphlet, waving it in the air. "We should do this," she says, fanning herself as the heat starts to build around us. A warm breeze flows through the quiet street, and the sound is like hundreds of popsicle sticks raining to the street as the stiff branches of the palms trees hit each other. I duck without thinking.

"We could, I guess," I say, noncommittal. I can't think right now. Too tired…

Suddenly, Langley grips my arm and pulls. "Look. Let's see if we can stay there," she says eagerly, finding some extra reserves of energy, which is good because my legs are like lead and she has to drag me toward the entrance.

The hotel markets itself as 'old Hollywood'. It's kind of cool with its kidney-bean pool and fifties architecture. We slip through the gate and into the oasis-type garden, Langley pulling me up the path like a reluctant toddler.

The man at the desk gives us a regretful expression when I ask, "I don't suppose you have a room we can check in to right now, do you? We've been driving all night."

He shakes his head. "I'm sorry, sir," he says, staring at his leather-bound booking folder. He taps the page with a pencil. "The best we could do would be twelve thirty."

My sigh is loud. I hadn't realized how desperately tired and in need of a shower I was until I stepped into this dark, plush room, with clean, blue water shining at me through the window.

Langley sticks close to my side, her head gazing around the lobby decorated with old Hollywood memorabilia. She's starting to slip, too, tiredness pulling her shoulders down. Her eyes blinking slower and slower.

The desk manager takes pity on us. "I tell you what. How about you book in now? Go park your car and get your bags. You could go for a swim while we get your room ready. I'll let you know as soon as it is," he says, a genuine smile on his face.

Once I've checked in and paid, he hands me a keycard and two clean towels, so fluffy and warm I want to wrap myself in them and close my eyes forever. "Here. This will give you access to the change rooms." And then he adds, "There are no other guests so we shouldn't be long."

I nod. I think I say *thank you*. My brain's so sluggish I wouldn't be surprised if I tipped the large ceramic statue of a black panther instead of the concierge.

53. LANGLEY

The Blue Flamingo Motel, Palm Springs, CA, 2015
WEATHER: HOT, HOT, HOT!

SARAH RUNS OFF THE minute we get to the hotel. It's okay, though. I know she'll be back. There are few patterns in her behavior, but this is one. New town, she likes to explore. If she knows where I'll be, she always returns.

We park the car and come through the back entrance. The pool calls to me. As soon as we open the gate, I peel off my jeans and wade in. Tupper looks abashed, turning his head. "I forgot to pack a bathing suit when I was fleeing from the loony bin," I say, shrugging. I don't get the big deal. Bathing suits are pretty much underwear anyway. But I keep my T-shirt on so his head doesn't explode.

He wanders into the change rooms.

As I sink below the water, I feel refreshed. Layers of dirt and oil pulling from my body like the jeans I just shed. My hair swirls around me, seaweed bobbing rhythmically with the bounce of the water.

When I come up for air, Tupper is already in. Just his torso showing. He sees me and sinks below the water shyly, though he has nothing to be shy about. I smile mischievously.

"What?" he says, water lapping his chin.

I splash water at his face. "Oh, nothing! I just expected you to be like really ripped or something, you know, because of the football thing…"

He raises an eyebrow. "Did I disappoint you?"

I bite my lip. *Far from it.* I like the fact he looks fit, but doesn't look like he overdoes it by spending all his time working out. I imagine if Tupper has free time, he draws. He strikes me as someone who doesn't even notice what his body looks like to others.

I roll my eyes. "Totally disappointed! Where's your eight-pack?" I ask, trying to see his wobbly form beneath the water.

For that, I get a large splash of chlorinated water in my face. I cough and splutter, swallowing some.

"Shit, sorry," he says, wading closer.

This feels like two bad ideas making a good one. The closer he gets, the more it feels like something other than water is between us. Something electric.

I laugh. It pulls strips from my armor. Bark falling from a tree.

My T-shirt sticks to me as I rise slowly out of the water. I take a weightless step toward him, and he just stands there like one of those flood markers in a river. Telling me all the bad things that have happened and how many bad things could still happen. But I'm finding it hard to care.

I'm not sure if there needs to be a deeper meaning to what I want right now. *I want connection.*

I close the gap between us until we're chest to chest. He seems to cave in a little, letting me in. He exhales tiredly, like he can't be bothered fighting either. I press my lips to his wet skin and smile. His hands slip around my waist, and I let go. I let him hold me up.

"I'm so tired," I whisper, burying my face in his neck.

He holds me close. His breath tripping me up. It's fast, hitched. "Me too."

Pressing my ear to his chest, I listen to his heartbeat. Enjoying the way it's forever in time, counting down.

Pressed against each other, we're waiting for some outside force to either pull us apart or hold us together. I feel his lips touch the top of my head. His hands start to wander under the hem of my shirt, but then go still. He yawns.

I lean back, gaze into his drooping eyes. "Am I boring you?" I say teasingly.

He smiles sheepishly, and his head drops a little. He moves closer, sewing our mouths together like the pull of a thread by the needle. Closer and closer.

It's a lazy but beautiful kiss. Slow and warm and promising. And I want to stay in it. Wrap it around my shoulders and live inside it, but he's gone, disappearing under the water and paddling away.

When Tupper's head pops up at the deep end, the desk

manager calls out to us from the open door. "Your room is ready." His voice is the musical equivalent of a knowing smile.

Tupper jumps out of the pool. I stare at the ribbons of water draining from his toned back, hiding like a frog beneath a lily pad with just my eyes above the water.

He grabs the towels and brings one to me.

I climb the stairs, knowing I resemble a drowned beast. Heavy water splats on the sandstone from my wet shirt as I exit the pool.

Grabbing the corner of my T-shirt, I squeeze out what water I can, secretly thankful I'm wearing black underwear. When I look back up at Tupper, he averts his eyes quickly. His mouth is open slightly and he jumps back, pushing the towel into my hands. "Here," he says gruffly, his cheeks red. As I dry off, he retrieves our bags. He drops them at my feet. "Got something to take care of. Meet you back at the room."

Pulling the towel tighter around my body, I leave, carrying all of our bags. Sarah appears from behind a bowing palm leaf and follows Tupper into the lobby.

54. TUPPER

THE BLUE FLAMINGO MOTEL, PALM SPRINGS, CA, 2015

WEATHER: WISHING IT WOULD RAIN

AN IMAGE OF THE Flash pops into my head. His winged ears shake back and forth in disappointment.

If there's a right way to behave, I'm super sure I'm doing the opposite. I just knew if I didn't put some space between us, I was going to move too fast. And it's not only for her benefit that I want to slow it down. I need a second to breathe, to take her in, not rush toward something neither of us is ready for. No matter how much I can't stop thinking about it.

55. LANGLEY

The Blue Flamingo Motel, Palm Springs, CA, 2015
WEATHER: SETTLING

WHEN I COME OUT of the shower, Sarah is perched on the edge of the bed. She seems upset or maybe disappointed, her knees up under her chin, her arms wrapped around her legs.

I come to sit beside her. "What's wrong?" I ask.

She just shakes her head, staring at the wall.

"Do you want to watch TV?" I ask, searching for the remote. Her eyes light up at the suggestion. I open the bedside drawer, finding it resting on top of Tupper's sketchbook. Two movie star tour tickets stick out between the pages. I flick the TV on to Cartoon Network. Taking Tupper's book out, I open it to the last page. There I am. Damp hair looking slick in black ink. A wet T-shirt hugging my body tight. My expression a little scary. Too secure. I look like the creature from the deep that walks out of a muddy river, set on murdering all the cheating boyfriends in the area. I grin. It's pretty cool.

"Is that why you're upset? You want a picture?" I ask Sarah, who's glaring up at me. She nods. "I'll see what I can do, okay?" She smiles.

The door opens, and Tupper pushes through just as Sarah slips through the gap. "Were you talking to someone?" he asks, his arms full of bags of food.

I knock my head toward the episode of *Uncle Grandpa*. "Just the TV," I say.

He dumps the food on the bed and shrugs. The smells of burgers and fries makes my stomach gurgle, and I hold it.

When he sees his book open, he flips it shut and gives me a nervous stare. "Sorry," he whispers. He snaps it up, clutching it to his chest like he's ashamed of it.

I smile widely. "Don't be. I think it's amazing. You made me look like some bad-ass creature from the black lagoon. I love it!"

His face seems to open up, a proud glint in his eyes. "Really?"

"Really, Tupper," I say, placing my palm on the book that's covering his heart.

His hands drum over the cover as he contemplates something in that quiet brain of his before he moves to puts the book away.

I get dressed in the bathroom. After, we eat burgers on the bed.

"So movie star tour tomorrow?" I ask for something to say. "Mhmm."

I SCRUNCH UP THE grease-stained paper and throw it the bin. Tupper leans against the headboard, his eyes slits as he fights to stay awake.

Standing at the foot of the bed, I'm not entirely sure where to go. I bounce the mattress with my hands, and Tupper's eyes fly open. "Uh… where do I… Do I…?" I ask, feeling a little unearthed, my eyes flitting to the warm space beside him.

He flips back the covers. "If you want," he says quietly, nervously.

I crawl onto the bed. He folds the quilt over me, getting under himself. I glance at the red digital clock staring at me with one evil eye. It's only seven. Light still shines around the edges of the curtains. But as soon as my head hits the pillow, my body just releases. I sink so fast I almost fall.

Tupper turns away from me, but shuffles backward so we're still touching.

We are two sides of a very strange coin, Tupper and I. Chances are there's only one like it in the whole world.

I AWAKE TO A slice of light across the bed and sounds of scratching. Deep rhythmic noises that sound like nails biding their time outside my hospital room door. I flinch, my knees flying to my chest, my head folded under, rolling myself into the protective ball that never really shielded me from anything.

The scratching stops, and a hand cups my shoulder gently. His voice is a beacon, a call home. "Langley," he says. "You okay?"

Rolling over, I stare up at the white stucco ceiling and re-member where I am. I breathe in to the point where my chest feels like it might burst and then I exhale. *It's okay. I'm okay.*

Sarah sleeps in the chair by the desk, curled up like a cof-fee-colored cat.

"Sorry I woke you," he says. "Couldn't sleep."

The clock reads four am. I shuffle up to sitting, my foot grazing Tupper's bare leg. He shifts.

The pencil spins in his fingers, and I realize the sound that woke me was the scratch of lead on paper. I peer over his shoulder. "What are you drawing?"

He lets me look, and it feels like a special privilege. It's a picture of a scrunched-up piece of paper, half-soaked in a dirty puddle. It's so intricate. As I stare at it, I notice the shape of a star coming out of the shadows.

"Sometimes it's the ditch with the trash blowing through it…" I whisper his mother's words.

He continues to shade the corners as I watch, my chin resting on his arm, bouncing up and down as his muscles flex with the movement of the pencil. "It's the first thing she's said that makes any sense to me." He speaks to the page. "It feels like something I would say, I guess."

I lift my finger to the page. "It's about ordinary things. Beauty in simplicity."

He stops drawing and turns to me, his eyes bordered with small parts of disbelief. "Exactly." I just stare at his lips as he says the words.

Taking his hand, I kiss his knuckles. "Tupper, I'm worried about us."

He nods like he knew this was coming. "Me too." He leans in, his lips brushing my cheek. His words tattoo my skin as he speaks. "But it's too late, isn't it?"

I rub my face against his. "Yes, it's too late."

We stay like that for a while. Just breathing. There are so many things to say, but neither of us really wants to speak. No one ever wants to talk about the end. Not when the story is just getting good.

"Tupper, could you draw me someone if I describe her to you?" I ask.

I like the way he sounds when we're so close. Like rocks

tumbling down a mountainside. "I'll try," he mumbles.

He lifts me into his lap and wraps his arms around me, settling the book on my legs. "Could you draw my sister Sarah? It would be so cool to give it to her when I see her," I say.

"Do you have a photo?" he asks.

I shake my head, lies coming so easily. "I did. Back in my hospital room."

Pencil poised, he whispers, "Okay, describe her to me."

56. TUPPER

THE BLUE FLAMINGO MOTEL, PALM SPRINGS, CA, 2015

WEATHER: PEACEFUL

I THINK THIS IS the part where I fall.

Langley taps her chin, tips her head to the side. "Well. She's two years older than me. We look pretty similar, but her face is thinner. Her nose is a little more turned up. Her eyes are a slightly different shape."

I start by drawing the outline of her face. "Whoa, slow down. One thing at a time."

Our arms are tangled, and she moves with me as I start to draw the shape of Langley's eyes. She puts her hand over mine, helping me change the shape.

"More almondy rather than archy."

Erasing the corners, I start again. Leaning over her shoulder, I breathe in the clean smell of her skin. She's taking the most private part of me, the part I don't share, and she's just embracing it. Holding it, not like a peculiarity, but with love and respect. She's fitting inside me like she was always supposed to be there.

I try to rein my feelings in, but I'm floating in midair. I've got nothing to hold onto.

"Her lips are just like mine," Langley says, anticipating where I was going next. I draw Langley's full but small lips. Heart-shaped. Dark pink.

She takes a sharp breath in. "Wow."

Yes, wow. I'm finding it so hard to believe. This language I speak, the one that has always made me feel like I'm standing on the edge of a cliff while everyone points at me, she seems to understand it. She doesn't speak it, but she understands it.

I fill in the spaces, listening to her instructions. Hair shorter. No freckles. Ears slightly bigger. It takes us about an hour, but at the end we have a picture of Langley's older sister Sarah. She is understatedly beautiful. Not like Langley, who looks like she stepped right out of a graphic novel. But I can definitely tell they are sisters.

Langley leans her head against my arm. Her tears roll down my skin and onto the bed. "Thank you, Tupper. You have a gift," she whispers. "You have no idea how much this means to me."

Putting the book to the side, I turn her around to face me. She doesn't seem sad, just thoughtful. Wrapping her legs around my waist, she holds me tight, just rocking slightly and allowing herself to feel what she needs to feel.

I want to say that she has given me the gift. But instead, I say, "You're welcome."

If I'm standing on the edge, it feels like maybe she's standing one step to the left of me.

While she's resting against my chest, buried warmly in my arms, my head turns to the portrait we just created, this woman who left Langley on her own to suffer in a hospital when she could have helped her. Langley's sister Sarah stares across the room, a strong defiant look on her face. She better have had a damn good reason.

57.LANGLEY

The Blue Flamingo Motel, Palm Springs, CA, 2015
WEATHER: DISAPPOINTING

I'M STRETCHING. BRIDGING THE gap between the real and unreal. Sarah tugs my hand. Tupper holds it. Soon, I will either split in half or let go, falling through the earth.

The hotel room is stuffy. I get up, dressing while Tupper snores softly, a pillow half over his head. I take the picture of Sarah, the one that breaks my heart more than it's already broken, and tear it from Tupper's book, carefully folding it and putting it in my back pocket. Tupper's phone vibrates next to his head. He emerges, hair scruffed-up at funny angles, eyes sleepy and adorable. He holds the phone close to his face, squints, and then puts it back down.

"Who was that?" I ask, sitting on the edge of the bed.

"My mom," he replies croakily. "She texts me every couple of days."

I pick up the phone. It reads, *How's it going?* and then there is a smiley face followed by a flower and a heart. I raise my eyebrows.

"She's just discovered emojis," he says, like I should know what that means.

"Oh, okay," I manage. "You should write back before she starts to worry."

He slides out of bed and walks to the bathroom, throwing over his shoulder, "Can you? Just tell her I'm in Palm Springs and I'm staying a couple of days."

I nod nervously, not wanting to show him how technologically challenged I am. I skipped out before they'd covered the cell phone part of Life Skills!

It takes me the whole time Tupper is in the bathroom to figure out how to text his mom back. I add a few emojis at the end. I even find a flamingo.

The phone buzzes her reply, and it makes me jump.

Are you feeling okay honey?

I reply, *Yes. Fine.*

Okay. Ran into your Kris yesterday. She told me to tell you hi! Waving hand emoji. Another heart. Then a weird grinning face that looks sheepish or angry, I'm not sure.

Putting the phone down, I wonder who Kris is and why she is *his Kris*, then shove it under a pillow because it's still vibrating and I've had enough.

Tupper emerges from the bathroom dressed. "You ready?"

I nod eagerly. "Ready."

He hears the buzzing and finds the phone, picking it up and giving me a questioning look.

I shrug. "It wouldn't stop."

He scrolls through the texts with no expression. But when he looks at me, he seems worried. I think he might tell me who Kris is or ask me why I am so bad at texting, but he doesn't say a word. Just grabs the tickets and holds the door open for me.

I register that Sarah's not around, but only fleetingly. My mind is distracted by the fact that as we leave the hotel, Tupper slings his arm over my shoulder and pulls me closer. We walk like this, like a couple, to the bus stop where the tour of movie stars' homes will begin.

THE WINDOW IS SMEARED with Tupper's fingerprints. He leans over me to add another to the collection, eyes wide and child-like, voice giddy with excitement. "Did you see that?" He points to yet another beautiful home with stone walls and a raked roof, a water feature dribbling down the side next to the front door. "Marilyn Monroe lived there." He keeps glancing down at the pamphlet and fact checking. He points to her name. "Yes, Marilyn Monroe." He grins.

I elbow him. "You're being a massive nerd, Tupper." He gives me a cheeky smile and continues to gush. Reading specifics from his little pamphlet and jumping up and down in his chair. It's sweet.

"Now this is a sad story," the tour guide begins, talking in hushed, overly dramatic tones. The bus stops at the front of a home spotted with cacti and leaning palm trees. "This place belonged to a very promising writer, Sean Ford. At the peak of his career, he sold five screenplays in one year." The guide went on to list some really famous movies from the fifties and sixties. Some of which I'd actually heard of. "But, you know, sometimes, fame and fortune can be a curse rather than a blessing…"

The whole bus goes quiet, all knowing what is coming. Tupper grips the glossy pamphlet in his hand, scrunching it at the bottom so it looks like a fan. "Ford considered himself an artist first, and he struggled a great deal with the way his scripts were Hollywoodized to fit the studio's idea of appropriate entertainment. That and his feelings of isolation led to his tragic end. He wished to produce something ground breaking, something truly honest and gritty, but his last work was never finished."

Tupper stares at his hands. I stare at the tour guide using someone's tragedy to entertain, and I want to slap him.

"Tragically, Ford hung himself from one of the gorgeous, exposed beams in his five bedroom, four and half bathroom home complete with lap pool and spa." I start to wonder if we accidentally got on the wrong bus and this is a real estate tour, but then the guide says, "The note he left read only—*I am but trash blowing through a sand-filled gutter.*"

The guide shakes his head solemnly, touching where I guess his heart would be. He gives Sean Ford a few seconds of false respect before he shouts, "Next stop is Casa de Liberace!"

Tupper has turned to stone beside me. I hold his hand as the bus lurches away from the writer's home, giving it a squeeze, but he doesn't squeeze back.

"I wanted it to mean something good," he whispers to himself. "Not this."

58. TUPPER

PALM SPRINGS, CA, 2015

WEATHER: ALL GLITZ AND NO SUBSTANCE

I FEEL LIKE I'M sitting in Anna's chair. An intrusion. Where I was hoping to find some peace, I keep running into sadness, loneliness. Big words that stand up on their own like the Hollywood sign.

When the bus stops, Langley yanks me from my chair and out into the sunshine. She tells the confused guide she's not feeling well and that we'll get a cab back to the motel. The bus leaves and we sit in the damp grass, the sun warming the top of our heads as she waits for me to talk.

Cars speed past. She ties her shoelace in a double knot. I breathe in. Breathe out. Try to collect the words into a sentence.

Langley pulls a Blue Flamingo Motel pen from her pocket and hands it to me. I twirl it in my fingers.

"I wish I had a memory," I say, my thoughts just slipping off my tongue. "But all I have is a police report." She touches my arm, coaxing the words out one by one. "I want to hate her. I want to understand her. But she's a stranger. A ghost. I'm not sure I'll ever get any closer."

Linking her arm in mine, she leans her head on my shoulder. "Memories aren't all good you know."

"I know. I'm just…disappointed. I'm not finding what I wanted to find," I say, sighing.

She raises her head suddenly. "Tupper, you have a unique opportunity before you."

I lift my eyes from staring at ants pulling something gross out of a crack in the sidewalk. "Yeah?"

"Yeah! You can make up your own memory. No one can tell you it isn't true. For all you know, it could be," she says animatedly, her hands chopping through the air like she's conducting an orchestra.

"Close your eyes," she orders.

I close them, pink light filtering through. "Are you going to disappear?" I ask, trying to be funny, but there's a hint of hysteria behind my words.

She laughs and finds my hand. "I'm not going anywhere. Now, picture the day you were found, this scrawny, screaming baby in a cardboard box."

Picturing it causes a sickening feeling to creep up my spine because my thoughts turn to—*how could you leave me there? What kind of person leaves a baby in a hot car and doesn't come back?*

Langley squeezes my hand and says, "Stop. Strip away your judgments about her. Really try to see a good reason for why she did what she did. It can be anything you want."

It takes a while for a story to form. But she's right. I can make up my memory. I can pretend I'm Superman, well, Kal-El before he was Superman. I imagine that she kissed me, she looked at me with love, and then she closed the lid of that cardboard box, my spaceship, and walked away because she had to. Because buildings were crashing, things were exploding. She was protecting me from something or someone. I can make it anything I want, and it will be mine.

"Got it?" she asks, when I've been silent for a long time.

I nod. "Got it."

She doesn't ask me to share it. Just musses my hair and stands. "We should head back."

Langley starts walking, even though she doesn't know which direction we should go. I grab her hand, pulling her back to me. "Thank you."

She smiles, pale teeth glinting in the harsh light the color of lightning. She makes me feel like maybe I am Superman. Or, at least, I could be.

IN THE NIGHT, SHE finds me, her hand creeping up my back like a tiny mountaineer. She threads her arms under mine to pull closer. Her chest pressed to my back, her legs cut to shape.

She thinks I'm asleep when she presses her lips to my back and whispers, "I'm starting to want more."

I close my eyes tighter. Try to stop my body from reacting to her words, because I want to shiver and turn, clasp her face in my hands and kiss her until we both come undone.

It's the way she says it that makes me hesitate. It's regret.

It's the words she leaves out, but I know are there… *I'm starting to want more… but I don't want to.* I just don't know why, and I'm terrified to ask.

59. Anna

Palm Springs, AZ, 1997

WEATHER: ALWAYS HOT AND DUSTY BUT I LIKE THE
CHANGE

ANNA WONDERS IF *HE* will love her if she stops using. He opened her mind, her heart, her body, but now she feels like the process of opening left a hole and now every part of her is leaking away. She thinks about Alcatraz, how she almost left Tupper sitting there crying on the filthy floor of an old prison, and she is disgusted with herself.

How could something that used to make the mundane more beautiful turn so ugly?

The wheels spin outside of herself, her heart working so hard. She touches her chest, and it bites at her ribs. It never used to work this hard.

Chewing her lip, she squeezes her shaking hands tightly together. She can't tell if the hotel bed is vibrating or it's her skin rippling. She needs to move. She's been lying here for what feels like days. Food wrappers rise to bury her. She needs to get out.

She opens the hotel room door and walks outside, light searching her out and finding her like a prison camp spotlight.

With the baby in her arms, she wanders down the street. It's cool for the desert, but sweat pours down her temples, soaks the back of her shirt.

Her eyes strip the corners of everything except the possibility of a hit. People fall like cards before her eyes. She blinks hard, trying to clear her head.

Tupper squirms and she grips him tighter.

She stopped it. But now her body is protesting, jerking around. She's a puppet with no control over her limbs. She looks up at the sky to find the strings, staring blankly into the burning sun. The sky rotates like a twirling plate, and suddenly the strings are cut.

She falls to the ground, her cheek smashing, marrying the pavement, Tupper rolls from her arms. Her body continues to shake as Tupper pulls himself to sitting and begins to scream. She takes a breath. Tries to take another. Her mouth tastes bloody and dead and coated with asphalt.

Spreading her fingers on the warm concrete, she thinks she could stay here. It's as a good a place as any to give up. To let *it* win. But Tupper's screams fill the wavy air. They wrap around her soggy head and slam it down, bury it deeper into the earth. He reaches over, takes a fistful of her hair, and pulls.

Closing her eyes, she gives herself a weak moment.

When she opens them, a warm breeze is channeling through the gutter and she watches as a gum wrapper skates across the sand, dancing in a light, graceful way. It's beautiful and simple. She doesn't need the drugs to appreciate it.

A tightly closed memory starts to un-scrunch, the writer who couldn't make life work, who couldn't stop the sadness from overtaking the good. She remembers stumbling through that tour, muttering bad words at the people who stared as she slipped down the bus stairs. She is so ashamed, but the message seems clear to her now.

A tear slides down her cheek. It waters the desperate weeds growing between the cracks in the concrete.

She must get up.

Gently untangling his fingers from her hair, she grasps Tupper around his middle and pulls him to her. Together, they watch the wrapper dance, watch the rest of the world moving with the breeze.

The palm trees clap their hands, impressed by this change in her.

She will get better. She understands now that if she doesn't, her heart won't survive.

60. LANGLEY

Palm Springs, CA to San Francisco, CA, 2015
Weather: Drifting, changing

Sarah is scarce. Appearing briefly and then disappearing again. She does little. Like she's sleepy. Lifting her limbs slowly. She's more of a vision than an interaction, and I miss her.

Tupper throws our bags in the trunk and slams it shut. He looks at me with an unspoken question in his eyes, but doesn't speak.

I am always surrounded by silent companions.

We unfold the map and study our route. The next town circled is San Francisco. Tupper informs me that when he looked this up at home, Google Maps said it was a seven-and-a-half-hour drive. "Which means it's more like nine or ten hours," he says.

"Well, what's the point of Google Maps then?" I ask.

"Good question," he mutters, starting the Chevy and rolling away.

Sarah slouches in the back playing with her hair. I lean over the seat and pat her head, forgetting I'm not alone, nor in the company of other crazy people who don't bat an eyelid at me patting the air since they're too busy dancing with their own delusions.

I try to pretend I'm just stretching my arms. It's not very convincing.

"Look at that," I point out my window where tiny tornados scuttle across the desert floor, twirling red dust into the sky and then disappearing. One crosses the road in front of us, and the car shudders and bounces like it hit a soft wall.

Tupper curses, brakes suddenly, and then continues on.

Without thinking, I reach for a strand of hair that's fallen across his brow and sweep it back into place. He relaxes, and I stroke his head a couple of times before my hand settles down over his.

We drive for hours, silently, hands together except when he has to change gears. Connected and quiet. Comfortable.

After we pass L.A., we pull into a gas station for fuel and snacks. It's only then that I turn around and see Sarah, arms crossed, eyes fuming. Tupper's paying inside, so I reach for her. She darts out the way.

"What's wrong with you?" I ask, surprised by her behavior.

She huffs, uncrosses her arms, and then crosses them again, blowing her dark hair from her eyes.

"Sarah?" I ask, now leaning over the seat. I lower my chin to try to catch her hurt blue eyes.

She points at Tupper, standing with his hands in his pockets, waiting in line at the cash register. I smile dreamily when I see him hunching over, creating as much personal space as he can between himself and the other people in line, his scruffy blond hair falling over his eyes. Sarah makes a face that looks a lot like a growl, and my teeth retreat behind my lips. "Tupper? I'm sorry…I…"

Before I can finish, she runs from the car, tearing across the dirt parking lot to the rough patch of dead-looking bushes right at the back. I chase after her, watching her climb behind a rusted gas bottle. When I finally catch up with her, she is huddled down, her back pressed to the metal frame, crying.

"What's going on, Sarah? I thought you liked him," I say, squatting down next to her. She nods—yes, she does like him, but she's worried I'm forgetting about her. She feels it. I feel it, too, the pull toward the real world, which means a pull away from hers. She's scared. She doesn't want to disappear. "I don't want that either, Sarah. Please believe me."

I reach out to touch her. This time, she lets me.

"Remember when you had a crush on Jacob Miller?" I say, thinking back to that time when she was the older one educating me on the nature of boys.

She sniffs. Nods her little head.

"Remember how much you liked him? How you couldn't stop thinking about him? You told me you would give anything for him to ask you to sit with him at lunch." She glances up at me with some understanding.

"I know I'm a bit late to the game, but that's how I'm

starting to feel about Tupper. I *like* him. Can you understand that?" I ask my hallucination, who is so real I can touch her tears, feel them wet the tip of my finger.

She rolls her eyes. Which means that she does understand. "I'm trying, Sarah, trying really hard to get this right. To not lose you or him and not feel split down the middle. But this is all so new. I need you to cut me some slack, okay?" I place my hands on her shoulders.

She offers her tiny hand for me to shake. It's so I promise not to forget her.

I take it, though it scares me how much she's drifting. I'm not entirely sure I can control it.

"Langley!" Tupper shouts, and I hear him crunching across the gravel. He pokes his head around the gas bottle, perplexed. "What are you doing back there?"

Sarah giggles. I stand up suddenly, acting like a school kid who just got busted smoking. "Uh… I was following a prairie dog…" I manage.

Tupper looks out across the field. Thankfully, a couple of prairie dogs lift their furry heads out of the long grass like hairy periscopes. Their noses twitch, their heads dart left and right, and then they drop out of sight.

"Aw, they're so cute," I say, leaning over the grass.

Tupper grumbles. "Fat rats are what they are."

"Cute, fat rats then," I say, smiling up at his cranky expression. He gives me a sharp grin.

Sarah winks and runs into the long grass, her dark head streaking through the fields, scattering the little rodents in her wake. I pull my shoulders up, shuddering. Tupper throws an arm over my shoulders, and we walk back to the Chevy.

"Only two hundred miles to go," he says with a sigh.

61. TUPPER

PALM SPRINGS TO SAN FRANCISCO, 2015

WEATHER: CAR AIR CON, SO STUTTERING AROUND 65F

LANGLEY STARES OUT HER window, stretching her arm because she doesn't want to let go of my hand. I don't want her to let go either. It makes changing gears pretty awkward, but it's mostly coasting down the highway.

We pass a beat-up minivan. Its tires look as bald as the man driving. I could draw that head by just making a circle… I glance at them, doing a double take when I see a woman on her knees straining to reach a screaming baby while sort of staying in her seatbelt, though I doubt it would do any good if they crashed right at that moment. She pulls her hair from her face, her expression creased with tiredness, impatience, and stress.

It makes me think about Anna, my age, driving down the highway with a screaming kid sliding around on the backseat. If I cried, what did she do? Throw her hand behind her and try to comfort me? Pull over? If she was alone, it must have been tough to manage. I imagine this mother with stretchy limbs like Mr. Fantastic and shake my head.

I catch a glimpse of the mother in my rearview mirror. She is seated again. Her eyes on the road ahead. She smiles sweetly and I smile, too, hoping the baby has stopped crying and all is well inside the minivan.

I nod to myself, understanding a little.

62. Anna

San Francisco, CA, to Palm Springs, CA, 1997

WEATHER: DAMP

ANNA CLOSES HER HEAVY eyes. She thinks it's brief, just a second. She scares herself when they open, and she is driving up the ass of a truck. She brakes suddenly, putting distance between them. The box in the rear hits the back of her seat, and the baby screams. He doesn't cry—he screams because she has hurt him.

Biting down on her bottom lip, she keeps driving. Using one hand to right the box and fumble around for his pacifier, she keeps the other hand on the wheel. She brushes his wet lips, feels the dampness of his cardigan, and sighs hopelessly. He's vomited on himself again.

The nurse called it posseting, which makes it sound pretty, like a basket full of flowers. When in reality, it's smelly and disgusting.

Popping the pacifier in his mouth, she returns her scattered attention to the road. Just another hundred miles or so and they can rest.

She thinks about them, as briefly as she had closed her eyes. Her mother folded on the lawn like she was praying. Her father shaking his fist in frustration.

Did she have to leave?

She tells herself, *yes, she had to.* They couldn't understand. They wanted to change her, and they were too late. Some people can't get along. They just can't. She wonders if that's her and the baby. Maybe they're destined to not get along. They're trying, but when he looks at her all desperate and helpless, sometimes she thinks maybe he should be looking at someone else.

These thoughts are damaging. Good for nothing, like her. She reaches into the ashtray and pulls out a small tin. Touching her fingers to the powder that's still stuck in the corners, she rubs them over her teeth. Lights get brighter. The world spins faster and at a pleasing angle. The night seems filled with possibility now. Tupper's cries sound like music, and she moves her arms up and down like a conductor.

Following the taillights in front of her, trailing red like blood through the night, she grips the wheel like a demon.

Eventually, the baby stops.

Anna winds down the window and laughs. The cold air will steal her voice; carry it down the road to her destination. When she finds *him*, she'll know that's where she's supposed to be.

63. TUPPER

SAN FRANCISCO, CA, 2015

WEATHER: INVADING WINDS

I'VE MADE IT FROM the middle to the West Coast. Undamaged but not unchanged. My life has shifted with the road. If this is my origin story, I wonder where I go from here? What tragedy is up ahead?

I text Mom to tell her where I am. I haven't told her about Langley. I don't intend to. She'll freak.

We find a small hotel on the wharf. It's very nautical, with ship wheels, bits of rope, and large glass bottles everywhere. Langley laughs at the fish net and wooden seagulls suspended from the ceiling. "Awesome!" she whispers.

Her enthusiasm for the crappiest things is mostly funny. But when I stop to think about why, then the feeling twists into sadness, sidestepping pity. She's like this because she's never been anywhere. Most of her life has been spent in hospitals or facilities or whatever they call them. Her world has unlocked like a cracked-open treasure chest, and I feel bad for her that all that's inside it is a bunch of tourist junk and an old map that's been scribbled on.

Scanning the corners, she sucks in every odd detail. She doesn't seem disappointed, so then maybe neither should I.

We step into the elevator, and the doors close. And then it comes out, the question I didn't know I had to ask. "What are you planning to do when you get to Canada?" I ask.

She seems stunned by my question, but recovers quickly. "Well, I guess I'll stay with my sister until I can get a job. Then I might find a place of my own."

The lights flash one, two, three and the doors open. I want to smack my head because, of course, the next thing she says is, "And what about you, Tupper? What are you going to do?"

We walk to our room. Stand at the door, both facing it like we expect someone to open it for us. "Don't know," I say, my eyes wandering so I don't have to see her reaction. It's the truth. I really haven't got that far. My future waits for me back at home. Although the smart thing to do is take it, I'm kind of hoping this trip will give me the permission I seek to not take it.

Langley opens the door, shrugging. "Well, at least you've got a solid plan," she says sarcastically.

I hold up my map and point at it. "This is my plan."

We spread the map out across the bed, tracing how far we've come. "Where's your other map? The one you've been writing on?" Langley asks.

I've been hiding it. Embarrassed of the list I wrote about her. After unzipping my backpack, she pulls the map out without acknowledging the list. Just moves her finger to Flagstaff.

"Pen," she demands, hands out.

I hand her the pen from my pocket. Under Flagstaff, she writes in very pretty script.

Broke into someone's house.

She slides her finger down the highway, tracing our route. At Williams, she writes,

Langley had her first date!

I take the pen from her and add,

TUPPER GOT DRUNK AND MADE AN IDIOT OF HIMSELF.

I draw a small, stumbling man, mouth wide open, expression obnoxious.

Somewhere between Grand Canyon and Palm Springs, after a shy peek at me, she writes two sentences.

Tupper and Langley had their first fight. Langley had her first kiss.

I draw fireworks and balloons over her writing, teasing.

TUPPER HAD HIS 1000TH KISS!

She elbows me in the side for that. Snatches the pen back. "Congratulations," she says sarcastically, and I chuckle.

She goes back to the Grand Canyon, scrawls her next statement.

Tupper talks dirty to the canyon.

"I did not talk dirty to the canyon," I say with mock offense, trying to get the pen back. She hides it behind her back, grinning.

"I seem to recall a lot of curse words flying out of your mouth that day," she says.

I lunge at her, trying to wrestle the pen from her hands. Pinning her arms to her sides, I stare into those muddy-brown eyes. "That's not what talking dirty means."

She tips her head to the side, her cheeks flushed. "No?" she asks innocently.

We're kneeling on the bed, facing each other. *Please don't ask me what talking dirty means.*

"No," I say, trying to cut the end of the rope of this conversation

On her knees, she shuffles closer. "Then what does it mean, Tupper? Tell me."

I feel a little like someone pushed me onto a stage half-dressed and unprepared, but expected to read a Shakespeare monologue by heart. I stumble over my words, the color disappearing from my face. "It's uh…um…" I stare down at the nautical-themed bedspread with anchors on it.

When I look back up, she's biting her lip to stop from laughing. Then she bursts like a bubble, giggling hysterically and holding her stomach as she rolls around on the bed.

"I wasn't kept in a nunnery, Tupper. I know what talking dirty is. Geez, half the inmates used phrases you've probably never even heard before."

I grab a pillow and throw it at her head, which only makes her snort and laugh harder.

Folding up my map, I allow myself a small laugh. She is a strange, pull-you-to-her-just-with-her-eyes beautiful kind of girl.

Unfolding Anna's map, I find her caption for San Francisco. She's circled Alcatraz, which we can see from our window,

SOME PEOPLE ARE IN A PRISON OF THEIR OWN MAKING. SOME ARE LOST AND WANTING TO BE FOUND. THEN THERE ARE SOME WHO NEVER GOT OFF THE ISLAND. BE THANKFUL. FREEDOM'S WORTH MORE THAN YOU REALIZE.

She sketched prison bars over her writing.

Langley leans over my shoulder, her chin grating against my collarbone. "Alcatraz, huh?"

I place my hand on hers, a cold shiver running through me. "Guess so."

64. LANGLEY

Alcatraz, San Francisco, CA, 2015
WEATHER: HARSH

I've been in prisons *before. Whether it's an island or the lock on the outside of a bedroom door, it will probably always feel the same. Tupper's mom is right. Freedom means more than you realize. It means everything, when it's taken away from you.*

More and more, I've been thinking about telling Tupper the truth. The idea strips me of all confidence until I'm red and bleeding, but he deserves to know. I know if I want things to grow between us, I should. I stop and try to picture how that conversation would go, but I can't. It's a blank page with a few words scribbled at the top that don't finish or go anywhere.

My hope is that it will come to me.

The ferry ride to Alcatraz is rocky. I stumble up to the deck for fresh air so that if I hurl, I don't hurl on the group of Japanese tourists I'm sitting behind. They're wearing raincoats, but still...

Tupper follows me up and stands behind me as I grip the railing and feel my stomach bouncing around like it has got room to move inside me. He places an arm on either side of my body, hunching over me to shield me from the wind. Salt sprays my face, and I shiver. He pulls closer.

Maybe I will tell him. I could, tonight, after the tour. It's getting too hard to hide it because we're not fighting the closeness anymore. It's just kind of implied now. And secrets are the shadows slotted between our bodies. If I want to be closer, I have to share those darker parts of myself. But they could swallow him whole.

Nuzzling into his neck, I try not to throw up on his shoes.

As soon as the boat docks, I stagger slash run down the

bridge to land, beautiful, rocky, bird-crap-covered land. Finding a less wobbly section of grass, I brace myself against my thighs and breathe hard. Tupper joins me, rubbing my back as I try to gain control of my nausea.

"I think I'd rather swim back than get on that boat again," I say quietly between dry swallows.

"I'm so sorry," Tupper says, looking very guilty.

I try to suck it up, for his sake. It's not his fault. "We can write *Langley's first boat ride* on the map when we get back," I say, straightening, the island tilting.

We look up at the white buildings bleeding rust, the sky almost the same color as the roofs. This is not a nice place. I imagine there are ghosts in every shadowed corner, chains scraping across the filthy floor.

Tupper takes my arm, holding me up as my knees weaken. "I already think this was a bad idea," he says, his voice soft in its strength.

I place one foot in front of the other, following the group of tourists up the concrete path, with Tupper behind me. He hovers too close like he's waiting to catch me. It makes me walk faster, pushing my way through the huddled groups to put distance between us. I worry he thinks I escaped from somewhere like this. I can tell by the look on his face the thought has crossed his mind. I feel like explaining and then like I shouldn't have to.

He pushes through the people to catch up with me. "I'm okay, Tupper," I say, staring up at him with eyes like mirrors. Hoping to catch some of his normalcy and reflect it back to him. Searching the room for Sarah, I'm relieved to find she's not here.

"You sure?" he asks, bending down and trying to fan out to stop the people from pressing up against us. "You could wait on the boat."

My stomach heaves just thinking about it. I shake my head. "We're trapped on this island, Tupper. Didn't you read the signs? There's no escape." I wink at him, and he seems to relax.

We follow the group to the tour guide, keeping to the back.

———∽———

IT'S VERY DARK AND wet, which I guess is on purpose to add to the scary atmosphere. Squares of white light puncture the black in small angular spaces. Small glimpses of the outside world must have felt like torture to the inmates.

The tour guide makes jokes about locking someone in a cell. A solitary "ha," echoes shamefully over the top of our bowing heads. The feel of this place is so oppressive, dark and depraved, stinking of mold and rust. There's no room for humor.

Toward the end of the tour, we stop at something called The Hole. "If an inmate had been particularly badly behaved they were sent to The Hole, or solitary confinement as some prefer to say. Times varied greatly from one day to months at a time. It was the most feared punishment. To be completely isolated was a terrifying notion. Many came out changed. And by changed, I mean crazy. It did strange things to a person. Things that often could never be repaired."

I expect the guide to waggle his fingers he's so cheesy in his delivery. But the irreparable part strikes a lonely chord across my chest. It rings out in this hollow, deathly place and speaks true.

Tupper stands behind me, listening intently. When the speech is over and we move on to the next horrible cubicle, he leans down and whispers in my ear. "Think I'd go crazy too if I were them. I'd be seeing people and hearing voices like a total nutjob." His innocent chuckling runs up my spine and turns my body rigid, each vertebra locking in. I walk quickly to catch up to the others, needing to get away from his voice, from his lack of understanding.

I tell myself it's not his fault, but his words hurt me to my core.

65. TUPPER

ALCATRAZ, SAN FRANCISCO, CA, 2015

WEATHER: UNPREDICTABLE

STANDING IN THE GIFT store, I feel split like Twoface. Langley is upset, and I know why. I said something stupid. But I didn't mean anything by it. The other part of me keeps dragging back to the past. I think about Anna riding that rocky boat over here with a baby, wondering why the hell she would bring me to this place? I run my fingers over name tags and prison onesies. Did she buy me one of these?

I do understand what Anna was saying. Being here, in this horrible, impenetrable place, it does make me thankful for what I have. I take out my phone and text my dad.

Have you ever been to Alcatraz?

The gray dots come up showing that's he's reading it and writing a response. I stare at it for a long time, tiny tourists shoving past me in their desperation to get the last *I escaped from Alcatraz* shot glass.

The gray dots jump excitedly once but then fade away. He doesn't write back.

Grabbing a couple of bags of chips, I pay and leave the tourist frenzy behind. I search for the lone person. The one standing away from the crowds in a place she's probably not meant to be.

I find her slim form standing on a smooth boulder, on the wrong side of the barrier and warning sign. The wind is harsh, shoving my chest like it's threatening me to get back. I step over the swinging rope and the sign that reads *please stay on the path*, then walk to Langley, her dark auburn hair whipping upward like a tornado.

She hears me approach, cutting back to me with a dark look on her face. She doesn't seem angry. The darkness is coming from within.

I hand her the cheesy puffs, and she takes them. "Battled it out for the last bag. I know how you love orange snacks," I say, trying to lighten the mood and elbow the cloud that's hanging over her head away from us.

She smiles briefly and opens them, eating and licking her fingers. "I love how they get stuck in your teeth."

I chuckle. "Weird thing to love."

She sighs, bunches up the bag, and stares out to sea. "Yeah, well, I'm a weird person. A nutcase. A total psycho."

My shoulders sag. I start to apologize, but she cuts me off. "It's okay, Tupper. I know you didn't mean it. It just stings a little."

I've made her sad. I hate that I've made her sad.

"You're not like that anyway," I stutter. "You're traumatized by what happened to you. Anyone would be. But it's not like you're talking to people who aren't there, seeing things…" I'm babbling and backtracking and making a mess of what I'm trying to say.

She steps back from the water. "No. I guess not." Her voice sounds as hollow as the insides of those cells. "But if I did, would that make me beyond repair? Would you be afraid of me?"

I consider her question, trying to find her eyes but only catching the side of her face. She swipes her face with the back of her hand. "No." I shake my head. "But you'd need help. I'd make sure you got help."

She laughs. Just once. It's as bitter and cold as the sea spray.

"Yes. I suppose that's what people do…" she says, mostly to herself.

I reach out to take her hand. She resists but then takes it.

I lied. I would be afraid. Because there'd be a part of her I couldn't see and couldn't reach.

------᪥------

ON THE WAY BACK to the mainland, she curls into my lap, riding at the front of the boat but inside. She closes her eyes, trying to pretend she's not on the water.

"I'm on a bed, and you're jumping up and down on it," she whispers into my shirt.

Smoothing her hair, I watch the waves. Feeling uneasy.

Like we left something important back on the island.

"I'm in the bath," she states, still not moving her face from where she's buried it.

I lift my eyes to the ceiling, trying to remove *that* image from my brain.

She brings her hand to her mouth, stifling something rising from her stomach.

"If you vomit on me, it's going to shatter several illusions all at once," I say, leaning down to whisper in the ear nestled into my arm. Her body vibrates like she might have just giggled. "I'm not lying, Langley. I may never be attracted to you ever again."

She blinks up at me, her greenish face holding up innocent brown eyes. "You're attracted to me?" She pokes my chest.

Rolling my eyes, I don't answer.

She pulls her knees to her chest as the boat hits the last few waves before the shore.

66. Anna

Alcatraz, San Francisco, CA, 1997
WEATHER: CHANGING WINDS

SHE'S GETTING A LOT of funny looks. Apparently, the Alcatraz tour is no place for a baby. When an older lady came up and told her so, Anna argued he didn't know what was going on around him. According to the books Mama forced her to read, he can't see past his own nose at this age anyway. Besides, he's her baby. She decides where he goes and what he does.

The Rock is a strange place. A beaten-down place. It seems so sad, and she can imagine what it must have been like for the people in here.

The wind swirls between the buildings and hits her like an icy slap.

It would never be quiet. There would be no peace even in solitude.

She had been thinking of her home as a prison. She feels like this is some kind of wake-up call. Yes, she was controlled, but she was also cared for.

For the first time since she left, she feels homesick. She misses the warm timber table, the silverware, and the eyes staring at her as they tried to read what was a very messy book. She had food, love, and shelter... and she threw it away.

She misses them in her heart. In a hurting way she doesn't think she can stand.

Waiting until they've all passed around the corner, she places Tupper on the dirty ground, desperately fumbling through her purse to find the small tin she needs. She pants. Her forehead grows sweaty even in this dark, cool prison.

It's not there.

She left it in the car.

Tupper's arms reach for her, and it strangles her heart.

For a brief moment, she considers leaving him there.

Running away a second time. Finding freedom.

The thought almost makes her vomit right there on the sign that says *Al Capone was in cell B-206*. The black and white print of his face seems so elegant, like he was a movie star, not a criminal.

She covers her mouth. Feels her desperation pushing at her closed fingers.

This has to stop.

She has to stop.

Picking her child up from the floor, she joins the rest of the tour, determination flowing through her veins.

67. TUPPER

SAN FRANCISCO, CA TO HUMBOLDT STATE FOREST, CA, 2015

WEATHER: ISOLATED SHOWERS

LANGLEY SAYS SHE'S FINE, but the quiet she's wrapped around herself in is hard to penetrate. Whatever she's thinking, she doesn't want to share. I know I should be more understanding, but it's hard. It's how I am a lot of the time, and I'm just now realizing how annoying I must be.

We strolled along the wharf, looked at, and smelled the stinky seals, and now here we stand. Facing each other on either side of the made-up bed.

She stares at me and then turns away, her hands diving between the cushions of the sofa. She sighs with relief when she discovers it's a sofa bed.

Shrugging, I go to the bathroom to brush my teeth. When I return, she is curled into one corner of the mattress like a postage stamp. Facing the window and away from me.

I shudder as I enter the bed. The sheets are cold and empty.

I want her next to me, but I won't say it. That's me.

For the first time in a long time, I don't reach for my pencil and paper. I just roll in my sadness and disappointment. I wallow.

The night drags like a reluctant tide.

--------♔--------

WHEN I WAKE UP the next morning, still feeling empty like I'm starving, I see the map unfolded and Langley's writing over Alcatraz.

Langley's first boat ride.

Smiling, I write my own caption.

TUPPER PUTS HIS FOOT IN HIS MOUTH.

I draw a small figure, Langley, on the boat holding her

hand over her mouth. Then I draw me, with one of Langley's sneakers in my mouth.

Wet hair drips onto my arm. "Make the shoe bigger," she says without malice and without humor. It's like she's not quite here.

Sighing sadly, I fold up the map and pack our things.

I don't usually mind the silence, but not like this. This silence is filled with unspoken words. They bounce around the cab, hit the roof, and get sucked into the air conditioning only to be blown back out again.

I groan and flick the radio on, finding that now she's decided to stop talking, I miss the noise. I just don't know exactly how to say that to her. I don't know what to do. My brain draws lines in the sky. Speech bubbles and frozen expressions. That's my language. But I can't say, *Here, you take the wheel while I sketch out my feelings.* So I don't say anything. I force my mouth into a neutral expression, stare at the road, and try to ignore the way she gazes out the window with big, sad, round eyes.

ABOUT THREE QUARTERS OF the way up the 101 to Humboldt State Forest, I snap. Slamming on the brakes, I pull over into a rest stop. Langley's eyes shoot to the backseat. She purses her lips and then turns back to the front, crossing her arms over her chest.

She looks ready to burst, but she's holding it in. Whatever she wants to say, it's pushing against her mouth to get out. "What's your problem?" I ask, exasperated. "I thought we were okay? I said sorry. You, you…" I throw my arms in the air before bringing them down on the steering wheel. This makes her jump. Seems to stun her from her silence.

"I just needed time to think," she says weakly.

My heart does this backing up and out kind of thing like a truck reversing. People say that when they're about to break bad news. I don't feel like I'm ready for her bad news. The words that go a little like, *I think we should go our separate ways.* I know. I've used them before.

Taking a deep breath, I sigh hard and get out of the car. I need to count to ten or something, let my anger settle. I don't even know why I'm so angry. I shut everyone out. *What gives me the right to be upset when someone does it to me?*

I hear the car door open and shut and she appears, staring at me from across the roof of the car. She puts her arms up and folds them, resting her chin and waiting.

"What did you need to think about?" I ask shakily.

She blows words at me, skating across the roof like leaves across a driveway. "We don't know each other very well…"

I wait for the and… I don't wait long.

"And… well…"

I start to walk around the very solid barrier between us, feeling panicky and not liking that I feel that way. I'm just not ready to say goodbye to her yet. I haven't had a chance to change her mind…

I round the hood as she says, "Don't you think it would be better if…"

Wait.

I hurry to her, grab her face, and kiss her, thinking, *This is the last time, try to make it count.* I hear brakes squeal. Taillights smash. I think of the world ceasing to spin, and it seems like a fair description.

She makes good noises like she's enjoying the kiss before she pulls back. "Well, that was unexpected." She touches her fingers to her lips, which are almost bruised from the intensity of what I just did.

"I don't want to split up. Not yet," I manage, my voice about two octaves higher than normal.

She smiles. "Me neither. I was just going to say that the reason you said what you said and the reason why I got so upset is the same. I think it would be better for us both if we got to know each other a little better, don't you?"

I'm some sort of idiot. An idiot who can draw a nice picture, can manage to feed and clean himself, but apart from those meager accomplishments, I'm a giant idiot.

I run a hand through my hair. Land a palm on my hot cheek. "Oh."

She smiles sweetly, nervously. "I warn you, it might get kind of ugly."

Yeah, it very well might.

68. LANGLEY

Humboldt State Forest, CA, 2015
WEATHER: CLEARING

DRIVING UP THE 101 is like pushing back dirt to reveal the treasure. The further north we go, the more gold glints through the gloom and the prettier the scenery becomes. And at each marker, each thickening pine forest and fog-soaked beach, we uncover more of each other.

We get so close to the truth of me. Skimming around the edges until the distance between Tupper and Sarah is paper-thin. But I can't do it. It feels like too much for him. It's too much for me. Because I know what he will say, and I'm not ready to hear it.

"So how old were you when you were adopted?" I ask. He's cooperated, but only offers me short answers. I understand that's all he's capable of. It gives me enough material, enough spare paint, to create a very rough picture.

"One, I think," he answers slowly. Words and numbers reluctantly given up like change from a child's pocket.

It's midafternoon, but as we drive closer to our destination, the sun seems to whimper and disappear. Great pines rise and lean over the road, shadowing everything. Even our conversation dissipates, and we drive several miles without speaking. Distracted by the outside world.

Sarah has her own questions. She wants to know how many girlfriends Tupper has had. She's feeling protective today, which is unusual.

"Do you have anything else you want to ask *me*?" I say after we've passed another exit, ignoring Sarah's prodding of my shoulder. I shuffle forward out of her reach, pretending to hover over the air vent. He glances at me and then grabs his sweatshirt from the backseat, placing it on my lap. I pull it close, up and over my body. It smells like brightly floral laundry powder, fresh. Yet around the collar, it smells distinctively Tupper-like. Inhaling deeply, I feel warmth spreading through my chest.

"Your monologue was sufficient," he says with a light chuckle at my very informative biography that omitted the most important detail. "I hope that son-of-a-bitch Johnny gets fired. If I'm honest, I kinda hope he never woke up."

I shake my head. I don't wish that. Johnny isn't worth it.

His fists clench the steering wheel a little too tightly. I put my hand on his. Sarah reaches over and pokes me again, harder, sending me lurching into the dashboard.

All right!

Before he can react to my odd movements, I ask the question she's been dying for me to ask. "How many girls have you been with, Tupper?"

He pauses, his eyes looking to the side like he's searching for a number. "Hmmm, let me think… There's been so many I lose count," he says with a smirk. I punch him lightly in the arm. "There was…" He counts on his fingers, snatching glances at me as he holds up all ten fingers, steering the car with his open palms. I give him an incredulous look, and he rumbles with laughter. "I'm kidding, I'm kidding! There were two. One girl I only dated for a few months. The other was more long term than that."

I want to glare at Sarah. I didn't really need this can of worms opened. "How long term?" I ask.

He says it flatly. "Two years."

My eyes roll to the window, to the framed view whirring past. The world is changing. Striking up all ancient and mysterious. Green moss licks the trunks of the trees, trunks that are as wide as the Chevy. Light filters gracefully through branches I can't even see. It calls to me in a primitive kind of way. Sarah bounds up and down in the backseat, also feeling the call.

"Stop the car!" I shout suddenly.

He pulls aside carefully into one of the many widened parts of the road made for just that purpose. Pulling over to marvel at this natural beauty.

I jump out of the car and tread on the soft ground laden with pine needles. It's spongy and feet deep. Tupper follows me, more slowly. "Wait, are you upset?" he shouts after me, his hand out in front of him.

Shaking my head, I say, "No!"

Sarah tears into the forest, weaving between the large trunks, following the dribbling paths that run circles around the trees. She is a white streak, a ghostly apparition that would fit nicely in a horror movie. I grin, her joy catching. Climbing onto an enormous fallen tree, slippery with moss, bark decaying around my feet, I hold my arms out and run the length of it like I'm doing the world's longest balance beam. I can't imagine being upset about anything in this place.

Nothing matters.

This place has robbed me of any anger, distrust, or insecurity, and replaced it with quiet awe.

When I get to the end, I stare down the trunk at Tupper, who is wandering through the forest, eyes up, trying to find the sky through the closely laced foliage. He squints, hand over his eyes, his mouth turned up in a quiet smile. He starts to say something, motioning toward the car. I nod. I know what he needs. He walks away to get his sketchbook. He'll settle against a tree, pixies watching through knotholes or peeking out beneath the ferns.

I jump down, following the sounds of water, creeping up behind Sarah, who is throwing pebbles into a brook.

"Wanna play hide'n'seek?" I ask, pinching her shoulder. She spins around, eyes so lively sometimes it's hard to remember she's not really here. Covering her eyes, she starts counting.

69. TUPPER

Humboldt State Forest, CA, 2015

Weather: Clearing

Pulling the map across the front seat to find Anna's caption, I glance up to see Langley quite literally prancing through the forest like a child hyped up on too many Twizzlers and then look down to read my birth mom's words.

I DO BELIEVE IN FAIRIES, I DO, I DO, I DO...

Around her words are small winged creatures and dots of exploding pixie dust. I can imagine all she meant was that this place is magical. I agree with her there.

I pause for a breath, a moment alone to digest all the information Langley shared with me in the last few hours. Some of it scared me. Some of it surprised me, like the part about her mother being Malaysian. She also told me her parents met in a bookstore. Her dad is a Civil War nut, and he took offence to one of his favorite books drowning in a sea of trashy romance novels in the bargain bin. Furious, he dived in and retrieved it, arguing to pay full price despite it being marked down to a buck ninety-nine. When she refused and told him that a buck ninety-nine was actually pretty expensive back in the 1860s (the era the book covered), he asked her out on the spot. It's cute. But not as good as our roadrunner escape story.

Mostly, it made me feel too much. It's an uncomfortable feeling, kind of like I ate a lot at the buffet. She's been through so much. Even though it's impossible and out of my control, I am pissed at myself because I can't go back in time, stand by her side, and help her through it.

She waves at me, beckoning with her hand. I watch her dance through this majestic place, and my feet push against the soft earth. She is wild here, part of the wind, the dark, the earth, and I wish I could join her. But I can't. Shyness makes me grab my sketchbook and shuffle through the pine needles. I find a good spot and settle, listening to the music of her laughter, and I marvel, not at the trees, but at Langley. For everything she has had to endure, she absolutely amazes me.

She is supernatural, and seems to belong to a place like this.

My eyes follow her flitting from tree to tree. Kicking off her shoes, she ties her hair in a messy knot on top of her head.

She should have wings.

I draw her body on the page. Wild and naked and free. Huge dark wings spreading from her shoulders.

If she was with me, I could belong here, too.

———✎———

LANGLEY PULLS DIRTY CLOTHES from her bag, transferring them to a plastic bag. "I need to wash some of these clothes," she says, twisting her nose like they smell. "You want me to throw your stuff in, too?" She holds the bag open, and I dump my clothes in there. I should be uncomfortable about her washing my boxers and stinky socks, but I'm not. I smile to myself, thinking how this is some next-level relationship stuff. *The laundry phase, followed quickly by the peeing with the door open phase… Nope. I won't be doing that!*

"Thanks," I mutter, spreading our array of packaged food over the table. "I'll start dinner."

She smiles and leaves.

Cooking for each other probably comes before peeing with the door open.

After our dinner of two-minute noodles with cans of tuna stirred through it, Langley pulls me from the table and out the door, dragging me down a sandy path to the blue-green river that runs through the park.

When she reaches the water she sits down, toying with the flat purple stones of the beach. "This place…" She sighs, lying back, the stones sounding like ceramic beads clinking against each other as she wiggles into a comfortable position.

Maybe there's something more to say. There always is. But I'm content in this moment. I lie next to her and she rolls closer, draping her leg over mine. I draw a circle around us in my mind. A way to capture us, keep us still. I don't want time to intrude. I don't want to forget how happy I was, lying with the wild girl by the river.

70. Anna

Humboldt State Forest, CA, 1997

ANNA PLACES TUPPER ON the damp earth, the smell of mushrooms and compost rich in the wet air. He comes up like a bridge, attempting to crawl, mud soaking the knees of his pants, and she briefly wonders whether she can jack the washing machine, get it to work without putting any quarters in it.

This place is beautiful. Otherworldly. It's the place she knew she would go once she got away from them.

Anna likes the paths, the way they squirm happily and seem to lead to nowhere. They are rambling trails made for exploring. They are chaotic like her thoughts.

She glances into the piercing light that splits the leaves apart. Her eyes water and yet she still stares. She should feel pain. Her eyes could blister and burn. She smiles, walking away from her child. He seems content plunging his hands into the mud and tasting his fingers.

The light calls to her. She hears music, chimes, and wings beating.

What *he's* given her has opened her mind to possibility. To fantasy becoming real. Fairies flit in and out of bushes; they laugh, and she laughs with them. The small buzz in her ears grows to a loud strumming. She holds her hands out to touch one, spinning around and around. *She feels so alive!*

One lands on her forearm. She can feel a pointed toe pressing lightly into her skin. Her eyes widen in wonderment. She dares not move. She doesn't want to scare it. The fairy tiptoes up her arm, smiling, vibrating, and changing color until Anna can no longer help herself. She reaches out and taps it.

"Ouch!" she shouts, hers and the baby's cries mixing together.

It scratches at her arm, creating a long red line.

The creature takes a bow and disappears, leaving her alone in the forest, searching for Tupper as the leaves seem to brown and the darkness grows.

The thick stick in her hand and the blood dripping quietly to the forest floor tells her, just as much as the feeling of sinking into the ground, that she's coming down.

HUMBOLDT STATE FOREST, CA, 2015

WEATHER: COMFORTABLE

LANGLEY COLLAPSES ON THE bed, glances up, and draws in a shocked breath. "I'm not sleeping under that," she says, pointing up at the tiled mirrors on the ceiling. "It's too creepy!"

I laugh, stopping on a breath when I see her expression. She's terrified. Her eyes blinking, her arms moving around as she watches her reflection. I gesture around the tiny room. "There's nowhere else to go," I say.

She sits up suddenly. "I'd rather sleep in the car!"

I shrug. "Won't matter once I turn off the lights." I put my hand down on the mattress, trying to stop her from tugging all the sheets off.

I yawn. I really don't want to sleep on the floor.

"Do you have anything we could cover it with? Any paper and tape or something?" She shudders when she catches her reflection again.

"I left my wrapping station at home," I say sarcastically.

Huffing, she pulls the top blanket off the mattress. Folding it over, she wedges it between the table and the end of the bed, pushing the chairs out of the way.

After snatching a pillow, she throws it down on her makeshift bed.

"Turn off the lights," she orders. I do as I'm told. Moonlight plus the bright safety lights marking each RV parking space make lines fall across the bed like an exercise book page. Lying on the bed, I stare up. I can see a dark blue and white version of myself on the ceiling, and I sigh. It *is* creepy.

Langley messes around with the blankets, apparently trying to get comfortable, and then she is quiet. I breathe in and out, try to force myself to relax, but I keep opening my eyes to check on my reflection. I wonder how anyone could sleep like this and then I chuckle, realizing sleep is probably low on the priority list with mirrors on the ceiling.

Her muffled voice comes from the floor. "It's creepy, right?"

Shuffling to the edge of the bed, I lean over and stare down at her curled-up form. "Yes." She opens her arms, inviting me to join her. "There's no room," I say, wondering how we can fit in such a small space.

"I'll make room for you, Tupper," she says, grabbing my arm and pulling me down.

Something like relief blooms inside my chest when she welcomes me into her arms, the night spent apart making each touch even more special. I curl around her, and she fits into me.

I have a mouthful of her hair and my back is contorted, but there is no way in hell I'm moving from this position. Sleep unknots my fears, and I am safe.

HUMBOLDT STATE FOREST, CA, 2015

WEATHER: DREAMY

THIS IS A DREAM. *I see the cartoon clouds and capital 'z's that get bigger and bigger, winding in a line to the sky. There's also the pin, poised ready to pop the illusion. But the sharp point hasn't touched the edge yet. I have a little time before the line is broken.*

We wander. There's not really anything else to do. The paths remind me of Dr. Octopus' arms. The way they swirl in and out and around everything and link back together. We follow them lazily, bee like. Poking our heads into holes, touching the tips of the root systems that spread like starbursts from fallen trees.

Langley can't help herself, standing at the base of every tree and stretching her arms wide. "Look. Look how small I am and how big they are," she says, pressing her back against the trunk and staring up into where the sky might be if we could see it. She does look small. Even I look small against these giants. But Langley doesn't disappear. She doesn't seem unimportant. She is the opposite of that. Standing next to these huge trees, she looks like part of the family. Like they have secrets to tell her, but only her.

She skips to the next sight, a giant fallen tree; a platform beat down in the center of its roots from millions of tourist sneakers. She climbs up and stands there like she's in the middle of a cartoon punch. "Come up here," she demands, pointing at a small space beside her.

Crawling into its shadow, I hunch under its ledge of complicated, twisted roots, so dense and deep I can't quite tell where the trunk begins.

It feels like we're posing for a photo, but there's no one to take it.

"You know you're a bit like this tree, Tupper," Langley says, leaning her head on my shoulder as we stare out at the quiet woods.

"What, dense and moldy?" I ask, putting my arm around her waist and pulling her closer so our hips are touching. I rest my chin on the top of her head, breathing in the smell of hotel shampoo and Langley.

"No," she says seriously. "So much going on beneath the surface. But the only way to reach it is if we pull you violently from the ground." She mimes yanking a weed from the earth.

People have tried.

I sigh, waiting for what's next. The part where she says, *If only you'd open up more…*

She turns me around so we're facing each other and carefully balanced. Her eyes all kinds of earnest, she says, "You know I won't do that to you, don't you?"

I know now.

I want to kiss her. I move in, hover close to her face, but she makes a strange expression, her eyes darting to the side, and I get the sense she doesn't want me to. Not right now. She takes my hand, and we jump down from the platform together.

"C'mon! There's still so much to see," she announces, galloping down another path that leads to nowhere. I race to catch up, reaching her just as she steps inside a rotted trunk, the hollow looking a lot like a cave mouth that might take us to another world. I linger outside, hands in my pockets. Her arm comes out from the darkness to beckon me. "Come inside, I want to see if you'll fit."

Stooping over, I enter the tight space. "This is stupid," I say, maneuvering myself until my back is against the trunk and Langley is pressed tightly to me. She pushes her back against the other side of the trunk until there is a small amount of air between us. I wait one second, one breath, and then say, "Right. I fit. Can I get out now?"

She doesn't speak, her slow breaths increasing in frequency like she's building on something. She's so close I can feel them on my face. I go to step out, and she stops me. Holding my arms tight, she stretches up on her toes and brushes my jaw with her lips. Just a graze that makes me lean into where it had just been.

"There's no room for anyone else in here, though, just us," she whispers.

She is part shade and part shadow, all warmth. "I know," I say, confused.

"We're alone," she says in a darkly soft voice as she takes my hand and moves it to the small of her back, urging me to pull her in. My knuckles graze the inside of the tree as I move under her shirt. I think about my inky hands leaving smudges on her back and press into her skin a little harder, making her gasp and throw her head back. It gives me the opening to kiss her neck. Rolling her shirt down to reveal her shoulder, I touch my lips to her collarbone.

My fingers roam the waistband of her jeans, just gently brushing over her hip bones and moving to the front. She shivers and bucks, moving her lips over my neck, crushing closer, clinging to me as she lets herself explore my upper body with her hands. She moves up under my shirt, digging her fingers into my back, the pressure lopsided because of her weaker hand. She touches as much as she can, greedily, like she's plotting a course she intends to come back to later when she has more time.

I try to rein myself in, wary of what might be new to her, trying to be gentle, but I'm breaking the ropes that bound me.

It's more than difficult, and it becomes impossible when she pushes me against the wall and makes sounds that tell me she wants more than I'm giving her.

Mud seeps through my clothes, but I quickly forget when her hands guide mine under the front of her shirt.

I know I am supposed to be careful, take my time, but when my hands sweep the soft swell of her breasts, I do what she wants. I let her guide the pace and the closeness. She moans as my fingers graze over the top of her bra and dip under the lace, emitting this low gasp that makes it hard to control myself. She presses so close she squashes my hand, and I can't stop myself from making a weird noise.

She seems to want it all and all at once and the lapse, the injury, makes me stop and think and then slow down. I hold her but bring my hand down to her hip, clasping her against me and then leaning down to kiss her gently.

I give her time to break away.

She pulls back and knocks her head on the wall, laughing. "I don't think I ever read *this* version of the Faraway Tree," she says, wrapping her arms around my waist and leaning back to look into my shaded eyes.

"Yeah. Don't think the dirty version did so well," I say through the dark, leaning down and kissing her cheek softly. The moment passes, and an awkward silence grows between us as we untangle and slow our breathing.

"What was that?" she exclaims. "I, um, I'm kind of embarrassed."

I chuckle, holding her hand up to my lips. "Believe me, you have nothing to be embarrassed about."

Exhaling kind of happily, she steps into the light. "Okay. I'll believe you," she says, holding her hand out to me. I decline.

"Now I'm embarrassed," I say, glad I'm in a dark hole in a tree trunk where no one can see me.

She bends down to peer into the hollow. "Why?" she asks innocently, a quizzical expression on her face.

"I, uh, need a minute before I can come out," I say through gritted teeth.

Throwing her head back, she laughs, finally understanding why I might need a second to recover from our faraway tree make-out session.

She walks backward and sits on a log. Tears in her eyes, she manages to say, "Oh. Sorry. Take all the time you need. What is it they say? Think of baseball and kissing your grandma." And then she proceeds to rest her chin in her palm and stare at me with a big damn grin on her face.

73. LANGLEY

Humboldt State Forest, CA, 2015
WEATHER: THE WARM BUZZ ANTICIPATING SUMMER RAIN

HE MAKES ME FEEL *unshackled. Like maybe I can have those things, those normal things, like kisses and hands on my skin in a safe and warm way. I blush at the thought of my sudden almost-attack on him in the tree hollow. It was a desperate need to be closer and an I'm-running-out-of-time action, too.*

I wanted all the things, all at once. I wanted to collect those teenage memories I've missed out on until now and hold them. Feel them. Store them.

It was perfect and awkward, and his heart felt so good under my palm. I sigh. I'm going to dream about that heart and those hands for years to come.

Sarah impatiently waves a hand in front of my face. I would tell her about it, but I don't think she'd understand. She's too young. But she was once my older sister, and the need to confide in her is strong.

I pull the clothes out of the dryer, socks and pants twirled together in one large static ball. It zaps me as I try to separate the items. I pull out a pair of Tupper's boxers and lay them on top of the machine, continuing to pull apart our things. I touch my lips, bruised and battered in a good way, and think of his hands under my shirt, the ink smudges left across the white lace of my bra. It was so hard to stop, and it will only get more difficult.

Sarah jumps up on one of the machines, swinging her legs and looking at me questioningly. "It's Tupper," I say as if that explains everything. She sighs, puts her hand on her heart. And I nod. "Yes."

She looks sad, staring at her feet, twisting her ankles around in circles. Hands planted on either side of her, she looks up and points to her heart. I shake my head.

"There's still room for you. There'll always be…" A tear slides down her cheek, and I reach out and grab her shoulders. "Sarah. Please don't be sad." She shrugs, trying to appear brave. The truth is I don't know how this works. I don't know what happens if I open my heart completely to Tupper.

I'm crossing the rope bridge between panic and love, and the planks are coming loose. I can't lose Sarah. She is the only family I have, and she needs me. Problem is my heart started to open when I wasn't paying attention. The door is ajar, and new light is flooding in. I touch my chest. An ache growing there. I want uncomplicated, but it's not my world.

She jumps down from the machine and goes to leave. "Wait," I say, pulling the picture Tupper drew of a grown-up Sarah out of my back pocket. "I forgot to show this to you before."

I hold it out for her to see. She stares at it a long time, tipping her head left and right. And then she shakes her head.

She pushes the picture back toward me as if to say, *That's not me.*

I feel a sharp twist in my chest, a longing for something that doesn't exist, because she's right. That's not her. It will never be her.

"You're right," I say. "I'm sorry. You know I love you just the way you are, right?"

She nods, her hand trailing along the door as she tries to escape. Just as she slips away, I say, "Please. Promise me you won't go far. I'll work it out. I'll find a balance."

She nods. Turns back and embraces me. She draws a heart on my back. I feel it burn into my skin. When she draws away, I ask her, "Do you mind if I let Tupper in?"

She shakes her head vehemently and stands up straight, telling me I don't need her permission.

The washing machine beeps, and I turn. When I turn back, she is gone, the picture of a beautiful woman who can't exist lying on the floor with the lint and scattered washing powder granules.

———✥———

TUPPER'S WATCHING TWO LINES bounce up and down on the TV when I get back. One arm folded behind his head, the other flipping through the nonexistent channels. He jumps up when I pass through the door, then helps me sort through the clean clothes and put them away.

The map sits open on the table. I see that he has immortalized our fooling around in the tree hollow, adding elements of the Faraway Tree. I think of it again, and my breath tumbles out of my throat like a bubble.

"You okay?" he asks as he rolls back the covers.

I want to tell you things. I want to share my secrets, all of them. Maybe together we can sort them like the laundry, find a place for everything.

"Yeah, fine," I manage.

He pats the bed and says, "Come here, I want to show you something."

I gulp, which makes him smile. When I crawl onto the bed, he puts his arm around me. "Tupper, I…" I start.

He puts a finger under my chin and lifts it. I think he'll kiss me. I've already forgotten everything. *What's the rest?* My eyes are closed, waiting. His body rumbles with small chuckles. "Look up," he says, raising my face to the mirrors on the ceiling.

Gasping, blinking, I feel my heart trying to grow, trying to fit him in. There has to be a way. He's drawn scenes on every tile, and it reads like a comic book.

I get up on my knees, hands clasped in front of me as I follow the story. Me, running down the road, fleeing from the hospital. Him stealing glances at me in the rearview mirror. The caption reads,

HE THINKS SHE MIGHT BE THE TIREDEST AND MOST BEAUTIFUL GIRL HE'S EVER SEEN.

He watches me take in what he's done with a quiet nervousness. It's part of our story. Our fight. Our kiss in the paddock. The last tile is full of sentences.

HE NEEDS TO TELL HER SOMETHING. HE JUST DOESN'T KNOW HOW. WORDS ARE HARD FOR HIM. SHE SEEMS TO UNDERSTAND THAT, AND HE'S STARTING TO LOVE HER FOR IT.

When I turn to him, he's staring at his blackened fingers. "It's okay," he mutters. "I used a water-based marker."

Crawling into his lap, I straddle him so I can stare deep into his shady gray eyes. "Me too, Tupper." I lean in, our noses touching. He needs me to say it. I can tell. His face is so imploring, so heartbreakingly honest. "I think I might be starting to love you, too."

He pulls me close and we just sit there for a while, heart to heart. Mine is stretching, straining toward him, and being pulled away at the same time. His is calm, steady.

Leaning back, I kiss him softly. He smiles as I do. "This is such a bad idea," I say, whispering against his skin.

"The worst," he replies.

I leave his lap and slide down so I'm lying flat on my back, staring up at his masterpiece. The messy representation of us. He does the same.

I hope there are more tiles in our story.

Pages and pages of them.

74. TUPPER

HUMBOLDT STATE FOREST, CA, TO PORTLAND, OR, 2015

WEATHER: REFLECTIVE

SOMETIME DURING THE NIGHT, I reach for Langley and she's not there. Getting up, I bash around trying to find the door. I find the window instead and part the curtains to see her sitting at the picnic table, legs crossed, staring at the empty seat in front of her.

I close them just as quickly because I swear, even though there was no one else out there, she was acting like she wasn't alone.

––––––⤳––––––

I'M SAD TO LEAVE the redwoods. I don't know whether it's Langley or the magic of the place, but I feel a little closer to Anna here. Maybe it's just in me, some inherited memory, I don't know. I just feel like I'm getting closer.

We leave early for Portland, the car taking a while to warm up on this cold morning. Langley leans in close, telling me she needs my warmth. I can't say I mind, and I let her nuzzle into my side.

The question from last night is left hanging. I convince myself that I was being crazy. That I was tired and that whatever I thought I saw was really nothing at all.

A hundred miles into our drive, I ask, "How are you feeling?"

She lifts her head from my shoulder to gaze up at me sleepily. "Caffeine deprived," she answers through a yawn.

When I see a little coffee hut, I hit the blinker and pull over. I try to keep my tone light, but it comes out more frightened. "Um. No. I mean, mentally. How do you feel mentally?" I tap my head like a weirdo and then roll my eyes at myself.

"I can count from one hundred backward, I know my

name and what year it is…" she says, purposefully misinterpreting my question.

I sigh, ordering two coffees at the window. The young barista smiles sweetly at me, rubbing grinds on her apron. "Where are you two off to?" she asks over the top of the milk-frothing squeals.

"Portland," Langley answers. "But I'm crazy, so I could be wrong. This could all be in my head," she says with a smirk, making the poor girl uncomfortable.

Throwing a couple of dollars in the tip jar, I say, "Ignore her," as I take our drinks.

As we drive off, I feel my aggravation building. Langley stares ahead, pouting.

I turn onto the I-5 and she grabs my sketchbook, flipping it to a fresh page. She scribbles furiously for a good half hour.

"Pull over for a second," she says. I find the next rest stop and park the Chevy.

She hands me the page of messily drawn stick figures and writing, pointing to a stick figure with long hair and circle boobs. "This is me," she states. The figure has a frown on its face and is crying. "And this is me." It's the same figure but with a smile on its face. She points to several drawings of the same figure, each with different expressions—happy, sad, angry, excited…

Flipping the page over, she points to two pills she's drawn. I'm kind of impressed with her shading and the way she's made it look three-dimensional. "This was my dad's solution. Or he wanted to cut my brain open, but I couldn't draw that, way too gory and past my stick-figure skill level."

On the neighboring page is another stick-figure Langley, this time with no expression, her hands hanging limply at her sides.

"I'm fine. I'm doing the best I can to manage my emotions, to live a normal life, whatever that means. It's not always easy, but do you find *your* life easy all the time?" she asks.

I shake my head, start to say *I'm sorry*, but she shushes me.

"If I thought it helped, I would do it. If I thought I was struggling *mentally*," she puts the word mentally in air quotes, "you would know." She stares at me. "Do I seem crazy to you?"

"No. But maybe you hide it well," I say jokingly, but she

seems un-amused.

"Maybe…" she says. "But you said you were starting to love me. That means you've already started to fall for this so-called *crazy* version of me."

We sit there in silence for a while as I try to find words I don't have. Try to make it better.

Finally, she speaks. "Look, I guess the thing is that you know where I've come from. You know why I was there, what I've had to go through. I have a brain injury and some sort of PTSD; that isn't going to change. This is me and my issues. You're the one who has to decide if you're okay with that."

"What would happen if you had the operation?" I ask, so neck deep in it I might as well ask.

She squeezes her right hand, staring down at it like it's not her own. "They can't tell me. It might make my hand better, it might make me feel better in myself, but they can't guarantee it won't change my personality."

"Damned if you do, damned if you don't," I say, understanding a little of that myself.

She nods. "Exactly. Except…"

I wait, see the words on her lips, the sadness in her eyes that I just put there. "Except?"

"I'd rather be damned and be me, you know?"

I know.

I start the car and she shuffles away from me, a distance made by my words. I hate my words.

"Just tell me if you need help, okay?" I say, staring out at the dark gray road, clouds gathering over the ocean, ready to come in and assault the land.

She nods. "Okay."

75. LANGLEY

Portland, OR, 2015
WEATHER: DIRTY RAIN

THIS IS WHAT HAPPENS when you let people in. They move into your space. Sooner or later, they start snooping around in your personal stuff. They go straight for the box that reads 'private' and go to town, reading stuff, misinterpreting, and throwing it all over the floor. Problem is I know I should have just given it all to him in the first place.

We arrive in Portland in the evening. The streets are dull and wet. There are people everywhere, and we realize we're driving in the city in peak hour. It's too hard to work out what's a hotel and what's a brewery through the dark curtain of dirty rain, so we decide to park the car on a side street and head down to the lit-up markets, sparkling like a purity beacon down by the water's edge. From there, we can find some food and then work out where to stay.

Tupper slams the door and runs over to mine. We have one umbrella to share, and he shelters me as I get out of the car. I'm hit with the smells of carnival food as soon as my feet hit the ground, sugar and cinnamon, batter and meats on sticks. "Mmm," I say, licking my lips.

Dancing around, Tupper hops from foot to foot. "I've gotta find a bathroom," he blurts, running me to the under-cover part of the market. Dirty water splashes up our pants, and we laugh at how soaked we are despite the umbrella.

He hands me his wallet and keys and backs away from me, making sure I'm under an awning, saying, "Get some food. I'll find you at the…" Someone walks between us, shaking a stick covered in tiny reindeer bells and shouting, "Jingle Bells! Jingle Bells!"

Find me where? I crane around the weird man, but Tupper is gone.

Soon, I'm distracted by the smells, sounds, and colors of

the market. I push deeper into the tented area.

TUPPER

I NEED TO PEE in the worst way. I run to the public restroom only to find it's being cleaned. When I poke my head in the door, a woman screams at me, "Didn't you see the sign?" She points at the sign I ignored telling me not to go in. I grimace.

"Sorry. Is there another restroom nearby?" I ask, in serious pain.

She shakes her head. "Try up the street at one of the restaurants."

I curse and she gives me a hard look meaning, get the hell out of here. I run up the street. There are people everywhere, hopping on and off buses, heading home for the day. I try to go into a restaurant only to have them tell me to get out unless I'm buying something. I put my hands in my pockets, realizing I've left my wallet with Langley. Cursing again, I exit the restaurant.

Moving up the street as best I can through the sea of winter-coated people, I see a shining beacon of hope. A red and white light. Target.

LANGLEY

SARAH HOLDS MY SLEEVE, not too happy about the crush of people. It doesn't bother me so much. I'm used to close quarters. We move to the back where all the food's supposed to be only to find that the cases are empty, just a sad spinning hotdog display with nothing in it. Cold oil sits in a vat with bits of blackened donut floating around in it. Sarah laughs and points at the donut, and I have to agree—it does look like a floating turd.

A man steps out from behind his stall and yells, "Closing time. Thanks for your money. Now everyone out!" He claps his hands and the crowd laughs, filing backward and out into the pouring rain, dispersing fast because they actually have somewhere to go.

Carried out by the crowd, the water hits me and I shudder, pulling my arms around my body and watching the tents collapse and the carts roll away.

I search for Tupper, his large form bounding across the now almost empty parking lot with a red umbrella over his head. But he doesn't come. I suddenly feel very vulnerable and lonely, even with Sarah by my side, as the fairy lights flick off in sections one by one, leaving me standing in the rain, black water reflecting the bridge lights behind me.

TUPPER

IS THIS A FUCKING maze? I saw the bathroom sign. It pointed down the baby aisle, but now I'm at a dead end. I find a kid dressed in red and black and grab his shoulder, shaking it a little too hard. "Where's the bathroom?" I ask.

The kid stares at me like I'm a crazed junkie trying to rob him. He puts his hands up. "I don't work here, man."

I laugh cruelly. "Nice outfit then."

The kid looks down at his black jeans and red polo shirt and gets it. He swears under his breath, making a quick exit.

Frantically running down aisles, I seriously wonder if today will be the day where I embarrass myself publicly in a way that I'll never ever live down.

When I finally see that little man, his round head and straight arms glowing on the blue door, I think I hear angels singing or something.

LANGLEY

I SHOULD HAVE CHASED after him. Made sure I heard what he said. I try to remember where we parked the car but in the craziness, with all the people pushing and shoving us, I just can't think what the street name was.

My hand aches, and I pump it a couple of times.

The parking lot is a shining black. I walk to the water's edge and grip the iron handrail, leaning over to listen to the water sloshing against the rocks and wait for him to come back.

It's so dark, black. I breathe so fast that not enough air is coming in. I attempt to open my eyes, but they are already open. It shouldn't be dark. It's like seven am.

"Mmm-mom?" I say into the upside-down, wrong-way-round blackness. I can only hear myself, my breathing, my voice that crackles and whispers. "Mom, Sarah, Mom?"

Nothing.

I find my seatbelt and unclick. I fall, my head hitting the roof of the car and my arms getting tangled in leaves and broken sticks. It makes no sense for leaves to be in the car. I'm not outside the car, am I?

Padding around on my hands and knees, I try to find the up and out of this vehicle that seems to be inside out. My hand touches things that are wet and warm, and I start to cry.

Soft at first but growing to deep hitching cries that push from my chest with so much pain I know, I just know, I will never feel this much pain again. That has to be the rule, right? If I go through this now, I will never feel this bad again.

I scream, "Mom, Saraaah!" the smell of gasoline making me dizzy and nauseous. "Mom, I think I'm going to be sick," I whisper, holding my stomach, spinning in tiny circles. They are empty words, said to nothing.

Curling into a ball, I'm too scared to move, to accidentally touch them. I can't, I just can't. I keep saying their names over and over, praying they'll answer, knowing they won't. I am alone. I tell minutes by the number of times I've said their names, counting them in small scratches over the car's interior.

In the dark for hours.

Sarah is afraid of the dark.

A window breaks, more leaves seem to push into the car, and then a hairy arm grabs me and pulls me out, my legs shredded by the broken glass.

I'm running without touching the ground, getting further away from them. Still screaming, "Mom, Saraaah," at the top of my lungs.

The sound and the force of the explosion forces us to the ground. It burns my mouth closed. The stranger holds me close and says, "It's okay. You're okay. I've got you."

But I know, even in this confused and bloody state, that I will never be okay. Never again.

I shudder and Sarah pulls me back from the edge, scolding me for getting too close to the water. She looks at me with that determined strength in her eyes, pointing to the cluster of port-o-potties under the bridge. I nod, and we run through the rain to find Tupper.

Of course he's not there. There's a sign saying they're closed for cleaning.

My guess is he said meet him somewhere in the market, but the market is no longer here. It's dark, and the few people who are wandering around make me nervous. A man stumbles down the alley in our direction, layered with dirty clothes, a dog on a lead in his hand. The dog looks like a muscled barrel on legs, and it barks at us once. The man swears at the dog, and I notice he's dragging a large chain behind him.

I turn my eyes upward to the stronger streetlights and walk fast.

TUPPER

Relieved, I head out and back down to the market on the waterfront. The street traffic has thinned to nothing, and people pool around the entrance to a red brick building that smells like yeast. I pick up the pace, feeling hungry and worried that she's been waiting too long for me already.

LANGLEY

I take a straight line up toward the city center, the signs of familiar brands bright and comforting. Sarah keeps tugging on my sleeve, pulling me left. It's an urgent tug and she pulls quite hard, sending me stumbling into a wall.

"What?" I mutter through gritted teeth, looking a lot like a crazy person and just as much like me.

She stares up at me with steely eyes. *This way,* she seems to say, pointing hard left.

I look left and right, searching for the Chevy. This isn't the street.

Gulping, I feel this hard thing rising in my stomach and creeping up my throat. *What if I can't find him?* I have no way of contacting him.

Sarah seems to understand. She reaches for my face. Smudges away a panicked tear. Again, she pulls on my arm, trying to lead me away from the city center.

I let her lead me. Still snapping my head back and forth, searching for his ashy-blond hair and eyes the color of shaded lead. He'll be worried about me. I hope.

TUPPER

WHEN I REACH THE waterfront, I swear. Loud. A man sitting in a vacant doorway jumps at my voice and a dog barks solemnly at me, its eyes squinted and judgmental. "Excuse me, sir?" The man scoffs at the pronoun. "Have you seen a pretty girl with long brown hair and big brown eyes walking around here? She would've looked like she was lost or looking for someone."

I bend down closer to the man. He doesn't seem to be paying any attention to me, patting the dog roughly. Smacking the palm of his hand down hard. I can hear this kind of hollow bone sound as he keeps banging on the animal's skull.

"Yeah, I saw them," he says.

Them?

Fear squeezes my throat. "She wasn't alone?"

He shakes his head and laughs wheezily. "No, she was alone."

I feel like shaking my head quickly, to clear it, to clear out the nonsense and find the truth. I sigh, exasperated.

"Which way did she go?" I ask, trying to resist shaking the old man until he makes sense. His beard is sharp and angular like the peaks of a mountain, his watery eyes seeming amused.

He points up. Like up to the sky.

A shiver runs through me, and I stare up into the starless night.

Langley, where are you?

LANGLEY

THE SOUNDS OF THE city dull as Sarah drags me away. The dark closes in, and I feel more and more nervous. More panicked as the minutes drag into hours. The cold seeps deep into my bones, reminding me of a darker time than this. I hug myself against the chill and look forward.

My feet ache in my wet rubbing sneakers. "It okay for you," I say. "You don't have the inconvenience of a body. You don't feel cold, feel pain…"

She turns and gives me a sharp look, rolling her eyes as if to say, *Yeah, I'm super lucky that I'm dead and just a figment of your imagination.*

I don't want to lose him. Not yet. I haven't said what I need to say. Done what I wanted to do.

I think back to the redwoods, the heat and closing distance between us. Tupper and I, we're not done yet.

TUPPER

THERE'S A TOURIST INFORMATION booth at the mouth of where the market stood. Now it stands lonely, like an opened milk carton in the middle of nowhere. I pull one of the maps of Portland out of the plastic holder and study it. Tracing my finger along the different tourist sights.

Where would she go?

LANGLEY

WE'VE BEEN WALKING FOR at least an hour, maybe two. I'm drenched and sad and lost and thinking we should turn back. I stop and do a three sixty. She's leading me into a deserted industrial area. There's a train line running through the road. To my right, there's a steep hill with carriages moving slowly up a wire. Sarah stops and points to the crisscross of iron beams and fluorescent lights at the base of the hill, empty carriages swinging sadly. "Did you lead me here just so you could go for a ride on an aerial tram?" I ask, hands on hips. Feeling pretty angry right now.

She shakes her head. *No. Tupper is here.*

We walk to the bottom platform, my eyes so desperate to see him that my heart doesn't want to hope.

"He's not here," I whisper, leaning down to her ear. She shakes her head and points up.

"Up there?" I ask, my finger following the aerial tram carriages that rise slowly up the hills of Portland. She nods.

TUPPER

I DON'T KNOW WHY, but I just feel like I know where she'll

go. The little blue carriage hanging from a wire seems to burn bright on the page. I don't think, I just run. Following the blue lines on the map with water splashing around my feet to the Portland Aerial Tram.

LANGLEY

WE HAND OVER OUR ticket and the carriage lurches from the platform, rising slowly, smoothly, into the sky. Sarah swings around the metal pole in the center, enjoying the emptiness of the space. I can't even enjoy the ride. I can only look down on the large city of Portland and worry. My fingernail in my mouth. My heart in my throat. *Find me, Tupper.*

TUPPER

THE WOMAN SHAKES HER head as I breathlessly try to jump on the carriage without paying. My red face and desperate expression are not helping my case. "Please. I need to get up there," I beg, pointing up the steep mountainside dotted with sweet little townhouses.

She gives me a smile, gives me hope, and then yanks it away. "Happy climbing, then," she says in a cruelly satisfied tone, crossing her arms over her chest and pressing a button, which closes the doors.

I could get there and this feeling, this unsubstantiated feeling, could all be bullshit. She won't be there, and I'll be left alone again. I'll be lost. I look out at the city and the million people who live here. *I need to find her. She needs to find me.*

Standing under the thick vibrating wire of the aerial tram, I watch it slide noiselessly up the hill. I start running, letting it guide me up the steep slope.

LANGLEY

I STEP OUT ONTO the concrete platform at the top. Its cold, bare floors sweep my insides with its emptiness. *What do I do?* I turn to Sarah. She's leaving me. I can tell. She wavers like a mirage, her image turning watery and then disappearing. I reach out, try to pull her back from wherever it is she goes, but it's useless.

Anxiety starts to bubble up and surround me, pushing like invisible bully hands. Shoving me back, back, back into a dark corner. A place to defend, a wall I can lean against, disappear into, wait for someone who's not coming.

Sliding down to the floor, I feel darkness crawling over me like mist. It sickly whispers in my ears, *He's left you. Everyone leaves you. Shrink down, make yourself small, cover your ears. Shut out the world and maybe the world will forget you, too.*

The air seems thin up here. I huddle down, knees up, head buried.

He won't come, and I'll lose the only thing that held me to this world.

TUPPER

This seems stupid. The bad idea laughing at a worse one. But I feel an unexplainable pull. A need to climb.

Digging my feet into the sloping sidewalk, I push, cold air burning my lungs, people giving me weird looks as I pass them. Because I know I look like a crazy person, focused on one thing, ignoring everything else around me.

I get to the end of the first block, and defeat claws into my shoulders. The top is so far away, stretching endlessly like an illusion. Cursing, I run a hand through my wet hair in frustration. I wish I had a better reason. Something more than a feeling driving me forward, but I've got nothing.

I start running. Putting all that athletic training to the test.

I focus on Langley, seeing her standing at the top, hands on hips, smiling wide and congratulating me for finding her. See myself scolding her and then taking her in my arms, a comic-book kiss flashing through my brain, where the two faces almost become one. She'll ask me how I knew, and I'll say, *I just knew. I could feel it.*

LANGLEY

I don't want to sink, but I'm sinking. The cold concrete around me whirls and drags me down. I want to be better than this. Not have dark hours. But I am sad and alone and it's overwhelming me. I have nothing to shield me, no one to care. Just like before.

TUPPER

REACHING THE TOP OF the hill, I glance at my watch. It's taken me over an hour to get here. My legs ache, my chest hurts from two different types of pain. The entrance to the aerial tram is through the Oregon Health and Science University building. There are signs saying only authorized personnel—students, doctors and patients—can use the tram from the top platform. I'm too tired to swear.

A man walks out of the hospital's sliding doors wearing a white coat. He pulls a contradictory cigarette from his coat pocket. With his Elvis haircut, he looks less like a doctor and more like a Vegas wedding chapel reject. But this is Portland.

Taking a deep breath, I approach him, wiping my sweaty hands on my jeans. "Hi. Excuse me. Do you know how to get to the aerial tram from here?" I ask, trying to sound casual, but it comes off more breathless and anxious.

He looks up from his phone and says, "It's through the doors to the left, but tourists are supposed to buy tickets at the bottom."

I breathe in a fat cloud of tobacco smoke and cough. "So how would I get in from here?" I ask.

"Are you a student or a patient?" he asks, knowing full well I'm not.

I shake my head.

He flicks his finger across his phone screen and mumbles without looking up. "Sorry."

Rage builds inside me, busting out like my skin's turning as green as the Hulk's. I have to get in. I have to. My fists shake. I want to pick this guy up by his shirt collar and shake him until he hands over that card dangling around his neck.

But I don't.

I walk away. Pace. I watch his cigarette burn down to the filter as it counts down my only chance to get through those doors.

My mouth wants to stay closed, the wire running loops through my lips. But my choices are pretty damn limited.

Storming up to the guy, I tell him the truth while he stares up at me, leaning away until the back of his head touches the glass behind him.

"I lost this girl. *My* girl. We got separated and I know it's crazy, but I just feel like maybe she's up here waiting for me." I throw my hands in the air. "She has my wallet, my keys, and my phone is locked in my car, so I have no way to contact her. I just need to get in. Please, can you help me?" He steps back from me, but he has nowhere to go, his back pressed against the glass. I sigh, giving him some space. "You don't know me, I get it, but I promise I'm just a harmless guy trying to find a girl, *the* girl."

The only girl.

It's more words than I've spoken in a long time, and I feel kind of exhausted from the exercise. I take another step back, my eyes on the sign behind him, embarrassed. Feeling like I wrote my heart across the sidewalk and I'm scared no one will read it.

He doesn't say anything for a while, just looks me up and down, once, then again. His nose twitches and then he puts his arm out, reaching up to pat my shoulder and ushering me into the warmth of the hospital.

"Intuition is a powerful thing, son," he says as he leads me down a corridor.

The doors to the aerial tram platform are wedged at the bottom of a long corridor.

I prepare myself. If she's not there, I'll go back to the car. I'll wait there until she turns up. If she doesn't turn up, I'll call the police. No, I can't call the police. I'll just wait. I will wait for her, for the rain to stop and the sun to appear. I don't feel like there is any other course of action.

I hear a beep, and the doors slide open. "Good luck," the man whispers, his words taken away on a breeze.

"Thank you very much," I say genuinely. The Elvis doctor snorts, tipping his head. He walks away and I take too many deep breaths in, forgetting about the breathing-out part.

This is like a movie I once saw. The guy runs to the top and finds the girl standing there, beautiful and lit by moonlight. She turns, her face changing from sadness to joy at the sight of her long-lost love.

She says, "I didn't think you'd come."

His eyes crinkle, he takes her in his arms, and they kiss with music playing heavenly in the background.

My head is in that moment as my eyes scan the area. My heart sinking lower and lower with every empty square of concrete.

And then I see her. Just a dark shadow pressed deep into the filthy corner of the platform. A mechanical whirring cycling over her head as the thick wire of the tram cycles through.

I run to her. Fall to my knees. Try to find her face under the curtain of hair and the arms up in defense.

"Langley?" I ask, because even though I know it's her, this soaking wet, shaking creature doesn't seem like my Langley.

She glances up, her bluish lips trembling. "You're not real," she says, swaying her head back and forth. "You couldn't find me."

She scares me. Her head not always here with me in the real world. She looks defeated. As gray as the concrete. Her sadness pulses out from her body, and I can almost see the cracks it creates in the floor. I understand the idea of falling into them. I do. I also understand that maybe there is a part of her I can't reach. That there are things wrong with her that I can't fix.

But I want to love her anyway.

Taking her cold hands, I place them on either side of my face. They touch me lightly, reluctantly. "I'm here. I found you. I don't know how I did, but I did."

Frustrated, I take her chin and lift it so I can stare in her eyes. "Look at me."

She finally does. "How?"

I close the distance between us, heat trickling like lava over the edge of a cliff. "I don't know," I whisper as our lips touch and the lights spark, the cable snaps and spider webs hold everything together on the verge of breaking.

She pulls back, warm breath blowing on my face. "Tupper. There are things I need to tell you."

"Not now," I say. "Not here." There'll be time later. A better time. "Let's get you safe and dry first."

She nods, unsure, her eyes sweeping the empty platform and landing on something behind me.

76. LANGLEY

Portland, OR, 2015
WEATHER: C-C-COLD

*I can't examine this too closely. If I do, my heart will start stammering violently in my chest, my breath won't sustain me. The word—*ghost—*floats up, a snake of smoke before my eyes, and I blow it away.*

She can't be. I can't think it... Believe it... Because if it's true, then I am the chains that hold her here.

I shuffle around on burger wrappers, my body racked with shivers. It's close to morning, and we decided it was too hard to find a hotel. I shake hard, not able to control my body temperature, and Tupper reaches for me.

The rain creates a solid, loud darkness around the car. The metal roof pelted with what sounds like bullets or ball bearings. He finds the skin under my damp clothes with his warm hand and swears. "You're freezing."

My teeth chatter as I try to say, "I...I...kn-kn-know!"

He tugs at my shirt, pulling it up, and I grab it, pulling it down. He laughs. "I'm not trying anything. You need to take this off. It's soaked," he says.

Pulling it over my head, I sling it over the headrest. "Jeans, too," he orders in a serious tone. I shuffle out of the wet denim with a sigh, and I hang them over the seat with a wet slap.

I'm so cold my body is doing weird spasms that are out of my control. It seeks heat. I climb into Tupper's lap, putting my arms under his jacket and around his back. He wraps the jacket around my barely clothed body and holds me close until I slowly stop shaking.

His strong heart lulls me. As I'm counting the beats, I start to drift.

Sarah's head appears in the window, and I jump with fright.

"Jeez, Langs, you're such a scaredy cat," Sarah teases, perched on the tiled porch outside my bedroom window.

I open my mouth to speak, but nothing comes out. Just a weird dry squeak.

Sarah smiles, nods like she understands me, and shuffles down the slope of the roof.

"You coming?" she asks.

Shaking my head, I try to say, Stop! Wait! But my voice is stolen.

I rush to the window just as she jumps from the roof. Disappearing into the impenetrable black ink that's surrounding the house.

I swing around when someone knocks at my door.

Tupper pushes me off his lap suddenly and I fall into the space behind the driver's seat, hands out before I dip head-first, ass up.

Through his teeth, he whispers tersely, "Put something on!"

I grab a shirt from the bag in the back, putting it on in-side-out as the persistent knocking gets louder. My jeans are still wet, and I just don't have time as someone from outside the car shouts, "Open the door!"

Tupper winds down the window very slowly, giving me time to grab a bag and rest it in my lap to cover my bare legs.

We squint into the slice of morning sun.

"Good morning." A curious face peers into the window, his eyes landing on my bare legs and then up to my inside out T-shirt. "Big night, eh?"

Tupper's hands are hidden from the cop, but they are scrunched into fists. "We're new in town. Got in really late last night and couldn't find a place to stay…"

The cop narrows his eyes at me. "License and registration, please," he demands, sticking his hand through the barely open window.

Tupper exits the car to go to the front door, swinging the back door shut on my frightened face. The windows are fogged up so I can't see what's happening, but he doesn't come back into the car to get his license. The cop laughs, and then Tupper's aggravated voice comes through clear. "What the hell?"

More laughing.

I'm desperate to get out and see what's happening, but I'm still without pants. I start throwing neatly folded laundry around the car, searching for something to wear and starting to worry. Wondering if my dad actually did what I asked him to. If he didn't, I could be in serious trouble. So could Tupper.

A loud bang on the hood. A lot of swearing.

Then Tupper gets back in the car and slams the door, starting the car and backing out of the alley.

"What are you doing?" I say, starting to freak out. "You can't just drive off. He'll see your plates!"

"Buckle your seatbelt," Tupper snaps as he tears down the wet sparkling street, eyes dark as the rain clouds.

Clambering over the seat, I bounce into my spot, buckling my belt and grabbing Tupper's jacket to cover my legs.

"Tupper?"

He stares straight ahead. "Frickin' Portland. Think it's funny to scare the shit out people by pretending to be a cop. You know he asked me what your rates were?"

He runs a hand through his hair angrily, the ashy-blond strands standing up on end.

I laugh.

"It's not funny!" he says, still staring straight ahead. "You're my, my… It's not funny." He shakes his head several times.

I touch his arm. "It's all right. Who cares what some random weirdo thinks?"

He blows frustrated air through his nose and blinks.

"You know, it made me think, though…" He glances my way and waits for me to finish. "I think I better call my dad. Make sure he hasn't filed a missing person's report or anything."

Tupper seems to relax a little, taking a few deep breaths. "Okay, that and I'm buying you a phone."

We drive in silence. Things hanging over our heads that we don't want to acknowledge or talk about. Sarah isn't here, but I don't feel the usual panic. I don't worry about where she is because a more pressing fear is creeping up on me, now that the quiet has surrounded us and I can think about what happened last night. I don't worry about where she is as much as I worry *what* she is.

77. Anna

Portland, OR, 2997

WEATHER: SHAKY

ANNA PARKS THE CAR in the street, staring vacantly out the window. Tupper seems to like watching the people walk past. He points at the crowd that looks more like a blob of flesh to her than individual people, and giggles. Someone lifts her wiper blade and puts a flyer underneath.

Shakily, she unlocks the car door and snatches the flyer from the window, chasing after the bearded man and waving.

She feels out of control. Her anger pulsing through her veins as cold as ice. She pictures her veins, hanging limp inside her, drying up from not enough blood.

She needs, she needs, she needs…

Catching the man, she grabs his shirtsleeve, swinging him around. Her mind touches briefly on the fact that she forgot to lock the door, that she left her baby in the car, but then the eyes of the stranger lie across her, appraise her, and seem to understand what she's asking for without her having to say a word.

He takes her wrist in his hand gently, and she wants to surrender to him. She wants to give him everything, if he would just take away the pain of her blood. Her shattered, icy blood.

"I can help you," he says, his eyes touching on the redness of her nose, the water seeping from her eyes. She looks at his large hand cradling her thin, thin wrist, and she bites her lip.

She has to say yes. She has to. Because she can't function like this. She can't be a mother. She can't be anyone when she feels this bad.

He pulls her into the alley, and she thinks about what she will do. What is she willing to do? She feels bile rising in her throat as she realizes *anything* is the answer. She will do anything.

He holds up the small bag. It drips from his fingers, pure and white. "Fifty," he says.

She nods eagerly, hands him the money, and snatches the bag in her cold pale fingers. Tears in her eyes. For how much she has lost of herself. For how relieved she is to have what she needs.

Now maybe if she can pace herself, she could work her way down.

The plastic bag burns a scar into her palm.

The man leaves her squatting in the alley to take it in.

———❧———

TIME PASSES. IT BUMPS over trash cans and drips down drains.

She stumbles back to the car, hears the screaming, and brings her baby to her chest, rocking him gently, kissing his forehead.

"Sh! It's going to be okay. We're going to be okay," she whispers, her voice as fast and as high as a condor.

78. TUPPER

PORTLAND, OR TO SEATTLE, WA, 2015

WEATHER: AIR OF CONFUSION

"**YOU KNOW WE DIDN'T** even have time to read what your mom wrote about Portland," Langley says, flipping open the map to find Anna's caption.

"What does it say?" I ask, not really that interested.

THERE ARE SAVIORS ON EVERY STREET COR- NER!!!

With three exclamation points," she announces animatedly. "Then she's drawn a guy with a beard."

I shrug.

I kind of want to put Portland behind us. Want to find a cozy, warm place to rest in Seattle. No more driving for a while. We need some time to just be her and me.

She fumbles with the crappy phone I bought her, and I know what's on her mind. "You going to call him?"

She nods, stares down at the phone in her palm like it's a spider sinking its fangs into her skin, and whispers, "Yes."

I watch as she dials each number slowly. Ten seconds or more between each button push. When she presses the phone to her ear, she suddenly looks tiny. Like she's a child ringing for her dad to come pick her up from the principal's office.

She worries her lip between her teeth and waits. I can hear it ringing for a long time, and she lowers the phone from her ear slowly. "He's not ho…"

"Hello?"

"Dad?" She's a child in this moment, scared and alone.

79. LANGLEY

Portland, OR to Seattle, WA, 2015
WEATHER: MISTING

"LANGS? IS THAT YOU? Are you okay? Where are you?" My dad's panicked voice is barely recognizable.

"Yes, it's me. I'm okay," I answer, not really wanting to answer the other question.

He sighs like he's relieved. It's so unfamiliar that I take the phone from my ear and check the number to make sure it's actually him before he says, "You know the hospital called me? They said there was an incident with an orderly, though they wouldn't go into the details… I said you were here with me like you asked. But you really put me in an awkward situation."

It's almost comforting for him to turn back into the dad that I know and understand. It pulls all the guilt away from me like a ribbon being tugged from my hair.

"Sorry, Dad," I say. "So no one's looking for me?"

"No one's looking for you," he reassures. The words bring sadness and relief in equal gushes. Because secretly, I guess I had hoped *he* might have been.

"Okay, good."

It's quick as a heartbeat, raw as the slice of a knife. Then it's over. "Look, I've got to get back to work. But please, be safe, kiddo."

I think this is him washing his hands of me.

My knees pull to my chest, my voice cracks unwantedly as I reply, "I will Dad. Promise."

The. End.

I turn away from Tupper. I don't want him to see my face, which must look like it's been rolled over by a steamroller and then stomped on. I want Sarah, but she's not here.

Tupper doesn't speak or pull me to him. He just brushes

the side of my leg with his pinky finger. It's a small touch, but it's enough to let me know I'm not alone.

I try to smile. Try to seem unaffected. "Well, that's that then."

He nods. Drives. Doesn't try to say something fake or comforting.

A full hour later, he says, "Langley?" Nudges me from a self-pitying stupor. "I don't think you should give up on him just yet."

My lips purse and then open. They're about to say something about *the end*, of it being final, but he gives me a soft look, his eyes round and concerned. "You said your sister Sarah is your only family. But that's not true. He's there. Maybe one day you'll work it out with him."

I'm a gaping fish. Words popping like bubbles on the surface of a pond.

"My birth mom, my grandparents are dead," he continues in a detached kind of way.

I swallow my words. *Maybe* hangs in the air, stretching and then falling apart. Nonsensical letters tumbling to my feet.

"CAN YOU DRIVE FOR a while?" Tupper asks after another half hour of silence.

Doing something sounds good right about now, and I jump at the chance. "Sure!"

He pulls over, and I climb over him to avoid the rain that's still persistently falling in misty sheets all over Washington.

"You're lucky I'm such a gentleman," he says with a chuckle as I stick my butt in his face.

I laugh. "You know you don't have to be," I retort. Putting myself in the driver's seat, I adjust my position.

"Yeah, I know," he says, rolling his eyes.

I think he's going to get out his sketchbook, but he picks up his phone and starts typing. My eyes keep sliding to the screen as I'm driving. More than once, he shouts at me to keep my eyes on the road.

Giving a self-satisfied sigh after about ten minutes, he puts his phone away. Glancing at me, he smiles, a warm heart-melting kind of smile that seems to reach out and touch me. "You okay to drive for a bit?" he asks.

I wiggle around in the seat, stretch my fingers, and nod. "Yep."

"I'm gonna close my eyes. I don't think I got a lot of sleep last night," he says, closing his eyes and putting his feet up on the dash.

"Feet off the dash!" I shout, startling him awake.

His eyes fly open, and he clutches his chest. "Jesus! You gave me a heart attack."

Snorting, I speed up to overtake a truck, water streaming behind me like I'm bookended with waterfalls. He closes his eyes again, sighing. "Tupper, how did you know where to find me?" I ask.

He doesn't open his eyes, like maybe it's easier for him not to look at me when he says this, "It's stupid, but I just kind of knew you'd be there. I felt it." He taps his heart, and mine stalls. "Why were you up there?" I watch his lips move, and I don't like the gravity of the words that come from them.

There are things. Things I need to tell you, Tupper.

Now would be a good time. I shudder as I think about last night. How Sarah dragged me to that aerial tram like she knew that's where he would go. My skin prickles, and my heartbeat sputters uncomfortably in my chest. I don't like this feeling, this unsure doubt creeping up my spine with bony fingers. She is supposed to be me, a part of my subconscious. Nothing more.

Tell him.

"It was the same thing, I guess. Weird, huh? I just kind of felt like that was where I should go. That if I went there, you would find me," I say like a giant coward.

I took so long to answer that he's almost drifted off, making small sleepy noises and muttering, "Mhm. Wake me when we reach the city limits," as he slips into unconsciousness.

Minutes later. "My sister led me there," I whisper, a deep admission to no one, because he's already asleep.

I curse my spinelessness, but it would change everything.

Is it okay to love him? Is it fair? I only have a little to give, and I'm sure it won't be enough. And it's ending, the ribbon of road is running out. Soon we'll be at the frayed end, the burned end. No matter how hard we hang on, it will blow away in the wind, dance across the pavement, and disappear.

Sarah appears as Tupper starts snoring. She shakes her head, disappointed in me. I turn my bleary eyes forward, finding myself a little frightened of her. My skin is cold and pulling in, worried that she might touch me.

I wish I could just throw my hands up and say, *I can't deal with it*. But she's here. She's always been here. Whether she's a ghost or a hallucination probably doesn't matter, because either way, I don't have a choice.

"Do you know what happened with Dad before?" I ask timidly. I never ask her things like this. I've always assumed she knew everything because she was an extension of me.

She nods. It should be reassuring, but it's not.

"Sarah?" I whisper, my head dipping down, my heart tearing open. "Please. Can you leave me alone for a while?" It breaks something inside me to say this to her, more than my heart, my own idea of who I am.

I stare at the road for ten breaths.

When I look back in the mirror, she's gone.

I put the radio on low and drive.

80.LANGLEY

Seattle, WA, 2015
WEATHER: CLOSING IN

"TURN HERE!" TUPPER SAYS excitedly, pointing to a very steep hill completely shaded by arching trees touching fingertips. The car struggles, and I have to jam it into first to make it to the top. The Chevy lurches. Our heads get thrown forward and then slammed back into the seat.

I park at the gate while Tupper jumps out and walks into reception, holding his phone.

Soon enough, the big white arm lifts like a skeleton's finger and Tupper hops back into the car.

The long, winding driveway leads us up to a huddle of log cabins on the back line of the sprawling property. "Number three." Tupper points to the biggest and most private of the cabins, set back from the others with two enormous trees folding over like they're embracing it. He turns to me. "Like it?" he asks enthusiastically.

Confused by his excitement, I take a while to answer. "Yeeeess," I say slowly.

"It's ours for five days," he says, gazing at me with hopeful eyes, his hand spread wide to show five expectant fingers.

My eyes fall. "Oh."

"I thought it would be nice to stop driving and actually relax for a few days." He seems hurt by my reaction, but this feels like a 'last hurrah' kind of thing to me.

Turning off the car, I watch the eagerness free-fall from his face. I want to lift it back up for him. "Sorry. I was just surprised, that's all. It'll be good to rest for a while." Leaning over, I kiss his cheek. "Thank you."

81. TUPPER

SEATTLE, WA, 2015

WEATHER: DARK AND COZY

SHE SEEMS SAD, WHICH is the opposite of what I wanted. This extension of the trip was supposed to give us more time before… Before the thing I'm trying not to think about.

I text Mom:

Thanks for organizing the cabin. Looks great! Will be hanging here for five days.

Her text back is a thumbs-up symbol. Then there's a long wait while she's typing something else.

Final settlement has been reached. They left you their house. It was tenanted. Trust has been managing it all these years. Address is…

I put the phone screen side down, unable to even look at the address. I can't deal with this right now, so I grab my sketchbook. Langley is in the shower. I leave her a note and exit the cabin, my fingers itching to draw. It's only been a day or so, but to me that feels like forever. I get my mom's map out of the car and walk toward the grassy hill, setting myself up at a wooden bench that overlooks the acreage. Water seeps into my jeans, but at least the rain has eased.

Finding Seattle, I read Anna's caption.

FREEDOM TASTES AS GOOD AS THE BEST CHEESEBURGER, THE BEST FRIES, THE BEST SHAKE. I'M GOING TO SAVOR EVERY LAST BITE!

Her picture is of a smile. A giant smile hanging in the air with big plump lips and perfect straight teeth. I trace the mouth with my finger, wondering if it's her mouth she drew or someone else's.

Using the free Wi-Fi, I search up the best burger joints in Seattle on my phone. There is one place that seems to have the highest and most ratings. I decide I'll go there with Langley tomorrow or the next day, smiling at the fact I have a few days to play with. I intend to enjoy them and her.

Thinking about the aerial tram, I start to draw. Langley starts out curled in a ball on the floor, but as I move through the pages, she unfurls, light emanating from her body as she stands tall. The look on her face is fierce, strong. She sweeps her hand in the air and the ground vibrates, trembles from her power.

I see so much power in her. See what she could be. I wish she could see it, too.

82. Anna

Seattle, WA, 1997

WEATHER: BRIGHT

THE FURTHER FROM HER parents Anna travels, the stronger she feels, like her bones are gaining layers, her skin is toughening. She has so much hope. It fills her until it's pressing against the car window.

She throws her head back and laughs, winding the window down to let some of the hope out, watching it puff out in cartoon clouds. *They* said she wouldn't make it. *They* said she was out of control. She thinks about her dad's sad face, his arms grabbing and trying to restrain her. She feels no guilt.

Glancing back at the safe, sleeping child, she drums the wheel frenetically with her fingers. *They're doing fine. Everything is going to be fine. Better than fine.*

She feels like she could fly. Spreading her arms wide, she crows, giggling when the car veers off course.

"We're free, Tupper." She laughs. "Now we can do what we want, what we need to do. And I say what we need is burgers and fries and a giant strawberry shake!"

SHE LIFTS THE STRAW to the baby's mouth, and he sucks on it happily. Pink milk slides down the corners of his mouth and onto his Spiderman T-shirt.

The waitress comes over to mop up some of the mess. Anna grabs the woman's shirtsleeve, pulling on it a little too hard. The annoyed waitress' expression softens when she sees the baby, sticky with sugar pink.

"Excuse me?" Anna says, blinking up at her with her dark blue eyes. "Do you know if babies can eat fries?"

She waves the fry in front of the poor child's face, and he snatches at it sluggishly with poor reflexes. This makes Anna laugh loudly, obnoxiously.

Heads snap in her direction. Someone whispers, "Junkie,"

but she doesn't hear or pretends she doesn't.

The waitress smiles at the baby before taking a fry from Anna's plate, breaking it in half. "Here you go, honey," she croons, turning her attention to Anna. "How old is he?"

Anna counts on her fingers. "Bout eight months."

The waitress pats the girl's bony shoulder and says, "Make sure to give him some formula as well as the fries, okay?"

Anna smiles and nods. She's too happy to be offended by the woman's condescending tone. She knows the kid needs milk. She's his mother. And when she finds *him*, he'll have a father, too, and they'll be a real family.

After she finishes her food, she throws a large tip on top of her greasy plate.

Today is the beginning of her new life. The life she's been chasing.

She opens the car door with a flourish. So amused at herself. So unbelievably happy.

She can't wait to start.

83. LANGLEY

Tall Chief RV Park, Seattle, WA, 2015
WEATHER: BUZZING

THE SOFT HUM OF the vending machine at my back is comforting. When I lean into it, the plastic dimples and resists. It makes a loud popping noise when I stop pushing, but there's no one to hear it. I do like this place. It's fuzzy and green and as quiet as being underground.

I had to leave the cabin. This dance we're doing of fooling around and pulling back is slowly tearing me open. There was a reason for it, something about getting too close when we are so close to the end, but I'm finding it hard to hold onto. We are a wave that never reaches the shore. Just crashing and receding, crashing and receding. I need to soak into the sand now. I need to seep gently down to that place I'm sure will feel like home.

Sighing, I watch the bugs dance over the grass. It's been three days since I've seen Sarah, and I find myself searching for her in the grass, under tables, and behind trees. I know I asked for the space, but now I miss her. I'm starting to forget why I asked her to leave in the first place. Gazing down at my twisted fingers, I pump the weak ones. I'm not sure I care anymore.

I look up, my eyes scanning the grass, and I catch the light bounce off the sheen of dark hair, a blur of white becoming solid as it walks toward me. Sarah smiles shyly, standing at the top of the hill, and looks to me for the 'okay'. At my nod, she runs down the hill, the nightlights streaming over her dark hair, lighting up her white dress starkly against the deep blue night and the tangled mossy trees. Laughing, I watch her roll down and climb back up a dozen times, wanting to join her. I squeeze my fingers together into a light fist, frustrated because it's all I can manage. Tipping my head to the side, I squint as she disappears below the rise. Bugs fly away in a cloud, reacting to her presence, and I shudder wondering if I'm hallucinating the reaction or if it's real.

When she doesn't come back, I stand. My heart doing that gulping thing. Walking forward, I find her lying in the long grass staring up at the sky.

I go to meet her.

Sitting down, I wrap my good arm around my legs. Sarah nuzzles into my side, and I wish it could always be like this. Happy, quiet. No one staring, evaluating, and prescribing.

"You scared me for a sec there," I say, searching for that Disney star, the one that grants wishes.

Glancing around, I check for watchful eyes. Tupper is sleeping, and the park is deathly quiet. Shaking my head, I try not to think about him wrapped in blankets, his strong arms reaching for me.

"I'm sorry I asked you to leave," I whisper.

She shuffles up to sitting and nods her wild head. I lift my hand to touch her hair, to push it behind her small ear, but I don't. Something has changed between us now, and I'm afraid to touch her lest my hand suddenly goes straight through.

"What do you think of this place? Do you like it? Tupper's mom found it online. I think he thought it would be romantic," I say, clasping my hands and batting my eyes.

Sarah thinks hard, nods yes to the first question, and then screws her face up at the romantic comment.

"Do you think you'll stay for a while?" I whisper. She fades in and out, staring at me with giant, sad eyes textured as velvet. I wish she would speak. I can barely remember what she sounds like anymore.

Hearing a rustle in the woods that hedge this park in on all sides, I freeze. This natural quiet amplifies the smallest noise. When no one appears, I continue. "Where do you go?" I say, my words reluctant because I'm terrified of the answer.

To the sky. To Heaven. To a place so dark and empty you can't find the corners. Can't find your way out until I call you.

She looks confused by my question, shrugging and winding her finger to the sky. I stop breathing. But then she opens her fingers and puts her palm in front of my face as if to say, *Stop.* She knows I shouldn't ask. It will only hurt me.

My head falls, eyes on the grass between my feet. I think

maybe I need to know. "Tell me, Sarah, please."

I hear shuffling as she stands, and I stare up. For once, I am smaller than her. Sarah just points at me, right at my temple. Then points to her heart. "I don't understand," I say, shaking my head.

She does it again, a frustrated expression on her face.

"Sarah, don't worry about it. Forget I asked," I say, dry tears in my eyes.

Stomping her foot, she points at my head and her heart again. Swallowing, I try to understand. "Your heart is in my head?"

She sighs, and I get it.

And I hate it.

She's telling me what I already know. She doesn't 'go' anywhere because she doesn't exist. Sarah is part of my fucked-up brain and when she's gone, she is nothing and nowhere.

"Well, just go then," I shout, splitting the quiet open with my hammer of a voice. "Leave me the hell alone."

Don't go. Please.

Our cabin light switches on, and shadows move across the windows.

I pick up a rock and throw it at her.

She is gone before the rock touches the earth.

84. TUPPER

TALL CHIEF RV PARK, SEATTLE, WA, 2015

WEATHER: A CHANGE COMING IN

LANGLEY SITS ON THE edge of the hill, head in her hands. The nightlights make her hair look redder than usual. Bugs swarm around the yellow bulbs, and I feel them feeding on my exposed skin.

I slap at my neck and she turns around, eyes so big and mournful I just want to wrap her up and tell her it's going to be okay.

I crunch over the gravel to stand over her hunched body, my arms straight at my sides. "Come inside," I say, swatting my arm. "The bugs…"

"You ever roll down a hill?" she asks without making eye contact.

I stare down the steep grassy incline. "Um, yeah, when I was a kid."

She snorts.

"Did you enjoy it?" she asks, staring straight ahead.

I try to remember. The giddiness comes back, the hysterical laughter as we got up and tried to walk straight afterward. I scratch my arm, remembering the itchy skin from the grass. Smiling, I crouch down by her side. "Yeah."

She smiles back, sort of half evil, half sweet, like a female Joker. "Lie down."

I don't know why I'm doing what she says, but I lie down across the hill. She moves behind me on her knees. Places both her hands on my sides.

"God, Tupper, will you relax? It's like trying to push a cart with square wheels," she says, her teeth clenched in concentration. Her hair flops over my face, smelling like fresh cut weeds, sour and sweet. I want to say she looks adorable and that I'm not a log of wood. But I don't say anything. Not sure I need to.

She leans down and kisses me on the forehead. I manage

to say, "Wait."

Before she wishes me "Bon Voyage!" and shoves me down the hill.

Rolling pretty fast, my cheek smashes into the earth over and over, my breath coming out in hysterical squeaks as I start to roll sideways. Every time my ear isn't crushed under my spinning head, I hear her cackling like a witch.

I finally come to a stop at the base; my legs and arms sprawled wide. I stare up at the white dot stars winking at us, and laugh.

Her body hits mine with a thud. We both lie there for a second, giggling. I find her hand and squeeze. I feel a weaker squeeze back.

She sighs.

Flipping onto her side, she places her other hand on my chest. "Your heart is beating awfully fast, Tupper," she says all breathy and sexy and then she grins like an eight-year-old.

Swinging her leg over mine, she pins me to the ground. Putting her lips to my ears, she whispers, "Again," and I shudder.

She jumps up and pulls me with her. We climb back up the hill. When she reaches the top, she stares at me, wide-eyed and flushed. "This time, when you get to the bottom, you've gotta stand up and run straight away." She touches my arm and giggles. "Tupper, it's so fun. You have to try it."

Grinning at her childishness, I rake a hand through my hair and shake the grass from it. She gives me a longing look. "You first," I order, pointing at the ground in front of me.

"No," she says excitedly, standing on her tiptoes. "Here, you lie with your toes touching mine. We'll go together."

We lie down, and she counts. "Ready? One, two, three…"

We roll apart and then crash about halfway down, tracing the shape of a heart. Standing up, we try to run, colliding with each other and collapsing on the ground, disoriented and dizzy.

Her head is on my stomach, and she complains when I chuckle. "Stop it…" She laughs, her head bouncing up and down.

We are in the shadows now. I look around to see if we've woken any of the other campers, but all is quiet.

I picture us from above, making the letter T. The dark trees hanging over our neatly placed bodies. I chuckle again, and she hits me. "Ouch!"

"So was that fun or what?" she asks.

I concede. "Yes. That was fun."

She turns her head toward me, her voice softer, darker than before. "So what should we do now?"

I have some ideas.

Putting my hands in her hair, I gently bring her face closer to mine. She is draped half on me, half on the grass. "What do you want to do?" I ask, attempting to sound sexy, but it's wobbly and unsure.

She snorts. "Tupper, I know you find this hard, but you can just tell me exactly what you want. I promise I won't laugh. I promise I'll listen."

Yeah, but you don't promise I'll get what I ask for.

Taking a deep breath, I open my mouth and then say nothing. I want my eyes, my hands, to do all the talking. I can't tell her what I want because it's too much. It's too much to ask her for.

She pulls back, sits up, and twirls her hair together over one shoulder. Her eyes stare intensely, darting back and forth as if she's speed-reading me like a book.

"Okay. Let's do this," she says before I can react. She bends down and touches her lips to mine, softly, but then they open, pushing the kiss into a place we haven't been yet.

I am stunned. Scared. Hopeful. All at once. I think she's going to pull away eventually, but she lingers, her lips between mine. Into my mouth, she whispers, "Are you going to kiss me back or what?"

I smile, and our teeth clash. Sitting up, I move closer and really kiss her, pulling her body to my chest and loving the gasping sound she makes as I part her mouth.

This kiss is going to kill me. This kiss is the gateway to another world.

She pulls back and gazes at me, her face serene. I want to draw that expression. I want to find each freckle at the end of my pencil.

"Now tell me, Tupper. Is that really *all* you wanted?" Her eyebrows are raised; her mouth parted, awaiting my answer.

Yep, it's going to kill me. Kill me dead.

85. LANGLEY

Tall Chief RV Park, Seattle, WA, 2015
WEATHER: READY

HE'S GONE TOTALLY STILL, and I'm worried I've scared him. Or he thinks I'm joking. But I'm not. My body pulses with the need to be closer to him, and I don't want to ignore it anymore. I don't need to.

He stares at me like he thinks I may disappear. A look I'm used to making myself. I move closer. "Tupper?"

He clears his throat, clearly flustered. "I don't know what to say."

He never does.

I feel strong. Ready. "That's okay." I hold out my hand, and he takes it. I make circles in his palm, and he shivers. Slapping at a bug drinking from my arm, I murmur, "Let's go inside."

———⌖———

WE CLIMB THE HILL in easy silence. He holds my good hand, and I feel like he holds the good part of me. He sees the good part of me.

Small doubt sits in our damp footsteps. *Can I, should I, do this without telling him the truth?* He looks down at me and smiles nervously. I squeeze his hand tighter. He could be the way through.

The road ends, and we stand at the door. "The key," I say quietly.

He chuckles. I find myself loving that sound more and more, wanting to live in it. Breathe it.

The door creaks open, and he lets me go in first. I move to the window and open the blinds, staring outside at the constantly lit park. He comes up behind me, resting his chin on the top of my head. Taking his arm, I wrap it around my waist.

"Touch me," I whisper bravely.

Steadily his hand creeps under my shirt, just grazing my skin softly. My hand goes to his hair, and I pull him toward my neck. I am want and need, and he is steady and sure.

He turns me around to face him carefully, waiting for permission at first. I nod, and he lifts my shirt up over my body painfully slow. I am less patient. I take his and try to yank it over his head in one go, snagging it in his hair. His deep chuckle moves through me as he takes the shirt in one hand and pulls it over his head easily.

I'm rushing. Am I worried I will run out of time?

He creeps his hands up my bare sides, his hands resting on the lace running under my arms. Standing in front of him in only a bra and jeans, I shiver. I press against his chest for warmth, and he envelopes me in his arms.

This could be enough. I could stand here pressed against him forever. I feel how much he needs me, and it makes me smile.

I kiss his bare chest, feeling heat grow between us. Kisses lengthen... deepen. Skin brushes against skin. I make sounds I've never made before as he unclasps my bra and moves his hands over my breasts. He is gentle and certain. When I moan with pleasure, his lips curve happily. It feels so good I want to pull away, but he holds me still as he moves on to the other. I arch my back, unable to stand it. These new feelings electrify my whole body. I find myself climbing him, pushing against him until he falls back onto the bed.

I need nothing between us.

Our breath mingles, speeds up, and hums with pleasure as we peel away the layers of clothing left and explore the parts of us we haven't touched before.

And then we're naked, facing each other, feeling the bridge between us building and burning at the same time.

Tupper whispers, his words dark and welcoming, "Are you sure?"

I am. I am more than sure. My whole body is racked with sure.

"Tupper," I whisper, feeling my heart slam against my ribs. My breath hiccupping. "Yes."

He fumbles around for what he needs in the bag by the bed as I wait, my leg slung over his warm body. My whole being thrumming with heat. I climb on top of him, easing myself down, thinking this should be more difficult. I should feel hesitant about what I'm doing, how I'm doing it, but I don't. He guides me onto him carefully. It hurts a little, and he pauses, making sure I want to keep going. I do, whispering, "I think I love you," as I press every part of myself to every part of him.

"Langley. I *am* in love with you," he says, his hands on my hips, rocking me back and forth.

Something rustles in the corner, and I stop still.

And then I hear it.

A powerful scream that fills the room and pierces my ears. I've heard that scream once before, and it marked the end of my world.

Tupper's hands are still on my hips, loving and wanting. Because, of course, he hears nothing.

"Oh my God," I whisper, pulling back and off, grabbing the sheet to cover myself.

Tupper sits up, his face stricken with worry as he watches me shuffle back from him in horror. I cover my mouth. *Oh my God.*

"Langley, what's wrong?" he says. "Did I hurt you?"

I shake my head, unable to concentrate, only able to hear Sarah screaming, "No!" her hands in her hair, her usually tanned face white as a sheet.

What have I done?

I've been waiting to hear her voice for so long. It was the thing I had craved more than anything. But not like this. This is darkness and jumbled feelings. Hurt and anger. I jump from the bed and scramble to dress, shouting after her, "Sarah, wait!" with my hands out as she steps backward, her shoulders hitting the wall. She stares at me like she's not sure who I am. And then it's my turn to say, "No."

I lunge to catch her, grabbing at her sleeve as she slips out the door. She shirks me off and tears into the bright night, sprinting down the hill into the thick woods below.

Barefoot and barely dressed, I chase after her, Tupper running after me.

86. TUPPER

TALL CHIEF RV PARK, SEATTLE, WA, 2015

WEATHER: METEOR SHOWER

I DON'T UNDERSTAND. ONE minute we were…happy. Together. Doing the thing I've been dreaming of since I kissed her in the desert. It seemed right and then…

I pull on my jeans, my heart hurting, my body unable to calm itself.

She just ran away from me, and I don't know what I did.

Following her out the door, I watch as she zooms down the hill. "Sarah!" she shrieks. "Wait!" comes out in a hollow thud as she slips on the wet grass and hits the ground chest first, hard. I scramble down to help her, my bare feet like ice on the wet grass.

Grabbing her under the arm, I lift her. She turns to face me, a horrible look of regret and fear in her eyes before she takes off running again, slamming into the fence and lifting her leg over to climb it.

"Langley," I shout. "What's wrong?" My voice sounds all kinds of scared. Scared of what I did, scared of what this means, and somewhere in there, scared of her, her wild eyes and disconnected voice.

"I have to find her," she cries desperately. "She doesn't understand. I need to explain…" Panic. Panic in every atom of air surrounding us.

She's over the fence, hand cut. She wipes the blood on her pants, her shirt only held together by one button. I jump the wire and land next to her, watching her sear the forest with her eyes, searching. I don't want to say it, I don't even want to think it, but… she's acting crazy. I grab her shoulder to hold her still. "What are you looking for?"

She looks up at me, her eyes vibrating in her small face, her lips quivering from cold and terror. "Sarah. I have to find

250

Sarah," she breathes.

Her sister?

"But I thought she lived in Vancouver," I say dumbly, my palms open and my arms at my sides, as Langley walks forward shouting her sister's name. I follow her because there's nothing else I can do. My feet sink into the smelly mud, my body shakes with cold as I shout, "Sarah," looking for a woman hiding in the forest, even though I know she can't possibly be here.

With every step I take into the dark, the branches hitting me in the face, slimy green stuff streaking my clothes, I start to really see Langley. I see the things I didn't want to see before. The questions I should have asked and never did. I ignored a lot, and now here we are. I feel grief pushing up from deep inside. This may be where I lose her.

Langley stops. Her entire body heaving with frightened breaths. "Sarah, honey," she whispers. "It's okay. Please…" She holds out her hand, crouches down. "Don't run away. I'm sorry. I'm so sorry." Her back is to me, but I don't need to see her face to know she has tears streaming down her freckled cheeks.

It hurts me more than I could have ever imagined to see her like this.

My Langley is broken. And I don't know what to do to fix it.

She walks forward very slowly like she's approaching a wounded animal. I stay where I am, my hand grasped around a small tree trunk, my fingers digging deep into the soggy bark. Because I want to grab her, pick her up and run somewhere with her, though I don't know where. I want this to be okay.

It's not okay. She's not okay.

Her hands are in front of her, palms out as if she's begging. I squint through the trees, hoping to see what she sees, but there's nothing but moss and decaying leaves.

A few paces and she kneels in the mud. "You spoke," she says. She lifts her hand. Strokes thin air. "You spoke, and I heard you."

I grip my stomach. I'm going to be sick. Everything's turning too quickly, too out of control for me to possibly hang on. I've never felt more out of my depth than right now.

I'm up to my neck in this spongy mud and although I feel like this is a private moment, I can't look away. So I stare like a gawking idiot.

"Tell me why you're so upset. Is it because Tupper and I almost..." She awaits an answer from the rustling leaves and faint traffic noise, then she nods. "Well, what then?" Her head tips to the side as she listens to something I can't hear. I feel shut out and boxed in. This is something I'm not a part of. A world I'm not in.

I should go up to her, shouldn't I? Take her away from this cold, filthy place and help her somehow. But I'm frozen in place. I grip the trunk so hard part of the bark comes off in my fingers. Again, this panicked nausea rolls through me. *Oh Jesus, what the hell do I do?*

"Because I said I thought I might love him?" she asks, and my words die on my tongue. Her head falls, and she tucks her hair behind her ear. "Oh." Her voice cracks as she shuffles in the mud, opens her arms. "Can I hear your voice again? Please. Just once."

I can see her crumbling. Her whole body crumples in until she seems so small and vulnerable I can't make myself stay away from her any longer.

As I approach her carefully, she whispers, "It doesn't mean I don't love you, too. I'll always have room in my heart for you. Sarah, you have always been my number-one priority. I'm sorry. Please, please don't leave again."

Tall chief RV Park, Seattle, WA, 2015

WEATHER: STRIPPED BARE BY THE BITING BREEZE

TUPPER'S ARMS WRAP AROUND me as I shake. As I watch Sarah turn and walk away from me.

She's gone. And I don't know when she's coming back.

I turn in his arms, the realization crashing down on me like that wave I was so desperate to see meet the shore. "I'm so sorry, Tupper. I've been lying to you."

He strokes my hair and whispers, "It's all right. Don't worry. It's going to be all right." His usually strong, deep voice is unsteady and unsure because of me.

Picking me up, he walks back to the cabin. The truth biting into our ankles like heavy shackles.

It's time to confess.

———————

THE BED IS ALL tangled, the sheet lying hopelessly twisted on the floor, and I bite my lip thinking about the very recent memory of us together. I mourn how we are unfinished. How we may never get the things we want.

Tupper sees me eyeing the sheets and pulls them up, roughly making the bed. He looks at me with nervous worry, runs a hand through his hair, and stares at the floor for what seems like a million seconds punching into the floorboards. When he raises his head, his eyes are clear. Sad but clear.

"You should get cleaned up," he says, glancing down at his own mud caked clothes. "I'll go to the camp bathrooms." He starts to walk away but then he storms back, standing over me so close I find it hard to breathe. "I'm not angry with you," he says, confused. His eyes tear up and his jaw tightens, and I hate myself for doing this to him.

I stare into his kinder-than-they-should-be gray eyes, hands clasped in front of me. "You should be," I say, lips bluish and chattering.

"I know," he says, grabbing a towel from the back of the chair and turning away from me. I let him leave. Give him the time and space to absorb what he saw. I know he needs to compose his questions carefully. That's Tupper. That's the man I love, and the one I am almost certainly going to lose.

I give a short sigh, and it hurts because there's no breath left in me. I stare at the closed door for a long while before I move to do as he asked.

Stepping under the shower is harder than I expected. Stripping off my clothing pulls me backward into moments I can't forget. I close my eyes and then open them quickly as the images of Tupper looking at my body, awed and peaceful, flash through my head. His loving hands touching me softly but hungrily. But those moments are gone. They are a sentence that will never be finished.

I take a long time in the shower, washing my hair twice, standing under the stream and wasting water until it starts to run cold.

When I finally come out of the bathroom in a towel, Tupper is sitting on the edge of the bed, sketchbook in hand. His hair is wet, a serious expression on his beautiful face. I dip down to get my clothes from the floor, and he turns around while I change. It seems so stupid when he saw me naked less than an hour ago, but this is where we are now. I'm the one who brought us to this place.

"You can turn around now," I say sadly.

Shuffling around, he pats the bed. His pencil is in his hand, and I notice he's been writing in his book. "We need to talk."

I nod and sit at the head of the bed, putting a few feet between us.

He turns so he's facing me, cross-legged on the mattress. Pointing down to what he's written on the page, he taps it with his pencil.

I'm so scared of what he might say, what everyone says, but I owe him an explanation.

"Tell me about Sarah?" he asks, staring down at the page as he speaks.

"Sarah is my sister. Was…" I correct myself. "Sarah *was* my sister. She died in the accident," I reply, talking fast.

He raises an eyebrow. "So you're not going to Vancouver to live with her, I guess." He crosses something out on the paper, which I understand is a list of his questions. It makes me want to smile, at his oddness, his sweetness, but I restrain myself.

"No. Tupper, I'm sorry. I know I should have told you sooner, I just..." He puts his hand up to stop me, pointing to the page again.

"So is your mom really dead or was that a lie, too?" he says, his voice a mask of steady and unemotional.

I lean forward, desperate to catch his eyes, but he seems unable to look at me right now. "Sarah is the only thing I've lied to you about, I promise. My mom, Sarah, and I were in a car accident when I was eight. They died almost instantly. I was the only survivor." He winces. Scrunches the bed spread with his free hand.

"So does she look like the picture I drew for you?"

I've shuffled forward, and I know he doesn't want me to. I can see his defenses rising. "No, not really. She died when she was ten. She's always ten," I say quietly. "I age, I grow up, and she stays the same."

My body is working up to full-blown shaking. The tears starting to slip down my cheeks.

He searches the corners of the room, almost reluctantly. "Is she here now?"

"No," I cry out, breaking into pieces. "Tonight is the first time I've heard her voice in ten years and now she's gone. She's gone, and I don't know if I've lost her for good now. Tupper..." I crawl forward and sit in front of him, a weeping mess. "She is the only family I have left. I can't lose her."

He stands up, takes a step back from me. "Please, Langley, give me a second to..."

88. TUPPER

TALL CHIEF... WHATEVER

WEATHER: WHO THE FUCK CARES?

To what? To start believing in things that aren't real? To be okay with the fact she lied to me, that she had this massive secret quite literally following her around all this time? This sucks! She's ruined everything. But then I look down at her shaking, frightened body, and I want to scoop her up. I want to help her.

"Wait," I say. "Let me finish." She stops, holds herself together for my sake. She's giving me space and time like she always has. The two things everyone else finds so difficult to give to me. I read the words on the page. Each question is as crazy as the next. "Is she a ghost?" I ask, my shoulders pulling in that icy feeling shivering under my skin. Because I want her to say, *Yes*. Even though it's terrifying, and changes everything I thought I knew about the world, I'm desperate for Sarah to be a ghost. Then what's wrong with my Langley is outside of her. Not inside. In a place I can't reach.

She thinks about her answer carefully, then she says, "No and yes."

"What does that mean?" I say, leaning forward over my book.

She plants her hands on either side of her body like she needs help holding herself up. "It means I'll never be sure. I know medication makes her go away, which makes me think she probably isn't a ghost. But sometimes, she does things that make me wonder."

My lips press together. That's not a real answer. "What do you really think, like in your heart?" I say.

Her head dips and so does her voice as she whispers, "I think she's only real to me. I feel like she's something, someone that comes from inside me."

I put the book down. Lay the pencil on top. "So you're…"

She smiles awkwardly, her eyes red from crying, her hair hanging wet over her shoulders. "A little more than just run-of-the-mill crazy? Yes."

I take a deep breath and release it. *Maybe if I can get her some help, get her to take the meds, things could be better...*

"Okay," I say on my outbreath.

She sits up on her knees, hopeful. "Okay?"

"Well, you told me you were crazy before, now I know what that means. Maybe now we can get you help. There's got to be a good treatment facility here in Seattle ..." I get out my phone, ready to search.

Moving from the bed, she shakes her head. "Tupper, no."

She starts to put things in a bag, collecting her meager possessions. "What are you doing?" I stammer.

She stops and comes to me, sitting so close I can smell her shampoo, feel her breath. "You didn't listen. It's not your fault. No one ever does. She is all I have. I won't give her up. I can't. So I think maybe it's better that I leave."

Grabbing her hand, I pull her back before she puts another thing in that damn bag. "You can't just leave. Give me some time to accept this."

"People don't accept this. They try and fix it," she says matter-of-factly, tapping the side of her head.

"Have you ever had someone say they were willing to try?" I ask, frustration rising.

This makes her pause.

I don't know what I'm doing, but maybe it's working.

"Never," she says like the idea is foreign to her, absolutely impossible.

"Let me try," I plead, not even sure I can do it.

Dropping her bag, she gives me a doubtful look. I stare her down, trying to inject all my sureness about my feelings for her into my eyes.

I pull back the covers, and she comes to me. We curl under. Exhausted. I flick the light off and let the darkness settle over us, still trying to brush away the creepy feeling. Like we're being watched.

"She likes you, you know," Langley whispers in the dark. Her voice calmer, almost relieved.

"Yeah?" *The weirdness will take longer than I have to get over.*

She finds my hand, squeezes it lightly. "She's the one that made me go to the aerial tram."

Shuddering, I pull her closer. I don't know what to think anymore.

She kisses my hand, mumbling against my skin, "You know, it's funny. All this time, you've been chasing a ghost and I can't get away from mine."

I want to find it funny, but I'm so not there yet. "Hilarious," I say, elbowing her in the side.

Freakin' hilarious.

89. LANGLEY

Seattle, WA, 2015

WEATHER: WEEPING

"Oh my God!" Sarah whines, dragging her hand down her face dramatically. "Is this it? There's like nothing here."

Dad gives my mom a sharp look, and she nods. "This is Fort Langley. The birthplace of British Colombia! Its historical significance is huge..." He begins another one of his monologues.

He keeps talking, but I'm distracted by Sarah's talking hand, which Dad can't see behind his seat.

Mom swings her head around and catches Sarah, but doesn't turn her in. Her beautiful brown eyes crinkle in the corners. "Listen to your father," she says with a smirk and a roll of her eyes.

He parks the car in a wet drive lined with pine logs and we jump out, desperate to stretch our legs. Sarah gives the place a quick scan and then announces, "There's no store. There's no café or anything. You said we could get something to eat." Her chin pushed out defiantly.

Dad pats her head, not really listening to what she's saying. He's too taken by the shabby brown cottages and old-timey artifacts. I follow him, and Mom grabs the back of my jacket. "Here, darling." She hands me and Sarah a granola bar each from her giant embroidered purse.

Sarah runs off to investigate at her breakneck speed. I hang with Dad, happy to read the plaques and soak up some of his enthusiasm. After all, I am named after this place. I guess I should learn a bit about it.

"You're such a dork," Sarah says, colliding with me and pinching my side. We lean over the fencing to look at some old pieces of equipment that I read were used to skin animals. I pull a face, and so does Sarah.

"Your namesake is gross," she teases.

Dad turns and snaps at her. "Sarah. Be quiet!"

But she's right. I can't believe my dad named me after a fur-trading post.

"Is she here now?" Tupper asks as we drive through the main part of Seattle, searching for this burger place he's intent on visiting.

I sigh. "How about I tell you when she *is* here rather than you asking me every five minutes?"

He closes his mouth and keeps it closed, and now I feel bad.

I wish she were here. But it's like admitting how I felt about Tupper pushed her to the side. She was right to be scared and upset with me. I don't think I know how to make room for them both, and I need to work that out.

We finally see it, glowing neon in the middle of the day, and Tupper parks the car.

He takes my hand and we enter the tiny diner, his eyes scanning the walls though I don't know what he's looking for.

A woman shows us to a booth and we sit opposite each other, staring past one another. Both in our own little worlds we're not sure how to leave.

When our burgers arrive, I take a bite and smile. "Mmm, tastes like freedom!" I say, repeating his mom's strange words. He laughs, and pieces of lettuce fall from his open mouth.

"More like tastes like unidentifiable meat products," he says after he swallows.

We both laugh and turn to our fries, suddenly uninterested in the burgers. "If she *was* here, I think we've learned one important thing about her," I whisper.

He gazes up at me, his gray eyes shining, "Yeah?"

I lift the lid on my burger and scowl. "The woman had no taste buds."

He gives me a soft smile, and I get all fluttery in the chest.

Stirring a shake that's got lumps in it and tastes like stale bubblegum, he mutters, "I just found out I inherited a house."

Milk snorts out my nose.

"Where? Whose house?" I ask. This is so not like Tupper, volunteering information. He pulls a napkin from the tin and starts drawing on it. He draws a burger with eyes. It's kind of muppet-looking.

"When I turned eighteen, all this money started coming. It had been held in trust for me from my birth mom's parents. The house is in Chilliwack," he says tiredly.

My legs brush his under the table, and he tucks them under the seat. "Is that why you're going up there?" I ask, desperate to keep him talking.

He shakes his head. "I don't even know anymore. At first, it seemed like a way to find out about my birth mom. Also a chance to get away from Kansas so I could decide what I wanted to do, you know, with the rest of my life." He rolls his eyes. "Now, I think maybe it was none of those things. Now I think it was so I could…"

He stops talking, looks down at his greasy plate of food, and sighs hard. He adds legs and arms to his burger drawing. "What, Tupper? You don't have to say it, but I'm listening."

Patiently, I watch him sketch a whole scene, talking burger, fries each with their own set of eyes. The shake talks through lips at the end of a straw.

"It was so I could find you," he mutters, glancing up at me all vulnerable. He freezes me in place with a stare that strips me, burns me, and breaks me all at once. "Look, I've been thinking about it a lot. And I've decided I don't care. I'd rather have you in my life as you are, with a ghost/hallucination sister or whatever, than not at all," he says quickly.

You say that now, but it will change. It always changes.

He reaches for my hand and grabs it, squeezing it strongly. "I'm scared you're going to break my heart, Langley. But I still don't care. You…" His eyes are so intense, silver and sparking. They search mine looking for hope, looking for a place that's just for him. "You inspire me."

Those words coming out of Tupper's mouth mean more than *I love you*.

I think I'm choking, or my heart is working its way into my throat. I want to say yes to what he's offering, desperately. But it's not fair to him. I'm not enough. At least not as I am right now.

His eyes are wide with fear because he knows what I'm going to say. I lean over the table, take his head in my hands, and kiss him gently but passionately. When I pull back, I say, "We have a couple of more days." Essentially stomping on his heart and working it deep into the floor.

I see the beginnings of the break starting to appear, just a small crack that will fissure and open once I do what I was always going to have to do.

"Maybe in those days, I'll change your mind," he says,

keeping my hand pressed to his cheek.

"Maybe," I say, smiling sadly.

I hope so.

90. TUPPER

TALL CHIEF RV PARK, SEATTLE, WA, 2015

WEATHER: UNCHANGED BUT WE CHOSE TO IGNORE IT

I HAD TO SAY it. It was as hard as finding that map. It was as hard as finding out I had grandparents only to learn they were already dead. I would have regretted it if I didn't tell her, didn't try.

But I saw the look on her face.

Love and leaving.

I get out my sketchbook, adding another likeness to the many I've already drawn of Langley since I found her. Starting with her big brown eyes, the love I see when she looks at me, and the twist in her mouth that holds in words she won't say, the ones that whisper, *I'm leaving you soon.*

How do I ask her to stay with me? To change for me? I can't.

The door opens and she glides into the room, two bags of laundry in her hands. "I think that will last us for the next few days," she says smiling, sweeping the bad things under the rug with her beautiful gaze.

I close the book, but she saw something and eyes me curiously. "Was that me?" she asks, moving to sit next to me on the bed.

I nod.

"Can I see it?" she asks, holding out her hand.

I hand her my heart, folded between the pages.

She flips through finding each picture I've drawn of her. Smiling, tracing the likenesses with her finger. When she gets to the last one, she says, "You know if you don't do something with this incredible talent, I'm gonna have to hunt you down and force you to!" She shakes her tiny fist.

"All the more reason not to," I mutter. She quiets, her hand falling to the side, the smile sliding from her mouth, and I wish it was as simple as leaving these drawings to die on the page. I almost convince myself I would do it for her. "You talk like it's over already, like you're already gone."

"I'm sorry. I'm just, I don't know, preparing you," she says, staring out the window at the hyper green.

"Don't," I say, stubbornly crossing my arms over my chest. "You said maybe. That maybe I could change your mind. So don't just give up."

She gets up and stands in front of me, gently trying to part my arms, working her way in until I'm open and bare and she's pressed against my heart.

"I'll stop," she says, kissing my chest through my shirt. "I promise."

I want to say *don't stop*, but I don't need to. It's like picking up where we left off. All the heat building back up to an instant fire like it was just smoldering in the background these last few days. Waiting for a tiny shred of paper to start it again.

"What if Sarah…?" I start as she peels her shirt off and stands before me, looking more beautiful than I remember. I blink slowly, not wanting to put darkness between my eyes and the girl in front of me. She's a super hero, or at least the beginnings of one.

"You and I have unfinished business." She quirks her lips, gives the small cabin a sweep with her large brown eyes. "We might get interrupted, but I'm willing to try." She gazes at me with a trusting expression. And I forget about everything.

I take her shoulders, hold her still, try to keep my eyes on her face. She breathes slowly, calmly, her lips parted and wanting. "You don't owe me anything," I say, trying to do the right thing.

My hands glide down her arms, her skin raised and bumpy. "You're wrong about that, Tupper," she says, sinking to kneel in front of me. "I owe you everything."

I can't stand the space between us any longer. Grabbing her face, I crash into her mouth, drawing my own patterns, my own designs on her skin. I pull her up and onto my lap. She is light yet strong. Her hair falls over my face as she pushes me down onto the bed.

Skimming the waist of my pants with her fingers, she fumbles for the button. I whisper in her ear, "I'm not going to rush." She exhales suddenly, like I've surprised her, and then laughs, her head falling back, her eyes to the ceiling. I could draw that laugh. It's like caged birds finding freedom. It's white and feathered and fills the room.

She leans down and kisses me as my hands make circles and pictures and question marks on her bare back. "Take all the time you need. I'm not going anywhere," she says in a shaded tone.

This night could change everything.

And as we come together, I start to believe that it already has. I can see the change in her, the love in her eyes as we change our space, as our connection strengthens.

This feels like nothing else.

Floating in Space

Weather: Perfect

I DON'T WANT TO speak. Those bubbles of animated words, exclamation points, and funny one-liners would crowd this space, because it is full. There is no room for anything else but her warm skin against mine, my breath grazing her neck.

The morning sun sets lines across the bedspread as it tries to push through the blinds. I smile, burying my nose in her hair, trying to remember what it felt like before Langley. Not trying very hard.

Taking my hand, she moves it back and forth under her lips. They are soft and dry, and I feel a rough part of skin scratch my knuckle.

"I don't just *think* I love you," she whispers with her back still to me. I'm not sure whether she knows I'm awake or not. I stay still. My ears straining to hear what she will say. She can probably feel my heart pounding out of my chest against her back. I take slow deep breaths, trying to calm myself down, but it doesn't work very well. "I know," she says.

I don't say anything. Just let her words float between us and then up. I see them bouncing against the ceiling like a balloon some kid lost their grip on.

92. LANGLEY

Seattle, WA, 2015

WEATHER: RAIN THAT EVAPORATES BEFORE IT CAN
REACH THE GROUND

SHE DID COME BACK, just briefly, in the laundry room. And I was so relieved. Then I asked her to leave. She stared at me with such sadness and rejection, then she nodded. I asked her where she would go, but she couldn't even look at me. It caused a twist in my heart I thought would never go away. It kept twisting and twisting, making it hard to breathe, to live. Until he held me. Until he peeled away every layer I had collected and let them fall to the floor. I forgot all about her. I forgot about pain and guilt and girls lost in the darkness. It was wonderful.

And it is why I must leave him.

His hand is draped lazily on my hip. I am caged in his arms, happily unwilling to move. Suddenly his phone beeps, and he rolls away from me. Lifts the screen to his face. Groaning, he taps out a message.

"Everything okay?" I ask, pulling the sheet over my naked chest and rolling to face him.

His scruffy hair is sticking up on one side, and he gives me a lopsided grin that makes my heart hurt again, saying, "Yeah, it's my mom again. She wants me to go check out the house when we get to Chilliwack."

I need to say something, but I can't find the words. They're glued to the floor, and I can't get a nail under to lift them. I don't want to. But there is no *we*. I will be leaving him in Vancouver. My eyes fall and he catches my chin, concern clouding his features. "You okay?" he asks, pushing his arm underneath me and pulling me to him. "You usually laugh every time I say that name."

His forehead is pressed to mine, and the mist that covers all the things I need to say but don't want to creeps over and erases my mind. He's too close and not close enough. I know

I'm making it worse, but I can't seem to drag myself back.

How can you love someone this much and leave them? His hands wander over my body. His lips press to my collarbone. *How can it be the right thing to do?*

It's agony to pull away. I'm so angry at myself, at my life. I've never had anything good and normal. I've never wanted anything so badly in my whole life. I want his words and his quiet. I love his focus and the sound of the pencil on paper when he's drawing. And I can't have any of it. I place my palms on his chest, push him back gently. I say, "Stop," in dead words from a mouth that's fighting against me. I think of Sarah waiting for me, shadows pulling on her, and I feel like I might tear my hair out in frustration. It doesn't matter if she's a ghost or just in my head. She is real to me. She is my sister, and I can't abandon her.

Tupper's confused expression breaks the broken pieces of my heart into dust.

I quickly dress before grabbing my phone. "Stay here," I order, pointing to the bed and walking outside before he can stop me.

After I sit down on the bench next to our bedroom window, I call Tupper.

The blinds come up, and his face appears in the window as he answers. "Langley?" He stands, and his bare chest is assaulted with sunlight.

I put my hand up, my eyes finding his and settling like leaves beneath a winter tree. "Don't come out here, please. Tupper, I need to talk to you. I'm scared if I try to do it when I'm close to you, I won't get the words out."

His expression changes. Sadness starting to take over his face, freckle by freckle. I did that. I made him look like he's been punched in the guts, and I haven't even started yet. "Okay," he says in a defeated tone. He sits back down on the edge of the bed, still gazing at me through the window.

I sigh, my fear building, my heart gone because he has it. It's back in the room. "I love you," I say, barely making a sound, tears pricking the corners of my eyes.

His mouth moves, his voice coming through the phone confused. "I love you, too."

"But… but…" A small hand slips into mine and squeezes.

I look down at Sarah.

She shakes her head, saying, *You don't have to do this. You can let me go.* But I can't. I won't. She's my sister. She needs me. She has been with me through my whole horrible life. "But I can't love you enough," I say, my hand shaking. "My heart is split. I'm in two different worlds." I clasp my head in my hands, wanting to shake it, change it, so it doesn't have to be this way. "I wish I was different. I wish my life hadn't turned out this way, but it did and you deserve better."

"I don't care about any of that," he says, putting his hand to the window.

"I care," I say, my voice a little stronger. "Last night was wonderful. But it left Sarah alone and in the dark. I know you don't understand, but I can't do that to her again. I need to find some kind of balance between her world and the real one. You've made me want to find a balance, find room in my heart for both of you. Until I do, we can't be together."

He hangs up the phone, staring at me for a long moment painted with sadness. I mouth, "I'm sorry." My body shaking, tears tipping from full eyes and pouring down my face. My head collapses in my hands and Sarah rubs my back, small circles like she always has. Then she stops, steps back.

When I raise my head, Tupper is standing in front of me, his face a torn picture of heartbreak and compassion.

He gathers me up in his arms. Holds me tight.

There's nothing left to say.

93. TUPPER

VANCOUVER, BC, 2015

WEATHER A SKY THAT DOESN'T WANT TO BE BLUE

I GET IT NOW. I get why they turn to evil. Why they fall in the rain and scream a name to the sky. Why couldn't I be enough? Why couldn't I fix her?

And now I'm just going to let her go, let her walk away.

I'm an idiot.

I don't know what I'm going to do without her.

"Anna wrote, **I CROSSED MY FINGERS, TOES, AND EVERY CROSSABLE PART OF ME AND IT WORKED!**" Langley says, running her finger over the drawing of a girl with her eyes crossed. I nod.

"I would try that, too, if I thought it had any chance of working," I snap, regretting it when I see her hurt expression. Crossing her arms, she looks out the window. This air of hearts tearing slowly down the middle fills the car.

Things calm as we drive through the city to the grand-looking Pacific Central Station. We've tried to talk, but every conversation goes around and comes back to the same thing. And I can't ask her to stay with me again.

The shitty thing is I do understand. The selfish thing is I don't care. I don't want to lose her.

We park the car, and I help her with her bag. My bag. I convinced her to take it. I can always buy another one, and she can't travel to Fort Langley carrying her clothes in shopping bags.

She stands at the front of the car, blinking back more tears. When she's not paying attention, I shove a thousand dollars cash in the front pocket and zip it up.‑

When I come to join her, she's frozen. Her lip sucked under her teeth. "I could drive you. It's on my way," I try.

She turns to me, her eyes making me doubt her resolution.

She shakes her head. "I can't do it."

Relief floods through me.

I put the bag down, and she picks it back up. "No, Tupper. I can't stay in the car with you for one more second."

This feels like when they try to set the bear free in the wild, and the kid has to yell at it and tell it to go to hell so it will gallop into the forest.

Shoving my hands in my pockets, I feel my jaw tightening, my words retreating. "Great, well, nice knowing you," I manage, a bitter taste on my tongue.

She smiles sweetly, and my head and heart start battling it out.

"You misunderstand me. I can't be in the car with you because it makes me *want* to stay."

I don't say, *Then do it. Stay.*

Hand in hand, we walk to the station like we're an ordinary couple. Not like there's a dead girl walking beside us. Between us.

After she buys her ticket, we wait on the platform silently.

She pulls my sketchbook and pencil from my bag, then hands it to me.

"I thought you might need this," she says, leaning her head on my shoulder and killing me with these things she does that let me know no one will ever understand me like she does. "Tupper. Draw our goodbye."

Flipping open to almost the last page, I start.

Langley jumps from the train, running toward a figure leaning casually against the wall. He steps out of the shadows and she grins, closing the distance between them. "Tupper. You waited for me."

They embrace. They kiss. They walk away together. An unwritten future ahead of them.

It's cheesy, but I couldn't draw our goodbye. I had to draw our reunion.

I hand it to her. "It's perfect," she whispers, sniffing.

The train pulls up. Suddenly, perfect moments and dramatic lines drain from the platform. My heartbeat speeds up as I start to panic. Because it's too soon.

Langley presses her hand to her chest, her breath coming in short bursts. She looks down and I know Sarah is there, holding her hand. Helping her do what she needs to do. And

I can't hate her for it.

The chime starts, and we glance nervously at each other. "I have to go," she says reluctantly.

I pull her in. Kiss her hard. I tell myself, *It's not a goodbye kiss. It's a promise.*

"Thank you," I say as she walks away. She gives me a weird look. It's for trying. It's for understanding me. Never pushing. Challenging me. It's for leaving so she can get her head right and come back to me. Then she nods.

"When I'm ready, I'll find you," she promises, though I know it's not really a promise she can make.

But I can have hope.

I stare down at my feet. Now I have to work out how to move as this empty shell, how to keep from breaking and disintegrating right here on the platform.

94. Anna

Vancouver, BC, 1997

CROUCHING DOWN, ANNA JIGGLES the fake number plate to make sure it's secure. Satisfied, she stands and lets the warm breeze tease her hair.

She wonders if she should feel a pull, or her heart stretching, the further away she gets from the white clapboard house where she spent her whole life. But she doesn't feel anything. She tucks her blonde hair behind her ear and her lips curve upward, nodding in agreement with herself. It must have been the right thing to do then.

As she rubs the space between her breasts, an icy pain shoots through her rib cage, but it doesn't last long. Soon, she is able to take deep contented breaths again. She shakes her head, smiles to herself. It was nothing.

Tupper is awake. Small gurgles come from the box as it slides slowly across the backseat when she turns at angles. She pulls over onto the road verge. Leans over to strap the box down with the seatbelt.

When he smiles at her, it makes her feel strange, conflicted, because he stares at her with *his* eyes. His blondish hair has already begun to darken to a more hazelnut-ash color. Tupper looks like his father. She sighs and strokes her baby's face, the softness of his skin reminding her how vulnerable he is. How much responsibility sits on her thin shoulders. Thinner than they once were.

"Don't worry, Tupper," she whispers, leaning down to kiss him. "I'm going to take good care of you. My heart is healing. I can feel it." She touches her chest again. "This is going to be good."

Tupper blinks, his gray eyes knowing. It makes her giggle. He can't understand her. She knows he just likes the sound of her voice, and love swells in her fast-beating heart.

Gazing ahead at the line forming at the border, she curses under her breath. She lifts the box from the seat and places it in the trunk, covering the baby with a blanket. Thinking about poking holes in the sides for air, she again giggles, covering her mouth, trying to plaster a serious, responsible expression on her face.

Carefully, she lifts the blanket and hands Tupper a bottle. "Sh! You need to be extra-specially quiet. Mommy only had enough money to pay for one American passport," she croons to the unaware child. She pokes his tummy gently. "Baby passports are really expensive." She winks and tucks him in, throwing a coat over the box for good measure. Then she shoves the small amount of baby paraphernalia under her seat and in zipped-up bags.

Just as she reaches the border control station, she glances down. White powder covers the corners of the center console. She quickly grabs a scarf, her wallet, and sunglasses, arranging them over the top.

Taking a deep breath, she drives forward, knowing this could mark the end of her freedom before it has even begun.

The attendant looks her up and down as he holds her fake passport in his hands. "Did you have a good holiday?" he asks politely.

She nods. "Yes, sir. But it'll be good to get home." She lays her Yankee accent on thick.

"Kansas, eh?" He glances at her passport briefly, and she holds her breath. He hands it back to her, ducking his head inside the car to give it a quick sweep.

"Mhm," she confirms, scared to open her mouth again and give herself away.

After he retreats, he taps the hood of the car. "Safe travels, Miss Barrymore." She smothers her grin at her new name, borrowed from her favorite movie star.

When her tires roll over the imaginary line between Canada and America, she feels a slice of her old life disappearing, flattening beneath the turning wheels.

95. LANGLEY

Vancouver to Fort Langley, 2015

WEATHER: CAN'T SEE THROUGH THE TEARS

THE RED EMERGENCY LEVER gleams at me as we pull away from the station. Sarah sees me staring at it, giving me a wicked smile. My hands shake, and I look up at the ceiling to stop myself from crying. It only makes my eyes fill with water. Spill big fat tears down my cheeks when I lower my chin. *I'm an overflowing rain gutter.*

I sit on my hands. Resist. Because I know I'm doing the right thing. I want to make room for love in my life. And to do that, Sarah and I have to make some changes. I just pray it doesn't take too long.

My phone buzzes in my pocket, and I pull it out. It's Tupper, of course.

Did they teach you how to mend a broken heart in Life Skills?

I laugh weakly, tapping out a reply.

Super glue and scotch tape?

He sends me a smiley face.

I hate this already.

96. LANGLEY

Fort Langley, BC, 2015
WEATHER: EERILY CALM

THERE ARE GHOSTS PEEKING out from every corner, streaking across the lawn, and knocking the air from my lungs. They've left their footprints in the mud. Their cold breath fogs the windows. Staring down at my now-trashed red sneakers, I see granola bar crumbs in the grass.

This is the last place my family was together.

Sarah hangs back, reluctant to push through the rough wooden gate. And it feels like a warning. But I shrug off the chill that's attempting to grab at my shoulders and walk in.

Memories of the day play like home movies in little lit-up spaces around the fort and I blink slowly, trying to work out if this is in my head or out of it. Pulling Sarah through the gate, I bring her to my side. She doesn't react to the sepia-toned Mom and Dad walking hand in hand across our path. I sigh, gripping Sarah's thin shoulder. I think this is just me replaying the past.

We walk to the center of the wooden fort. Sarah looks up at me questioningly, as if to say, *Why are we here?*

I don't know.

It seemed like a good idea, a way to connect to my past, to remember a time when I was happy.

I run my hand over the dark brown animal fencing and the various tools I no longer have to climb up on a railing to see. I understand there will be no particular peace for me here.

The past is a mirage I'll never reach.

Sarah pops in and out of the buildings quickly. Boring easily. She didn't like it the first time we came here. Nothing's changed there. I roll my eyes as she points at the newly appointed gift shop. She runs back to take my sleeve, leading me to it.

I step out of the frigid air and into blasted heat, smells of handmade soap and new fabric wafting past my nose.

There are the usual souvenirs, shot glasses and squirrels carved from rocks. But Sarah has found something different that she anxiously points at, her eyes wide with mischief. I turn the spinning display around to see what she's been pointing at. It's a simple plastic number plate with *Langley* written on it.

Taking it, I turn my head, opening my mouth to speak to the only person who would understand how special this is. But Tupper's not here, of course. The feeling leaves me empty. I place the name tag back on its hook, spinning it out of view.

Sarah seems upset by this and she stomps her foot, trying to drag my attention away from how I was feeling, what I was doing, but instead of letting her like I always do, I resist.

I take a huge breath, pushing oxygen into my lungs until they feel like they will burst. My eyes flick to the shopkeeper, who is looking at me like he thinks I might steal something, and then I release my breath.

I need to work this out.

I need to find a way to be more in this world and less in hers, without hurting her, without losing her.

The task seems impossible. I don't even know where to start.

I picture Tupper leaning over his sketchbook, stealing glances at me with his guarded gray eyes. I hear his chuckles, sense his awkwardness as he leans against a wall, trying to become part of it just so no one will talk to him, and my heart squeezes in my chest. Missing him was a given, but now I understand something deeper about myself—I can't do this alone.

Taking the phone out of my pocket, I dial the number. Hoping it's not too late, praying I can convince him.

"Hello?" His deep, worried voice questions me in more ways than one.

With a shaky voice, one that's used to fighting against everything rather than seeking help, I say, "Dad… I need your help."

97. TUPPER

CHILLIWACK, BC, 2015

WEATHER: LIKE YESTERDAY

IT'S BIG. IT'S IN a nice area. It's where Anna grew up, where my grandparents lived, but to me it just looks like a house. White weatherboards, a bright yellow door with a shiny black knocker.

The agent's footsteps echo in the empty home. Standing in the center of the dining room, he gives me a weird half smile. I don't return it. "It's a beautiful home. Do you think you'll want to continue renting it or sell?" he asks, rocking back on his heels expectantly, waiting for a potential commission to be thrown his way.

I rake a hand through my hair and rub the back of my neck, wondering what Langley would say. Probably something inappropriate about shacking up here, asking, *How thin are the walls?* Something that would make me laugh.

I try to picture the life they had, someone mowing the lawn, doors closing and opening as things change and people say hello and then… goodbye. It's a fuzzy, out-of-focus picture. Because I don't know them. And I will never know them.

I groan. I don't want this house. It seems as empty as my heart right now. I feel Langley's elbow in my side. *Don't rush. You don't have to decide right now.*

I've left the agent standing there for way too long. I mumble, "I, um, I'm not sure."

The blinding shine of his hair product makes him look like a Lego man, and the corner of my mouth lifts.

He seems disappointed, but nods and folds the wad of papers he was carrying in half, shoving them awkwardly in his back pocket. "No need to make a hasty decision, but just so you know, now is a great time to sell."

I shrug non-committedly.

The man keeps talking as we walk toward the front door. "This house has been in the Beaulieu family for a long time…"

I try to say the name, but it comes out very American and butchered. "But my last name was Barrymore."

He opens the front door, ushers me outside. "Yes, well, I don't know a lot about it really, but this is a small town, so you know, there are stories."

Shadowing him like Batman, I ask, "What stories?"

"Oh, just that their daughter was a bit of a hellraiser. She ran off when she was really young, took her baby, which she had out of wedlock, mind you, and never returned." His greedy eyes dart left and right like he's got the good gossip.

Squirming under my gaze, he says, "From what I gather, she stole a car, bought some forged documents, and disappeared. We only found out she died a few months ago. An old boyfriend came up here trying to make amends, part of his twelve-step program, I guess, and informed us of her death way back in '97."

I frown, hard, at his words.

That light bulb goes on in that dim brain of his, and he realizes I'm that baby. "I guess that's why it took them so long to find you. Your name was wrong."

My name is something I can't even pronounce. My life was already threaded so thin it barely held together. Now there are more holes. I can't hold water. I can't hold anything.

The agent glances at his watch and says, "I have another showing I have to get to. Er, when you decide what you want to do, contact the office." He hands me a card. "Lock the door before you leave," he throws over his shoulder as hurries down the neatly paved path.

A metallic streaking sound grates my ears, and I glance up to see an old guy running his finger across the hood of my car.

I walk toward him. "Um, what are you doing?"

His wrinkly mouth purses as he scrutinizes my face. "She didn't steal the car," he says, shaking his head as he surveys the thick layer of desert dust the car has accumulated. *Clearly, this man had his hearing aid turned way up.* "Things get twisted over time," he says, rubbing his dried-up neck. "It was a graduation gift. Doreen and Gill paid for half; Anna paid for the other half outta money *she* earned." His affection for the family is clear. He taps the hood. "You need to take this old girl through a carwash."

I nod, watching him hobble around the Chevy. The questions. I feel them working their way through my teeth. "So you knew them well?" I force from my mouth.

"Mhm. I've lived here forty years or so. They were good people. Sad situation but good people."

I'm not sure I can take any more sadness in my life. I curl over the rest of the questions. Keeping them covered, except for one.

"Do you know when Doreen and, er, Gill died?" I ask.

"1997, a few days before Anna." My head drops. He clears his throat, and I look up. The old man smiles at me with his crummy dentures. "It's a beautiful car, son," he says, slapping the hood.

I mutter, "Thanks," to his cardigan-clad back as he shuffles toward his house.

The sun's tipping to the earth, sending slanted rays down the road like cartoon punches.

Grabbing my bags, my maps and sketchbooks, I haul it all inside. At my hollow steps, the house moans and creaks like it doesn't want me in here and I pause on the stairs, trying to picture Anna flying down, running late for school, her mom warning her to get her butt in the car. I grip the banister, and my throat closes like I've been kissed by Poison Ivy. Anna, my grandparents, haven't stepped foot on these stairs in nearly eighteen years. Their ghosts don't even brush the walls or reflect in the windows. It was So. Long. Ago.

I get to the top and investigate the hallway, my sneakers dragging on the plush carpet and leaving wormy imprints. One door shows remnants of old sticker glue and a scratched name hiding under layers of paint. I put my finger to the indent of the name *Anna*, dug out in Freddy-Kruger-style handwriting just above the doorknob.

My heartbeat stalls as the door falls open.

I drop my stuff on the floor. I don't know what I was expecting. Posters, clothes in a hamper, an unmade bed, some evidence that she was here. But, of course, it's empty.

I run my hands over the clean white walls, searching for something, anything. Until I come to the partially open wardrobe. I peer inside. There's a change in color, a disruption to the perfect cream paint. Using my phone as a flashlight, I push aside the wire hangers. There, under the spotlight, is Anna.

Her nose is snub, fine featured, with long hair sweeping around her face. She looks pissed—a narrow-eyed, pursed-lip expression on her face. I duck down under the clothes rail and trace her figure, drawn in sharpie on the back wall. Following her gaze, I see... I see me. My hand withdraws. The baby's big eyes stare out into the blackness of the wardrobe, trapped in time and space. But he doesn't look scared. He looks at peace. Safe.

I check Anna's expression again. It's not anger. It's fierce protectiveness.

I found her.

My laugh is muffled by mothballs.

I found Anna in the back of a cupboard. That's it. That's all I'm going to get. I shiver, hearing Langley snicker behind me at the weirdness of it all. The mystery that will never be solved.

Backing away from the picture, I turn to face the blank walls of what was once my mother's bedroom, kind of amused. Kind of devastated.

I rush to flip open Anna's map to read her caption for Chilliwack.

I HAD TO GO.

The picture beside it is a heart-shaped flower, straining to push through dry, crumbling earth. And maybe she did. Maybe she didn't have a choice. Maybe she was protecting me, loved me. It's as good a story as any. And it's good enough. Whatever happened in the past, it brought me here. Hell, it even brought me to Langley.

It *could* be my origin story. Tragedy is always the beginning. But what turns an ordinary story into an origin story is the idea that tragedy breeds a hero.

Warmth blooms in my chest as words and pictures rain down from the ceiling.

Grabbing a marker, I drag it across the cream-colored wall, producing the long lines of Langley's body. It's easy to draw her. The lines that compose Langley are printed in my brain.

When I'm done, I step back, staring at the picture for a long time, feeling like something's missing. She has her polka-dot sneakers. I've added a cape and mask, her trademark freckles and long dark hair. And then I realize what completes her alter ego, and I press the sharpie to the wall.

Standing by her side is Sarah. She holds Langley's hand. Together, they are a formidable pair. I grin at the life-sized Langley, staring down at me. I see her now. See what she really is. A hero. Her superpower—seeing into two worlds at once. The living and dead. The real and the unreal. She is the Delusionist.

The space beside them pulls my pen like a magnet, and I draw someone I've never drawn before.

He's tall, lean, and a little stooped. He has no disguise. He can't hide his wired-shut jaw. He holds the source of his power in his right hand, a pencil. He can rewrite history; draw a new future. He speaks through his drawings. He is Iron Jaw.

They stand together strong, powerful. They tell me, *Keep going.*

I pull out a fresh sketchbook. Under the soft glow of oyster lights, pages and pages are drawn. With my back to Iron Jaw and the Delusionist, their willful eyes watching every sweep of the pencil, words fill the spaces above the characters' heads. The story grows. The romance, the banter, and drama all flows onto the paper.

For the entire night, all I do, all I hear, is the scratch of lead on paper. The filling of pages. The beginning of something important for me.

When the orange light of a sunrise pours through the arch window, Iron Jaw and The Delusionist have become real. I hold up two sketchbooks filled with drawings, dialogue, and narration in my weary hands, and I feel like crowing.

This is what I'm supposed to do. She knew it, she told me, and now I believe her.

I wish they could see it. Both of them.

Shutting the wardrobe door, I close the book on this part of the story. Anna's not really here. Who she was, why she did what she did, will always be a mystery to me. I have to be okay with that.

I pack my bags and throw them over my shoulder, running down the stairs without the past clamped down on me.

The door closes, the snap of the latch marking the end of one frame and the progression into another.

The Chevy sits dully in the shadow of the broad-leaf trees, shadows dancing over the roof like ink blots. I clean it out. Leave the keys in the ignition and the doors unlocked. Hopefully someone will have a new adventure in it.

I leave both maps, too. The last caption I write is simple. **BEST TRIP EVER!**

I miss Langley with every step. It's not as simple as moving on. She's still in my story. There are more volumes to come.

Picking up my phone, I know what I need to do. I punch in the numbers I've learned by heart.

It only rings twice before she answers, "Tupper?"

Her voice is comfort. It is home.

"Mom," I say, feeling emotion crack my steady voice in half. "I want to come home."

98. Anna

Cilliwack, BC, 1997

WEATHER: DRY AND SCORCHING

NOTHING CAN GROW FROM dead earth. And as far as she is concerned, every street they walked together, every tree he pressed her against as he made her see colors she'd never known before, has been sucked of life. Now that he's gone, there's nothing left for her here. If she doesn't leave, she will become undernourished and she will wilt. Fold down on herself and become food for the worms.

She runs from the family home, a blue blanket held by the corner nearly tripping her up as she hurries down the stairs. Jolted and too unaware, the baby just watches the performance from her hip, his big gray eyes on his grandparents, who have come to the bright yellow door and are now screaming as they follow her.

Her father catches her quickly, grabbing her arm and squeezing it too hard. He doesn't mean to hurt her. She knows this, but she shouts at him just to make him release her. "You're hurting me, Dad," she screams for the whole neighborhood to hear. When he doesn't let go, her voice wails like a horn blowing, "Get your goddamn hands off me!" She shirks her arm. His eyes widen and he releases her, looking at her like he doesn't know who she is.

She nods in a satisfied kind of way because he doesn't know her. He never knew her. All he's ever known is disappointment in her.

"Please, Anna, you can't take care of him. If you have to go, leave Tupper with us," he begs, standing in the wet grass, moisture soaking into his slippers, his pajama pants. She looks at him, and all she can see is an old man. Old and out of touch. She wishes he would try to understand her, but he won't. He is afraid of her. Of the kind of people she represents.

284

She sniffs, her nostrils burning. She can feel the pull to the dead earth, sludge-covered hands reaching up to grip her ankles. The need to lift herself up is strong. "He's my baby. *Our* baby," she screams, standing half in and half out of the Chevy wagon they helped her buy for her sixteenth birthday. "No one can look after him except me."

Mama can't seem to form words. Her heart is broken, and Anna can't look in her direction. It's too much. Too much guilt. Too much doubt. Mama sinks to her knees. Anna can tell she wants to scream, but soon people will be coming out to collect their papers and she won't make a scene.

"Please..." is the word that floats in the air between Anna and her father. It knocks on the window, and she quickly winds it all the way up and locks the door. She places little Tupper in a box on the backseat. Then she faces forward, stares down the street, and doesn't acknowledge the devastation she has created. She can't see it. She is blown apart, smoke billowing from broken windows, piles of rubble.

Her own father doesn't recognize her, and she is unsurprised. She doesn't recognize herself.

NINE MONTHS AFTER SHE LEFT ME

THE TABLE WOBBLES UNDER the weight of the books. I stand up, sit down, then stand again, shoving my hands in my pockets to try to subtly wipe the moisture from them. My parents hang back. They look as awkward as I feel, staring at the line of people waiting on the other side of the glass door. I take my hands out, rearrange the Sharpies again. Mom scurries up. She repositions the plastic frame that has a large, trying-to-smile-but-looking-more-like-a-serial-killer picture of me in it, my name written in big comic book letters underneath.

I breathe big, incredulous breaths. *I can't believe I'm here.*

The store owner opens the doors and people flood in, lining up at my table while I try to keep some non-existent personal space between me and my readers.

My readers.

My eyes do that thing they always do. What they've been doing for the last nine months. They scan the room, searching for long brown hair, dark arms, giant cartoon eyes held up by dainty freckles. Sighing, I try to listen to the person talking to me. *She's not here.*

My agent prods me in the back. My attention must go back to the girl in front of me who's clutching a copy of my graphic novel to her chest, grinning nervously.

Planting it on the table, she gives me her name. I sign it, thank her, and move on to the next one.

I get into a rhythm, signing, talking, smiling, and it gets easier. People ask me questions, and I find I can answer them. I actually want to answer them. Because I know this story. I know everything about it. There are no blank spaces, airy silences in the conversation, because I'm in *my* world.

I glance at my parents standing against a bookshelf in the cooking section. They watch me with a mixture of pride and confusion in their eyes. This is not what they had planned for me, but they're trying to understand. They're here.

Another book slides in front of my eyes and I sign it, talk a bit about inspiration and drawing techniques.

"Thanks, man," he says.

"No problem. Thank *you*," I say, tipping my chin and leaning down to get a bottle of water.

A loud smack jolts me upright as the table vibrates on its thin metal legs. I glance up into that super-villain smile...

One part devil and one part nervous.

ABOUT THE AUTHOR

LAUREN NICOLLE TAYLOR IS the bestselling author of THE WOODLANDS SERIES and the award-winning YA novel NORA & KETTLE (Gold medal Winner for Multicultural fiction, Independent Publishers Book Awards 2017), which is the first book in the acclaimed PAPER STARS SERIES.

She has a Health Science degree and an honors degree in Obstetrics and Gynecology.

A full time writer and artist, Lauren lives in the tucked away Adelaide hills with her husband and three children.

She is a proud hapa and draws on her multicultural background in all of her novels.

ACKNOWLEDGEMENTS

In 1992 MY PARENTS made the impulsive and brave choice to take me, my brother and sister on a the trip of lifetime. Scrounging every last cent and racking up credit card charges, they took us on a six week long road trip around Western USA. We travelled through small towns in our GMC people mover, roasted in the desert because mum maintained we had to experience the climate rather than use the AC, and argued about elbows in sides and knees in backs. We ate sandwiches on our laps layered with strange, orange-colored cheese as we crossed miles and miles of entrancing and foreign landscapes. It was amazing! And once I returned, that burning need to return never left me. So thank you Raelene and Bob Gaffney for taking a risk and giving us an experience we never forgot.

In 2015 I was able to take that same road trip with my husband and three children. We drove through redwood forests, saw a bear and her cub in Yellowstone, felt the dwarfing power of the Grand Canyon and made the terrifying climb to the Clifftop Palace in Mesa Verde. My heart aches in a good way, remembering all the incredible things we did.

We would not have been able to make this life changing journey if not for the generosity of my parents and Maureen (Nanna) Payne, a wonderful and loved matriarch whose insistence on using her gift for something exciting and fun led us to America. It is a true reflection of what she was like as a person and we miss her a lot. We will always attribute our enjoyment of this trip in great part to her kindness and advice.

These two trips shaped me as a person and inspired Travel Diaries of the Dead & Delusional. Even now, I dream of those immense mountains and carved ochre rock formations that you just don't see anywhere else in the world. I crave them.

As Gonzo sings in one of the best road trip movies of all time, The Muppet Movie, "I'm going to go back there someday."

CPSIA information can be obtained
at www.ICGtesting.com
Printed in the USA
LVHW022312080219
606968LV00005B/8/P